PATRIOTS
OF
TREASON

A Novel

David Thomas Roberts

This is a fictional narrative. The storyline of this novel is for
entertainment purposes only. It is not intended to imply any
real person actually made statements, nor acted in any manner
consistent with the storyline of this novel.

ISBN 978-1-936688-37-1 Hardback Edition

Also available in:
ISBN 978-1-936688-36-4 Paperback Edition
ISBN 978-1-936688-38-8 eBook edition

PATRIOTS OF TREASON

David Thomas Roberts

Dedication

This book is dedicated to my loving, beautiful and patient wife and my four incredible children who remind me every day how important it is to fight for the things you believe in.

Prologue

"A declaration of war limits the presidential powers, narrows the focus, and implies a precise end point to the conflict. A declaration of war makes Congress assume the responsibilities directed by the Constitution for this very important decision, rather than assume that if the major decision is left to the President and a poor result occurs, it will be his fault, not that of Congress."

~ U.S. Congressman Ron Paul

Six Israeli Kfir C-22 fighter jets roared down the runway two at a time at Israel's Palmachim Air Base at approximately 11:33 p.m. on September 21. Afterburners aglow, they screamed into the darkness to join four American-made F-151 Israeli jets launched from the same base less than eight minutes earlier.

There were more than seventy aircraft already in the air from Nevatim, Ramon, Ramat David and Hatzerim Air Bases. The Israeli first strike fighters streaked across the night sky to engage Russian-made ZPU-4 and ZU-23 Iranian anti-aircraft and radar defense positions scattered throughout Iran.

Less than twenty hours earlier, the Spirit of Texas B-2 bomber had lifted off, along with four more B-2s from the United States Air Force Global Strike Command at Whiteman Air Force Base in Missouri.

The flight decks of the American aircraft carriers USS Carl Vinson and USS John Stennis, already in the Persian Gulf, were a hub of activity as both F-151 Eagles and AWACS aircraft launched in synchronized, methodical intervals.

The USS Ronald Reagan and the USS Abraham Lincoln, positioned in the Mediterranean one hundred twenty miles apart off the coast of Cyprus, were also in full flight deck operations, with aircraft being launched in thirty-second intervals as the carriers churned headlong into a stiff 38-mph wind that provided maximum lift for their heavily-armed fighter jets.

On the decks of all four aircraft carriers were the newest highly maneuverable stealth fighters, the F-22s. They had never been used in combat and the Pentagon was eager to see them in action. More than forty F-22s were slated for sorties in the operation, mostly for air defense priorities.

Two weeks before, nuclear watchdog agencies reported that Iran had significantly increased its uranium enrichment processes at the Esfahan and Natanz nuclear facilities. Both Israeli and U.S. intelligence sources indicated it was highly likely this enrichment process had increased from 20 percent uranium enrichment—typically used for peaceful nuclear power plant purposes—to the almost 90 percent enrichment necessary for a nuclear bomb.

Most troubling to Israel were satellite images indicating large movements of earthen structures and visible signs of a yet unknown missile delivery system. Iran could be weeks or even days away from having nuclear missiles and the capability to arm ballistic missiles.

* * *

During the current election cycle, President Tyrell Johnson and his administration repeatedly called for more time for economic sanctions to work against Iran.

Israel warned the world that it would not wait for Iran to possess nuclear arms, while continuing to secretly prove to the Johnson administration that Iran was closer every day to nuclear capability.

The Johnson re-election campaign and Johnson's senior administration officials were deeply concerned an announcement could be made by Iran that it had become a nuclear power. The Iranians would allow the news to be confirmed by the world less than two months before the November elections.

President Johnson's election handlers and the Democratic Party thought this potential news would depict the president as weak because he failed to prevent Iran from obtaining nuclear weapons. The president already suffered low approval ratings over high gas prices and unemployment. Surely the GOP would capitalize on this news when it broke, and Senior White House Advisor and Democratic strategist Avery Smith and others on the president's campaign staff and in his cabinet knew it could be tough to overcome.

As the Johnson campaign and the president's senior advisors met in late August, Johnson was behind Republican presidential candidate Micah Logan in every major poll, including some polls showing a double-digit lead for the GOP candidate. Unemployment numbers that had improved in the spring reversed course and were now back over 8.5 percent nationally. Gas prices skyrocketed in some states to over $6.00 per gallon over the summer and there had only been a slight drop in the previous thirty days.

A global confirmation of Iran's success at acquiring nuclear weapons could be the final blow to Johnson's re-election campaign. The electorate had given Johnson credit for killing high value targets in the war on terror but, unfortunately for Johnson, that good news had been almost forgotten under the weight of a stumbling economy made worse by historically high gas prices. President Johnson's executive orders' history and his embattled Attorney General Jamail Tibbs dragged on his poll numbers.

As advisors strategized over the news from Israel and independent atomic energy commissions, Johnson's former chief of staff and current Chicago Mayor Davian Kyler called President Johnson to remind him that, "There is opportunity in every crisis!" Could the president have actually been blessed by the opportunity for an "October Surprise?"

If the U.S. participated with Israel and the mission was successful at knocking out Iran's nuclear capability, Johnson's status as commander-in-chief could leap his poll numbers by ten percent or more, effectively sealing his re-election victory. Additionally, Independents who were not enamored with Logan might see President Johnson in a new light as a definitive, confident world leader.

If the mission was successful, American pride and patriotism might overcome the current economic malaise weighing down Johnson's polling numbers. The defeat of Iran's nuclear capability could help President Johnson carry the day and win re-election.

If the mission was unsuccessful, however, the president's senior staff agreed the re-election campaign would be dealt a death blow.

The administration knew Israel would do whatever it took to ensure Iran did not possess nuclear weapons, at least in the short term, and they approved engaging the Joint Chiefs of Staff to work out a strategy with Israeli military. The Joint Chiefs were briefed over three days by the CIA, Mossad and Israeli military officials. The U.S. military had three weeks maximum to launch a successful joint strike. Given that information, President Johnson reluctantly approved the operation.

Despite not having the necessary defense intelligence clearance to be briefed on this type of operation, Johnson's senior officials were included in numerous debriefings of the operation, now termed "Operation Python." Typical of the president's first term on most foreign relations matters, members of the House and Senate Intelligence Committees were not briefed.

***

Israel convinced the United States to avoid seeking permission from Turkey, Syria and Saudi Arabia for the use of their air space, as there was a well-founded and deep distrust that any of those countries could keep Operation Python secret from their Muslim brethren. With the likelihood of being categorically denied by those countries anyway, the U.S. agreed with Israel that the mission must be unannounced.

Both countries agreed to fly over Jordan, which essentially had no air defense capabilities, and then over Iraq where the Iraqi military—without U.S. military assistance—was virtually unable to monitor and control its own air space. The administration decided to only notify the Iraqi leadership once the fighters were well into their air space so the Iraqis could deny to Muslim fundamentalists and the Arab League any advance knowledge of the operation or its tacit approval for the flyover.

The initial objective of the Israeli Kfir C-22 and F-151 fighters was to knock out known and newly identified Iranian air defense installations, including surface air-to-missile (SAM) sites and radar. The F-151s also carried one 5,000-lb. GBU-28 "bunker buster" bomb each.

The second wave of American F-151s was to strike any unknown air defense sites that emerged and provide air-to-air combat protection for the fuel tankers and heavily armored Stealth B-2 bombers.

The administration ordered four Los Angeles Class nuclear submarines with six San Jacinto Class nuclear cruisers positioned in the Persian Gulf, the Strait of Hormuz and the Gulf of Oman. Their Tomahawk cruise missiles had a range of fourteen hundred miles and were primarily used against mobile SAM sites and radar installations. The submarines carried up to twenty-one Tomahawks each, while the cruisers carried one hundred twenty-two Tomahawks each.

Adding to the complexity of the mission was the need to refuel fighter jets in mid-air due to the distance they had to fly carrying heavy armament and performing diversionary tactics needed to avoid surface-to-air missiles. The U.S. launched fuel tankers from various bases throughout the region to fly over Jordan and Iraqi air space at critical junctures to provide refueling for the F-151s and Kfir C-22s.

Operation Python was designed for three continuous waves of Stealth B-2s, each carrying two of the new 30,000-lb. GBU-57A Massive Ordinance Penetrator "bunker buster" bombs that joint intelligence determined would be necessary to penetrate the underground concrete-reinforced encapsulated Iranian nuclear facilities, which were reportedly at least fifty feet underground with nine feet of reinforced concrete.

Joint military planners determined that a single accurate strike would not be enough to ensure success. Contrary to common public perception, a "surgical" military air strike could not effectively eliminate hardened Iranian nuclear facilities. Annihilation of the sites could take one to two "preparatory" strikes to weaken and expose the bunkers for a second or third wave of direct hits.

Israel's two previous strikes on nuclear facilities were both surgical in nature, less complicated and significantly less dangerous than Operation Python. In previous Israeli strikes, the facilities were above ground, with less sophisticated air defenses and less distance to travel.

President Johnson, Secretary of State Annabelle Bartlett, the Joint Chiefs of Staff, most of the president's senior cabinet and senior members of the campaign staff were in the situation room as Operation Python kicked off.

Both Israeli and U.S. administrations and military agreed that Operation Python would be communicated to the rest of the world as a limited "surgical" strike; in fact, however, it would be a ferocious, multi-faceted knock-out blow to Iran's nuclear capabilities.

Chapter 1

"Stupidity is a luxury and you will find time and time and time and again that those who are overwhelmingly on the left are those who can afford to be."

~ *Evan Sayet, Conservative Jewish Comedian*

Rashid Safly-Allah, known as "Rash" to his friends, locked the door to his cheap third-floor apartment, bounded down the narrow stairs and headed over to a local coffee house.

Rash was born in the U.S. to Iranian parents twenty-six years ago. They'd emigrated from Iran to Dallas, Texas after the Shah of Iran was deposed in the revolution of 1979. Both parents had since died, and Rashid's only other close relative, a sister two years older, had moved back to Iran with her husband when she married at eighteen, nearly ten years ago. He hadn't seen her at all during that time.

Making his way to the shop on foot, he slipped through the back door, waving at Nouri, a friend of his who worked in his dad's shop. Nouri's father, like Rash's parents, had come to the U.S. years ago, and the two boys lived in the same neighborhood. They had even gone to the same high school and were both in graduate school at Southern Methodist University. Nouri was working on a Master's in electrical engineering while Rash was finishing his Master's thesis in political science. Rash's fascination with politics started at a young age when his parents told him stories about why they had to flee Iran.

Making his way to the front of the store, Rash slid into an empty booth and waited for someone to take his order. He liked the sweet, full-bodied Turkish coffee his parents had loved, and this shop, using traditional methods, brewed the best.

Molly Parker, a cute raven-haired co-ed from SMU, also a grad student, worked part-time at the coffee shop. Molly met Nouri and Rash at the Muslim Student Association meetings on campus. Although she wasn't Muslim, she was a devout liberal and supported any cause on campus she felt aligned with her political beliefs. Molly had worked as a volunteer in President Johnson's first campaign and was the campus liaison for his re-election campaign at SMU.

Molly strolled over to the booth, a steaming cup in her hands. She set it down in front of him. He picked up the cup, sniffed its contents, and smiled up at her.

"Why the big grin, Rash?" she asked, resting her hands on her slim waist.

"Nothing special," he said. "I just really love this coffee."

"I could have brought you some tea, I suppose." She was laughing, and he decided she was referring to his Tea Party involvement.

"Yes, I suppose so," he agreed. "Still, I'm done with the Tea Party. Found out they're not so bad, and they really aren't prejudiced against Muslims, or anyone else, it seems. They gave me a great subject for my thesis, although my professor won't believe a word I write about them."

"Uggh, you really think so?" she said, acting as if she could barely fathom the possibility that the Tea Party organizations Rash had joined weren't somehow diabolical.

She dropped his ticket on the table, noticing his laptop open to the last page of his thesis. "You're finally finished? Wow! How long did it take you?"

"Long enough," he told her. "My expectations were such that I had to go back and rewrite most of it. What I expected to find didn't happen and, the more I dug into the culture of the Tea Party, the more I realized they're pretty much okay. I don't agree with all their politics, but they're really just average Americans. So it took longer because I had to write two versions." He took a sip of the hot coffee.

"You don't agree with all their politics? Did they convert you?"

she teased. Then she noticed he didn't take it as a joke, and got serious. "When do you have to turn it in?"

"Next week."

"I bet you're excited," she said.

"I am ready to move on to the next chapter in my life," he told her. "Maybe I'll go visit my sister in Iran after I get my Master's."

"You promised you'd help in the campaign when you're done," she pouted.

"I will, I promise, as soon as I get back."

Her pout disappeared. "I already have you registered with the campaign. You'll officially be the co-chair of the Johnson re-election committee at SMU. I can get you into all the events, maybe even the inauguration."

"Don't forget about Nouri."

"He's a co-chair, too. No problem."

"Can the president do without me for a couple of weeks?" Rash laughed.

"Sure. How long has it been since you saw your sister?"

"About ten years. She even has a couple of kids now, so I'm an uncle."

"Oh, that's great," Molly said. "I'll bet she'll be excited to see little brother."

"No doubt she will," he said.

Rash closed up his laptop, gave Molly the money for the coffee, and headed for the door.

"Good luck again on the thesis," she called after him.

"Thanks, Molly. Talk to you soon."

Rash went back to his small apartment to finish the edits on his thesis so he could submit it next week. As he sat down to eat a snack, he turned on his television to see the breaking news. Israel and the United States had jointly launched Operation Python, a major attack on Iranian nuclear sites

Rash had always been proud of his Iranian heritage and always wanted to visit Iran, maybe even move there. His sister had married a devout Muslim and had written to Rash many times expressing her desire for him to become the same.

As he channel-surfed all the news channels and watched the live video feeds of Iran in flames, Rash became furious. He never agreed with the popular opinion that Iran be prevented from having its own nuclear weapons. He wondered if the operation might be the beginning of a war between Iran, the United States and Israel.

Rash tried throughout the night to call his sister in Iran, but couldn't get through. Because his sister and her husband followed strict, fundamentalist Muslim law, his sister was not allowed to access the Internet, making it impossible to communicate with her by email.

Rash laid in bed, thinking he had volunteered to work in this presidential campaign for the man who authorized the bombing of his homeland and his sister's home. He tossed and turned the entire night, not able to sleep because he tried to call his sister every half hour.

Chapter 2

"A good plan violently executed now is better than a perfect plan executed next week."

~ *General George S. Patton*

All major networks broke into regular television programming shortly after 7:00 p.m. in New York to announce that Iran had been attacked in coordinated "surgical" air strikes by Israel and the United States. White House Press Secretary Ted Duncan announced that a live national statement from the Oval Office would be made by President Johnson at 8:00 p.m.

Fox, ABC, CBS and CNN all reported the strike as "massive," with hundreds of sorties by both American and Israeli forces. Early intelligence leaks reported "likely" major damage at all suspected Iranian nuclear facilities and at military command headquarters in Tehran.

Political shockwaves reverberated around the globe as world leaders began issuing statements on the attack with the typical support from Great Britain and other NATO countries, and sharp criticism and dire warnings from Russia, China and most Arab League countries. Saudi Arabia even issued a protest and announced no attacks had been launched from Saudi bases, nor was permission given to use Saudi airspace—but both Israel and the U.S. knew the Saudis were secretly ecstatic that the Iranian regime and its nuclear capabilities had apparently been pulverized.

Sitting at his desk in the Oval Office and looking the most presidential since the announcement of the strike that took out the head of Al-Qaeda, President Johnson looked straight into the camera and, in a serious tone, stated, "Today, brave American and Israeli forces launched a necessary pre-emptive strike on Iranian nuclear facili-

ties. As the world knows, the majority of civilized nations have tried
for years to work with Iranian President Atash Shirazi and his government to allow independent nuclear inspections to validate Iran's
claim that its nuclear program was for peaceful domestic energy
purposes only." The president paused. "However, over the last few
weeks, intelligence sources have verified that Iran has successfully
enriched enough uranium to supply up to twenty-five nuclear warheads. With the recent delivery of North Korean intercontinental
ballistic missiles, Iran has obtained the full capability to arm those
missiles with nuclear warheads. Through diplomatic channels, Israel, the United States and various Arab League countries have tried
to reason with the Iranian regime. Iran's deliberate attempt to hide
uranium enrichment, coupled with the delivery of the North Korean missiles, was a provocation of our national security interests in
the region and a serious threat to Israel."

President Johnson, like other great orators, paused again for effect, then continued. "I have said many times that a nuclear-armed
Iran is unacceptable to the United States, Israel, the Middle East region, the Arab League and to most of the civilized world. President
Shirazi's regime has deliberately violated the trust of the world community and the actions we took were entirely caused by his regime's
continued threats to Israel and the region. Once Iran achieved the
enriched uranium and the ability to launch it with a missile delivery
system, we had no choice but to act.

"Make no mistake," the president went on, using his signature
phrase, "we have nothing against the Iranian people. They should not
consider this action an attack on Iranians, but rather an action made
necessary by an out-of-control zealot. God bless our military and
God bless America."

Throughout the night, reports of the attack were sketchy but, as
the night wore on, the size, scope and ferocity of the attacks became
clear. Reports about the various aircraft carriers positioned in the
region, the use of drones, hundreds of Tomahawk cruise missiles,

nuclear submarines, "bunker buster" bombs and literally hundreds of aircraft and fuel tankers surprised even military analysts on various news channels. With less than half a dozen sites targeted, it was clear this was a "scorched earth" strategy for the targeted locations.

Even more surprising were the looks on congressional leaders' faces when queried on news programs about how much they knew and when they knew it. By midnight, Fox News reported that no one in the congressional Republican leadership was consulted or even informed before or after the attack was launched. Most of the Democratic leadership seemed to be equally caught off guard, but they were more diplomatic in their interview responses, completely supporting President Johnson, with only a few raising concerns about the timing of unilateral action by the Executive Branch. Talking heads on most mainstream news channels claimed that, ultimately, secrecy was paramount for the success of the mission and that success trumped any constitutional requirement for advance notice of military action under these special circumstances.

Meanwhile, while agreeing action was necessary, Republican presidential candidate Micah Logan excoriated President Johnson for taking unilateral action without consulting Congress.

The next morning, the first images of the destruction hit the news wires and the Internet. It was apparent the destruction at the identified nuclear facilities was widespread. Israeli intelligence reported that all nuclear facilities were completely destroyed.

White House officials weren't quite ready to address the possible success of the sixteen-hour attack. Even Ted Duncan asked reporters to hold their questions because President Johnson would make a live statement at 10:00 a.m. EST. Before closing his press briefing abruptly, Duncan hinted there was an incredible and heroic story the president would communicate to the country at the news conference.

As the networks continued to get Republican reaction to the strikes, the GOP praised the apparent success of the mission but didn't hesitate to call out President Johnson on acting without Congress' blessing.

At 10:02 a.m. EST, President Johnson walked up the red carpet to the microphone in the East Wing of the White House. The White House only invited specific pool reporters for a very limited press audience, leaving out Fox News and the BBC, among others.

"Fellow Americans, last night I informed you that American and Israeli forces initiated necessary strikes on Iranian nuclear facilities. Today, the Joint Chiefs have informed me the mission was totally successful," President Johnson said. "Early reports are that Iran's facilities for producing and enriching uranium for nuclear warheads have been totally destroyed."

A somber look crossed the president's face. "Although the mission was successful, the United States lost seven airmen and Israel lost eleven. Our hearts and prayers go out to those whose family members have made the ultimate sacrifice for their country.

"During the mission," the president continued, "Iranian air defenses shot down two Israeli fighter jets whose four pilots ejected safely; they were captured by elite Iranian Revolutionary Guards. An American Recon and Special Forces team entered Iran and successfully rescued those pilots and extracted them to safety."

Johnson stated he couldn't take questions because Operation Python wasn't complete. Reporters shouted questions anyway. On his way out, Johnson walked over and shook the hands of several Joint Chiefs brass standing behind the podium. Their smiles made it obvious that top brass and the president felt the mission was a huge success.

Shortly after the president's announcement, Israeli Prime Minister Malachi Dayan conducted his own press conference in Jerusalem. The prime minister reported the mission was a complete success; however, he warned that, despite the destruction of Iranian nuclear facilities, Iran's knowledge on how to build nuclear weapons had not been impacted. He told his nation the attack was most likely not the end, but a continuation of the process to deny Iran nuclear capability.

"Every Israeli should be prepared for a future that requires protecting Israel's right to exist," he stated.

Dayan expressed deep gratitude for President Johnson and the United States for assisting with the mission. He said that, without U.S. support, Israel could not have carried out the mission successfully.

Iranian President Shirazi wasn't heard from for days. Operation Python had hit the military command building and the Revolutionary Guard headquarters in Tehran but, as news of Iran's president was non-existent, there was speculation he might have been killed in the attacks.

Through the Al-Jazeera news channel, Al-Qaeda and the Taliban vowed to exact revenge all over the world on the Zionists and the Americans, wherever they were, even in the United States. Hamas and other terrorist organizations were quoted as saying in videos and news releases that both countries could expect renewed terror operations as the result of the unprovoked attacks on a Muslim nation.

Finally, after three days, President Shirazi appeared before cheering crowds on state-run Iranian TV and swore a devastating revenge for the cowardly attacks. He also vowed to continue Iranian nuclear operations, and threatened that the Zionists and the Great Satan would not successfully deny Iran its rights.

Homeland Security in the U.S. raised the terror alert to its highest levels since 9/11. Pundits and talking heads agreed that terrorist cells in the United States might be activated.

Chapter 3

"A nation of sheep will beget a government of wolves."

~ *Edward R. Murrow*

At first light, Rash got up and dressed. Today, he put on traditional Muslim garb and went to the mosque, hoping to find a way to reach his sister. Several fellow Iranians at the mosque had relatives who knew Rash's sister and husband. He hoped they had news.

When he arrived, he was surprised to find a large number of the congregation there. Angry, they shouted epithets at Israel, President Johnson and the U.S. military. Rash slipped easily into the same angry and frenzied state.

Some in the mosque were like Rash and had family in Iran. Very little communication was coming from relatives of anyone in the mosque. Those who weren't Iranian were just as angry that a Muslim country was being bombed by the United States and, even worse, by Israel. The two families at the mosque who had relatives living close to his sister were frantic. Reports were that one of the heaviest hit areas was where his sister lived in Natanz.

For the next twenty-four hours, Rash remained at the mosque hoping for news of his sister. She still did not answer her phone. Other members of the mosque brought food in to feed those waiting for word. The local imam came to Rash several times to attempt to comfort him. After the imam had shown such compassion for him and the other Iranians in the mosque, Rash felt guilty for not being a devout Muslim and for his thoughts that the imam was a little too radical for his tastes.

Rash fell asleep in a corner of the mosque, only to be gently awakened by the imam and his friend Nouri.

"Brother, we have word from family in Iran," said the imam in a solemn tone.

Worry flooded through Rash as he saw their faces.

"What? What do you know?" he asked.

"My brother, your sister has perished in the Zionist attacks."

"What? Please, no." Rash begged them to take their words back.

Before he could comprehend what he was being told, the imam continued, "My brother, your sister perished with her husband and two children. They are with Allah now."

Rash, who had gotten to his knees as the two kneeled next to him, now fell to the floor. Many in the mosque came to him as Rash cried openly. Other members were again shouting "Death to the Zionists!", "Death to Johnson" and similar chants.

Rash remained in the mosque for two days without eating, mourning the deaths of his sister and her family.

For the next month, Rash locked himself in his apartment and had little contact with the outside world. Both Nouri and Molly came to see him, but he wouldn't let them in. The only person he would allow in to talk to him was the imam, who started to visit Rash daily, sometimes for hours at a time.

Weeks passed, and finally Rash came out of his apartment, showing up at Nouri's family coffee house, much to the surprise of Nouri and Molly.

"Oh, my God, Rash, are you okay?" asked Molly, dropping the dish cloth she was using to clean a table. She ran to him as he walked through the door.

"Yes, I'm good."

Both Molly and Nouri hugged him.

They sat at a table for next two hours and Rash took them through the events at the mosque and what he knew about the bombing. The small home his sister lived in had been completely leveled. It was less than a quarter mile from the Natanz nuclear facility. There were no remains.

"Rash, how do you feel now about America, Israel and President Johnson?" Molly asked cautiously.

Rash collected his thoughts before answering. "It's a terrible tragedy. It's hard for me to forgive Israel, but I understand why Johnson did it. The regime in Iran has to change. In fact, I want you to tell the Johnson people that, despite my sister's death, I still support him."

Molly was silent for a few seconds. "Wow, really? I don't know what to say. I thought you would hate him after this. Rash, they will want to hear from you if you really believe this."

"Tell them," he told her, "I want to work on the campaign. Everything else in my life is on hold. Do you think I could get to meet the president?"

"I promise you I will do everything I can. I will pass word up through the campaign about your tragedy and how you still support the president. I hate that you had this loss, but I'm so glad you are still with us!"

The three sat there and talked for another hour before Rash suddenly stood up and said he had to go.

As Rash walked out the door, Nouri said to Molly, "Rash has a different look in his eyes, and his demeanor has changed."

"Well, of course, he just lost his sister."

"I guess that's it. Did you notice his blank stare?"

"Nouri, he's in deep mourning," Molly said. "He'll come around."

"I guess so, because the guy that just walked out the door isn't the same happy-go-lucky Rash I know."

Rash went home and stayed to himself for the next two days. He hadn't seen the imam during that time. They spoke by phone and decided to meet at another café not owned by Nouri's family.

After their meeting, Rash and the imam took extra time to say good-bye, almost if one of them was going on a long trip or saying a final goodbye. They hugged again, kissed each other's cheeks, and Rash watched his new mentor walk away.

Rash stood on the sidewalk, looked at his phone, and crossed the street, heading west. Checking behind him occasionally, a habit he had developed during his Tea Party research, he made his way to a local pawn shop.

He browsed through the store, eventually making his way to the gun section. Rash wasn't the usual type people associated with Muslims; he was light-skinned, and avoided the hirsute custom of others in Islam. To the casual observer, he would look like a skinny college student, not worthy of serious consideration for anything related to terror.

The weapons locked in glass cases overwhelmed him. There were so many. As he paused there, a frown wrinkling his forehead, a young man approached him.

"Lookin' for a gun, sir?"

Rash looked at the clerk, then pointed to a revolver in one of the cases. "Maybe," he said. "Can I look at that one?"

"Sure." The clerk reached under the counter and pulled out a bunch of keys. He flipped through them to find the one he needed. Inserting it into the key hole on the case, he opened it and hauled out the handgun.

"Can I ask what you want to use it for?"

Rash shifted uncomfortably, and then looked at the salesman. "I just think I need some protection," he said. "I'm a student, and sometimes I'm downtown pretty late. Would this be a good choice?"

"Yep, it would work," the sales clerk told him. "Not too expensive and good bang for your money."

"You sell ammunition here, too?" Rash asked.

"Sure do." The clerk pointed at rows of ammo stacked in a case behind him. He slid the door open and pulled out a box of .45 shells and set it on the glass counter. "These will do the trick."

Rash picked up and pretended to look over the package, then set it back on the counter. "I'm going to think about it," he said.

He left the shop. Now he had to weigh his options for revenge. He'd been born in the U.S. and, for most of his early years, he'd heard nothing bad about America. His parents were grateful for the asylum they'd been granted, and they loved Dallas, which had been their home and his since they arrived.

As he came into his teens, he began to spend more time with other Muslims. At first, he felt like an outsider but, as he spent more time in the local mosque with some of the older boys, he started to absorb a bit of their disenchantment and even hatred for the U.S. Being late to this game, he didn't understand it all. Now that his only sister and her family were dead, some of what he heard at the mosque began to resonate with him.

The next day, Rash visited Molly at the coffee shop and went with her to a small Johnson rally at SMU, then to Johnson's campaign headquarters in downtown Dallas. He quickly became something of a celebrity with state and local campaign staff when they learned the story of his loss and that he was not only voting for Johnson, but working in his campaign. They promised Rash they'd get his story to the national campaign headquarters and they would be in touch with him, maybe even want to interview him for TV or an ad campaign.

Rash would only comment that his goal was to actually meet the president.

Chapter 4

"When liberty is taken away by force it can be restored by force. When it is relinquished voluntarily by default it can never be recovered."

~ *Dorothy Thompson, the First Lady of American Journalism*

The GOP's worst nightmare before the election had occurred. President Johnson's poll numbers, sagging four to six points behind Micah Logan's most of the summer, took a sudden and dramatic turn. Rasmussen and other reliable organizations reported polling numbers after Operation Python had done an about face.

President Johnson's approval rating had reached a low point of 41 percent in August, due to lingering 8+ percent unemployment, record-high gas prices and various scandals at the Justice Department. But those negative factors quickly became a distant memory. He surged ahead in most polls, with a favorability rating now topping 55 percent in most polls.

Logan and the GOP leadership found themselves in a precarious position. Most conservative leaders had called for action on Iran for more than three years, criticizing the administration heavily, but they never thought President Johnson would act. Now it was difficult to criticize the president without incurring major political damage.

With the close proximity of the strikes to the elections, President Johnson had essentially launched an "October surprise," even if it was still only mid-September. The momentum the president's campaign was now enjoying could be a tidal wave that swept him right back into office.

Logan and his campaign staff gathered at his headquarters. "You can always count on the president to pull off something to counteract his bad press," Logan barked, "but you have to admit this was a brilliant stroke. It took a lot of courage, because the downside would have been a disaster for him."

"Yep," one staffer agreed, "now he's back in the driver's seat. The public loves victory, and he managed it."

"This just means we must work to bring the big issues back into focus," Logan said. "Let's concentrate on the economy and jobs, and show that we know these are the real problems in this country."

"I hope it's enough," someone said.

"It has to be. We have to win, or this country's done." Logan leaned forward, placing his palms on the conference room table. "Right now," he said quietly, "we're all that stands between this country's grand history as the world's greatest government and a socialist takeover. It's up to God and us to bring things back into balance."

He went on to point out how the Democrats pounced on the momentum provided by Operation Python. President Johnson appeared at several Air Force, Army and Naval bases over the following weeks to greet returning warriors with a hero's welcome. The crowds were boisterous, jubilant and patriotic at every event, and the mainstream media captured every moment—the adoring crowds of supporters and the high-fives of the president with returning service members. New polling data showed the president's approval ratings soaring, especially on foreign policy and leadership.

Sensing the momentum being yanked out from under them, the GOP leadership and congressional candidates continued to blast the administration on the military action taken by the president without congressional authorization or consultation. Editorial opinions in most major newspapers and media outlets were unmerciful to the GOP, calling them insincere and guilty of talking out of both sides of their mouths. On one hand, Republicans criticized the president for not acting on Iran, then tried to politicize it when the successful mission had him soaring in the polls.

President Johnson traveled to Europe to meet with allies, conducting a good will tour to repair any damage done to foreign relations. During his visits in Moscow with Nikolai Federov, the president came off as a confident, capable and strong leader, which pushed his polling numbers even higher.

Despite the condemnation of the attack from Russia, China and various Arab countries, it was apparent that most global leaders were happy Iran's nuclear ambitions had been dealt a crippling blow.

With the general love affair the mainstream media had always had with the president, and less than forty-five days to the election, Democrats detected an opportunity to bury Logan. Effective, professionally produced Democratic PAC ads were laced with comments from key Republican lawmakers criticizing President Johnson for moving on Iran without congressional authority, interspersed with video flashbacks of the same lawmakers complaining about the administration's lack of action on Iran.

GOP political operatives were unsuccessful at turning the conversation back to unemployment, high gas prices, health care and other domestic issues. The fascination with Operation Python continued as in-depth coverage of the mission and the faces behind it dominated the news.

Chapter 5

"The people who cast the votes don't decide an election, the people who count the votes do."

~ Joseph Stalin

Rash couldn't believe his good fortune. The local Dallas Democratic Party organization promoted him to anyone who would listen, including major organizers at Democratic national headquarters and Johnson's campaign managers.

Molly was excited. She had gotten the ball rolling locally in Dallas, and it looked like it was picking up steam. She heard Rash might be interviewed and actually appear in a TV ad for the campaign. He was Molly's ticket to get exposure at high levels in the campaign.

The whirlwind came to a screeching halt one afternoon in Dallas. Molly and Rash were at the Johnson re-election headquarters when the city campaign manager, Jim, came into the small office where they were working and closed the door.

"Rash, I'm sorry to tell you this," he said, "but the staff has decided not to use you and your story for the campaign."

Molly was first to respond. "Why the hell not? Rash is Muslim, his sister was killed, and he believes the operation was justified. What would be better for the campaign than to tell America this story?"

"Yes, Jim, why the reversal?" Rash asked.

"First, polling on Operation Python's success is off the charts. The president's approval ratings have been up ever since. The campaign is afraid that, if we put a personal face and story to the fact that some civilians in Iran were killed, it will hurt the president."

"Wow, I never thought of it like that," said Molly.

Jim nodded and continued, "Because of the news blackout from

Iran, we haven't gotten any credible pictures or stories of civilian casualties. If we put Rash on TV, it personalizes the casualties and could actually have a reverse effect. People could be trying to relate to Rash and be asking themselves if they could still support the president after they lost a family member. We want them concentrating on the victory."

"So you don't want anyone to know people were actually killed?" asked Rash.

"We all know people died; we just don't want to personalize it. I know you are both very disappointed, but I do have some good news."

"Really?" Molly grinned.

"What's that?" echoed Rash.

"The state Democratic Party has arranged for both of you to be in Chicago for the re-election celebration and the president's victory speech in Lincoln Park."

"Oh, my God, are you serious?" yelped Molly.

"Yes, I'm very serious." Jim smiled at her exuberance. "On top of that, the DNC said they may want access to Rash later, so you both have standing invitations to the inauguration."

Rash smiled as he realized these two events could give him the opportunity to meet the president.

"You'll also have all-access passes as part of the re-election campaign to the victory speech. Molly, I've got you assigned to the volunteers tent and Rash, I got you assigned to the press corps tent next to the stage."

"Jim, I love you!" Molly jumped up and hugged him.

Jim turned to Rash. "Rash," he said sincerely, "I know this doesn't make up for your loss in any way, but I hope this shows you how much we appreciate your contribution."

"Thank you, sir. I look forward to the opportunity," said Rash, his response measured.

Chapter 6

"Tyranny and anarchy are never far apart."

~ Jeremy Bentham, 19th Century English Philosopher

Caroline Perillo was never much for politics. They annoyed and bored her at the same time. She always voted at her husband's insistence, but all the damned politicians seemed the same to her—just liars who said whatever voters wanted to hear.

Caroline's husband Nick owned a trucking company that had shrunk with the bad economy over the past four years. At one point, he had been able to cut back on driving one of his own over-the-road trucks as their fleet had grown to ten rigs. Now, they were down to two trucks, with Nick having to drive one of them. The bank had taken back the other trucks, and the family owed the IRS back taxes. Caroline kept the books for the company, so she was never insulated from the reality of the economic times.

Trucking seemed to be one of the hardest hit industries of the recession. Diesel prices jumped to more than $6.00 per gallon and now there were fewer loads, meaning increased competition for less freight.

Nick and Caroline's marriage had weathered the storm pretty well. The only serious disagreement was over Nick's decision to keep some of his drivers on the payroll longer than he probably should have. He hated to let good, dedicated employees go because he knew their prospects for finding another job were slim.

Still, Caroline was excited about becoming a grandmother, as their only child Jim recently married and announced he and his wife Donna were expecting. Caroline found it difficult to think of herself as a grandmother; she still had a good figure, and had her hair tinted so the gray didn't show. Working out three times a week and playing tennis when she could kept her in good physical shape.

Jim wanted no part of the family business and instead got a job out of college with an insurance company in downtown St. Louis. The Perillo family lived in Lebanon, Illinois, a bedroom community across the river from St. Louis.

Jim and Donna had come over for dinner right after work to watch the election returns with Caroline before they left for their apartment six miles from Jim's parents' house.

After dinner, Donna helped Caroline clear the table and put the dishes in the dishwasher. Jim slumped on the sofa, watching breaking news on Fox News' Election HQ.

"I bet he wins again, Mom." Jim sounded defeated.

"God, I hope not!" Caroline exclaimed.

"I bet Dad is fit to be tied."

"I don't want any part of that bet."

"Well, here we go again, only now it's going to get even worse," Jim grumbled.

"Jim, you sound just like your dad!" Caroline laughed, but she was worried.

Nick was on his way home from taking a load to Kansas and was still around Kansas City, Missouri, as the polls closed. He told Caroline he was going to drive a little further until the election was called while he listened on the radio.

"Your dad said he's really tired," she told Jim. "He'll probably pull over to sleep in his cab in Kansas City before coming home tomorrow."

After an hour of election coverage, Jim got up. "Come on, Donna. We've got to go. Mom, I don't know about you, but I can't sit here and watch any more of this. This whole things smells to me—I'd hate to be near Dad right now with everyone predicting Johnson's re-election." He gave Caroline a hug.

"Yes, I know that," she said.

"Goodnight, Mrs. Perillo," said Donna, yawning as she got up to follow Jim.

"Goodnight, kids."

Jim and Donna left right after nine-thirty. The TV commentators continued coverage, speaking glowingly of the president's chances for re-election.

"Yeah, right," Caroline said. "He's only the worst president in our history."

Chapter 7

"The Constitution is colorblind, and neither knows nor tolerates classes among citizens."

~ John Marshall, Chief Justice of Supreme Court, 1801-1835

It was over. President Tyrell Johnson won, and won big. The huge boost he got from the Iranian attack carried him to victory.

Chuck Dixon turned off Fox News shortly after 11:00 p.m. on November 6 when it became clear Johnson would win. It was only a matter of time before the election was called by the political pundits.

His wife Christy had gone to bed an hour earlier. She knew the outcome; it was obvious to her.

When he got home, as Chuck checked the locks on the doors and turned off the lights, he had a terrible sinking feeling. The unthinkable had actually happened. President Johnson had apparently won. America might not recover.

As he crawled into bed, Christy awoke.

"It happened," he snarled. "Johnson was re-elected. Unbelievable. What are Americans thinking? Again."

Christy gave him a quick kiss and rolled over in bed. "What did you expect?" she murmured.

Chuck tried to sleep but couldn't. Although he was a little overweight and had sleep apnea, these factors weren't keeping him awake. He was worried about the country and the path it had been set on by the re-election of Johnson.

At fifty-two, Chuck had built a successful business over the past fifteen years. His thirty-two employees depended on him making correct business decisions. He'd been fortunate and made good decisions and, despite the economy, his business wasn't affected like most, especially in other parts of the country. But the future of small businesses was uncertain, to say the least.

He laid there, staring up at the ceiling, his mind churning a hundred miles per hour. It seemed the entire Johnson campaign was targeting him as part of the 99 percent "privileged" class that made over $250,000 per year. That was the group Johnson wanted to pay more taxes—his fair share, according to the president. It seemed like half the country didn't think he was paying his "fair share," despite his 35+ percent tax rate.

A sleepless hour later, he got up and turned the TV on in the living room instead of the bedroom so as not to wake Christy.

He tuned into Fox News just as Special Report's Stephen Fletcher announced the president won by a comfortable eight-point margin in the popular vote. He carried the swing states of Florida, North Carolina, Pennsylvania and Ohio for a comfortable electoral vote margin, with West Coast states yet to fully report.

Chuck watched as Johnson came to the podium near 11:30 p.m. at the huge stage set up in Lincoln Park in downtown Chicago. The crowd was not as big as Johnson's first election, but this crowd was different. Where the previous election night crowd had come to see history with the first black U.S. president, a sense of relief permeated this post-election gathering by Johnson supporters.

Four years earlier, Lincoln Park had been a celebration. Tonight, small trash fires were being set all over the park. Several vehicles were overturned, and one was on fire. Most mainstream news channels didn't show these events but instead focused on the dignitaries, politicians and celebrities jammed together on the stage.

In many ways, the happenings around Lincoln Park, downtown Chicago and about a dozen other cities reflected that same "celebration" Americans had seen in the past after various sports championships. Looting, fires and violence were widespread. MSNBC and CNN didn't broadcast any coverage of the carnage; CBS and ABC made very brief mentions of the disturbances, but showed no live coverage. Fox News and the BBC were the only news outlets reporting the violence.

The media outlets declared the Tea Party a three-year "fad," with its high point the election of many candidates at the expense of incumbents in the mid-terms.

Chuck wondered if he could have done more. He got involved in the Tea Party when it first broke onto the political scene. He was concerned over the country's direction, the rising debt, taxes and unchecked federal spending. He and his friend Stan Mumford started a local chapter and began to actively recruit others. Like most Tea Party members, Chuck and Stan believed the country had abandoned the Constitution.

Chuck felt like the country had turned the corner for socialism despite the Tea Party's victories. With half the country taking money from the federal government, he knew his views and those of the Tea Party were now in the minority. Surely there were more people in America who believed in the same conservative and small government ideals he did.

Although the GOP seemed to close ranks around their candidate after the divisive primary campaign, Chuck knew neither he nor many of his friends, business colleagues or relatives were enthused about Logan and wanted a more conservative Tea Party candidate. Many who admitted they had to "hold their nose" while pulling the lever for the GOP candidate four years ago had to do it all over again. The GOP, whose establishment desperately needed grass roots support, nominated a non-Tea Party candidate. The Tea Party, which the GOP could have used to energize its base, wasn't enthusiastic enough to vote Logan in as much as they wanted Johnson out.

Chuck wondered to himself how this could happen after the Department of Justice debacle, socialized healthcare, the czars, the class warfare, high gas prices, and unemployment. The list of negatives seemed endless, yet the American people re-elected the guy.

How could this happen?

His shoulders slumped. It was too late now. Johnson was re-elected, and it really wasn't close.

The view on TV switched to show newly re-elected President Johnson take the podium to make his acceptance speech, dual teleprompters poised on both sides of the podium. He was flanked by First Lady Maggie Johnson and their daughters, Vice President Bert Doolittle and his wife Lily, Attorney General Jamail Tibbs, Treasury Secretary Benjamin Gould, their spouses, numerous Hollywood stars, union bosses, Democratic politicians, strategists and handlers.

As Johnson thanked his supporters, he went into an unrelenting verbal attack on Republicans and the Tea Party.

"Today, my fellow Americans, we have sent a message to all Americans. Fairness is alive and well in America. The politics of the past are gone forever. Voters have sent a message to the entire world. We are no longer a nation of the privileged few. It's time to restore the middle class and all working men and women to prosperity!" Johnson proclaimed. "America has rejected the politics of obstructionism. You have delivered the House and Senate back to a Democratic majority!

"This administration and the Democratic leadership have a very ambitious one-hundred-day agenda when the new Congress convenes to continue to repair the economic damage done by the previous administration and the do-nothing stalemate caused by the far right extremist Tea Party faction of the GOP. For important issues that can't wait, I will issue executive orders on matters of urgency to continue to support jobs and economic growth."

He paused as he was interrupted by thunderous applause, his head held high and his chin pushed forward. He basked in the response and patiently waited for silence before continuing. "This election validates that the American people have rejected outdated notions of privilege for those of us who can afford to pay a little more so kids get the healthcare they need, young people get a college education, and our social safety nets remain. I will end the subsidies for big oil and, through executive order, will take the necessary steps to lower gas prices.

"In the coming weeks and months, we will introduce sweeping tax reform to reflect the will of the American people. Everyone— and I do mean everyone—will pay their share. We will also address the crime associated with out-of-control access to guns!" The president's voice peaked as he finished.

Again, he paused, allowing the adoring audience to express their approval of his plans. He then went on to thank "working Americans," the unions and others for their support.

As Chuck listened to the rest of the election returns for congressional, senate and gubernatorial seats, it was obvious to him the rout was on. Many of the Tea Party candidates who were elected in the previous mid-term elections were defeated by Democrats. Some Tea Party and Conservative candidates were elected, but not enough to stem the tide. The Democrats again controlled all three branches of the federal government.

As he sat there dejectedly, Chuck wondered how this could have happened. Sure, the joint attack with Israel on Iran's nuclear facilities was a success, even though the timing less than two months before the election was suspect. And Johnson did get some of the most notorious terrorists. But the unemployment rate was still over 8 percent. The dollar continued to weaken. All Republican attempts to slash the deficit had failed. Johnson seemed intent on his own course now to fix everything through executive orders. He was riding a wave of momentum. Contributing to his cause had been the lack of enthusiasm for Micah Logan, even from within the GOP.

Chapter 8

"Those who stand for nothing fall for anything."

~ Alexander Hamilton

Fox News showed Johnson, the first family and their entourage leaving the stage after thunderous applause. Thousands of flash bulbs created a strobe effect as people left the stage, most stopping long enough to give the president and first lady handshakes, greetings and hugs.

Finally, First Lady Maggie Johnson and Lily Doolittle left the stage. Sharply dressed Secret Service agents helped them down the steep temporary metal stairs. There was only enough room for two people to descend at a time and, as President Johnson started down last, a Secret Service agent extended his hand to steady the president.

Suddenly, another flash, slightly different somehow, lit the black-curtained square where the entourage awaited the president and his party. A loud crack rang out, but was only audible for a second. Anyone more than ten feet from the curtained area couldn't hear it over the noise of the crowd.

A moment of confusion ensued in the staging area as two more flashes came and went in an instant. Then Secret Service agents, handlers and members of the entourage swirled in chaos. The crowd shrunk back.

The cameras near the stage shook and lost the picture for a few seconds. As the picture came back into focus, viewers saw police, Secret Service and unidentified men in suits, guns drawn, push spectators to the ground. The mass of humanity scrambled away from the area to avoid getting trampled. It was obvious something had happened, but the media could only say that the president and the first family had been rushed past the black-curtained area and out of sight.

Most of the networks continued their election coverage, switching from the site of the acceptance speech to their pundits in studio. Then cameras zeroed in on Senior Political Analyst Quentin Reynolds, the Fox anchor for election night coverage.

"I have been told by reliable sources that an assassination attempt has just been made on President Johnson," Reynolds said solemnly. "We have not been told if the president is injured, but police are reportedly clearing traffic to Children's Memorial Hospital, which is about two and a half miles from Lincoln Park. I repeat, we do not know if the president or any of his family was injured."

NBC was the first to report definitive news of the situation on the ground. Nightly News Anchor Jonathon Alcott reported, "President Johnson has been wounded by an assailant. He has been taken into surgery immediately at Children's Memorial Hospital. No one else from the first family was injured; however, we have an unconfirmed report that a Secret Service agent has been killed, along with the would-be assassin, who was killed by Secret Service agents in the president's body guard."

As the news swept across the nation and the world, the celebrations that had produced isolated cases of minor looting, fires and violence turned into massive demonstrations fueled by rage. Unsubstantiated news reports circulated that a white Tea Party member had shot the president, one of his daughters, or both. The news blackout for the next several hours only heightened the speculation and exponentially increased the drama unfolding in American urban areas.

In Chicago, Cleveland, Detroit, New York, Trenton, Atlanta, St. Louis, Los Angeles, San Francisco and Seattle, roving bands of blacks and others unhappy with the unexpected turn of events ransacked their own neighborhoods, then flooded into upscale business districts and began destroying, burning and looting businesses. Local authorities encouraged people to stay home. TV news coverage showed dramatic footage of burning businesses and houses that made the Watts riots of 1965 and the Los Angeles South Central riot of 1992 look like block parties.

Original plans called for President Johnson to attend various post-election parties held by influential donors throughout Chicago after the Lincoln Park appearance. Many news cameras and reporting teams were broadcasting from those sites as they anticipated the arrival of the newly re-elected president and his party. As word of the tragedy spread, video images of supporters collapsing in tears were shown, reminding many of the JFK assassination news reports.

At 1:46 a.m., it seemed the entire throng of supporters from Lincoln Park had migrated to the two-block area around the hospital. Many in the crowd, assuming the president was dead, mourned, wept and wailed. Some in the crowd began assaulting white Johnson supporters after hearing the unsubstantiated reports that a white Tea Party member had shot the president and one of the Johnson children.

Nation of Islam's Lewis Khoury, Rev. Russell Jones, Rev. Homer Baxter and Rev. Lloyd Dobbin were interviewed by numerous media outlets. Instead of trying to stem the tide of violence, innuendos, conspiracy theories and assumptions poured forth from these black leaders. It was obvious to them that this assault on President Johnson was to keep the first African-American president from serving a second term.

Unsubstantiated Internet reports, tweets on Twitter, and Facebook messages claimed the president had been assassinated. Violence in major urban areas increased with every new report. Many Northeast, Rust Belt and West Coast cities were on fire.

City and state officials across the country began activating emergency protocol to quell the violence. Governor Carey Chambers in

New Jersey called out the National Guard and dispatched thousands of troops to Trenton and Newark. Los Angeles and San Francisco appeared completely unable to deal with the massive riots as thousands poured into the streets within an hour of the assassination attempt.

City and state officials were caught in a Catch-22 position. If they begged the administration to make an announcement, and the announcement was of the death of President Johnson, violence would reach unprecedented heights. The administration was not prepared to make any statement, other than stating that the president was in surgery from a gunshot wound and that no member of his family had been injured.

As the drama unfolded into the early morning hours at Children's Memorial Hospital, the situation on the ground escalated. The anarchy in the streets of dozens of major U.S. cities grew in intensity and began spreading to others areas of the country.

In Dallas, several thousand black protestors converged on the swank West End retail, restaurant and entertainment district downtown, destroying shops and restaurants and starting fires in buildings and vehicles. Police were finally able to quell the riot, but three black youths were killed, along with two Dallas police officers. The mayor locked down the entire downtown district, essentially establishing martial law. No one was allowed in or out of the area.

The scene in Dallas was replicated in most major cities, but on a much larger scale. Texas and Arizona, as well as most major urban areas in the South—with the exception of Miami and Atlanta—did not encounter the mass destruction and violence burning out of control in other areas of the country.

In some Western states—where the polls had closed but election results were not final—numerous polling places were attacked and destroyed. California had been officially called for Johnson at 11:26 p.m. by all major news outlets with only 8 percent of precincts reporting, but with Johnson holding a 58-36 percent lead. California's electoral votes were a formality as it became obvious early on that

Johnson had enough electoral votes, even without California.

At 3:52 a.m. in Chicago, most Americans still did not know with any certainty the status of their president or the exact events that had occurred at 11:58 p.m. As each minute passed, most assumed the worst. Even in locations where no violence was reported, local officials called in all off-duty police, firefighters and emergency workers and activated SWAT and National Guard troops.

Meanwhile, all media outlets complained about the lack of information coming from the administration. The delay meant more violence pouring out into the streets of the nation. America still did not know for sure if their president was dead or alive.

Chapter 9

"Our government teaches the whole people by its example. If the government becomes the lawbreaker, it breeds contempt for law; it invites every man to become a law unto himself; it invites anarchy."

~ U.S. Supreme Court Justice Louis D. Brandeis (1856-1941)

Press Secretary Ted Duncan entered the emergency room at Children's Memorial Hospital within ten minutes of the motorcade's arrival. Bedlam reigned in the emergency room and adjoining waiting room, with Secret Service, police and various administration officials running everywhere but nowhere.

Duncan found Chief of Staff Cliff Radford in the hallway with former White House chief of staff and current Chicago Mayor Davian Kyler, U.S. Attorney General Jamail Tibbs, and Democratic strategist Avery Smith. Duncan prepared for the worst as he approached the small group.

"Okay, how bad is it?" he asked.

"He's alive," Radford said flatly. "He was shot point blank just above the heart in the shoulder region. Early news is no vitals were hit, but he's lost a lot of blood."

"Federal Judge Manning is in the adjoining waiting room with Vice President Doolittle just in case," Kyler interjected.

"Just in case?" Duncan looked puzzled.

"We sent for her as soon as the president was brought in so she could swear in Doolittle if necessary, just like JFK and LBJ," Radford explained.

Just then, operating doctor John Fagan arrived with two other surgeons. Tibbs asked if the group could be taken to a private area, and Vice President Doolittle, Secret Service, FBI, and several administration and campaign staff were ushered into a conference room.

The doctors waited for the large group to get settled before telling them that, despite a huge loss of blood, the president was alive and responding. Dr. Fagan stated that Johnson had been shot with a .45 caliber handgun at point-blank range; the bullet entered about four inches above the heart in an upward trajectory and exited in back of the left shoulder after breaking his collarbone and left scapula. The bullet, which had been recovered, had missed his aorta by less than two inches.

One of the other doctors continued. "The president was apparently shot as he came down the steps from the stage. His assailant was standing below him, shooting upward, which explains the trajectory. A total of three shots were fired, but only one hit the president."

"He's very lucky. If he had taken one more step down before being shot, it would have been a very different outcome," stated Dr. Fagan quietly.

After a few more questions for the doctors, administration officials asked the doctors to leave. Tibbs also directed Duncan to leave.

Duncan was irate and indignant. "Why can Kyler and these others stay?"

Tibbs looked grim. "Ted, you may need plausible deniability until we have all the facts. Bear with me. You'll be thoroughly briefed, I promise. Ted," he yelled to Duncan as he left, "tell the judge she can go home, but have the FBI speak to her first. She can't say anything to anybody!"

Duncan stormed out of the room.

Tibbs began to question the Secret Service and FBI agents. "Did we lose an agent?" he asked.

"Yes, we lost Agent Randy Miller," said Agent Patterson. Patterson was in his early fifties, with silver hair and the typical rock-solid Secret Service aura. "He was protecting the president and took the second shot from the shooter while getting two rounds off at same time. They were both DOA at the hospital."

"What do we know about the shooter?"

"He had no ID," Patterson said. "We're running checks on the guy."

"Black, white or what?" asked Tibbs.

"Arab or Middle Eastern probably," Patterson told him.

"DAMN!" yelled Tibbs and Kyler, almost in unison.

"Has that been broadcast in the media yet?" Smith demanded.

"Nothing's gone out yet, sir," Patterson said, "nothing."

"Get Duncan back in here," Tibbs ordered.

When Duncan returned, he was obviously delighted to be back in the "circle of trust" until Tibbs explained they still couldn't disclose anything to him. "The press will be in a feeding frenzy when you get out there, and it's best if you can just say you don't know any details at this point."

"Okay," Duncan said, somewhat dubiously.

"Ted, I need you to find out what the press knows. What are eye-witnesses saying about the shooter, any details you can find," ordered Tibbs.

Duncan looked confused, "Are you serious?" He saw Tibbs' face. "Okay, I'll see what I can find out."

After Duncan left, Agent Patterson told the small group the shooting happened in the holding area where the dignitaries exited the stage.

"Let's hope there's no public video of this," Tibbs said.

Maggie Johnson had been at or near the president's side since he arrived at the hospital. The Johnson daughters were close by in a private area.

The door remained closed for two hours, although updates were provided every thirty minutes on the president's condition. Tibbs, cabinet members and other staff were frequently interrupted with up-to-the-minute reports on the rioting and destruction occurring around the country.

At 6:23 a.m., Radford instructed Duncan to issue his first official statement to the press, despite the fact the president was shot before midnight and was out of surgery before 3:30 a.m.

Tibbs, Radford and Smith proofed the release before Duncan left the emergency room area.

"Eliminate this section." Tibbs pointed to a section that had been inserted asking the crowds to stop the rioting and destruction of property.

Duncan glared at Tibbs in stunned amazement. He acted like he might refuse, then he nodded and marked through several sentences.

He handed the paper to Tibbs. "Does this work?" he asked.

Tibbs scanned the sheet and showed it to the others.

"Yes, that'll do," he told Duncan.

Duncan exited the hospital at 6:45 and walked to the parking lot where a makeshift podium was set up. Dozens of microphones were draped over the stand, and hundreds of reporters and news anchors crowded close to hear what the press secretary had to say. The press was eerily silent, as if expecting the worst news since JFK was assassinated.

Duncan stepped to the podium, his classic black-rimmed glasses and nerdy persona looking tired and sleep-deprived as he read from a written statement. "On November 6, a night the entire nation was celebrating the historic re-election of President Johnson, our first African-American president, an assassination attempt was made on his life. No other members of the president's family were injured.

"Despite a heroic attempt by the Secret Service, President Johnson was shot once in the shoulder. He is alive and responding well. Doctors expect a full recovery. Unfortunately, in defense of the president, a Secret Service agent lost his life, but fatally wounded the would-be assassin." Duncan glanced at the crowd. "The president went through a short surgery to repair his wound and received a blood transfusion. While the president was in surgery, the United States government was fully functional and many of his cabinet members, including Attorney General Tibbs, Treasury Secretary Benjamin Gould and Vice President Bert Doolittle were at his side and remained at the hospital through the night. I want to assure the American people that the United States government was and is fully functional," he repeated.

"The FBI is in charge of the investigation into the assassination attempt. Please understand that, at this juncture, we cannot release any information about the assassin or what connections he might have to any group or organization. Because the assassin was fatally wounded, the FBI will conduct its investigation through clues they continue to gather since last night.

"We ask everyone to pray for President Johnson and his family, as well as the family of the slain Secret Service agent whose name has not been released yet," Duncan said. "We will have more information as the day unfolds. God bless President Johnson and God bless the United States of America."

The press secretary folded his paper and turned away from the podium to return to the hospital. Police restrained reporters who had more questions.

Chapter 10

"The Los Angeles riots were not caused by the Rodney King verdict. The Los Angeles riots were caused by rioters."

~ *Rush Limbaugh*

Nick Perillo pulled his empty 18-wheeler into the truck stop near Kansas City on I-70 East. He was dead tired and decided to stop for the night after the election was called for President Johnson near 11 p.m. central time He would get some much needed rest by sleeping in his rig's cabin.

He slept through the events that occurred in Lincoln Park and the ensuing chaos that enveloped the country during the night. At fifty-six, he was no longer the road warrior he was in his thirties, driving non-stop sometimes for forty-eight hours. Now he needed his eight hours every night.

He was driving home at a loss. The high diesel prices and lagging economy had taken its toll on the Perillo family finances. It had been the worst five years of his career financially. After leaving the Teamsters to start his own trucking company, he had built up his company to twelve rigs; recently, all but two had been repossessed. There simply were not enough loads or profit to sustain the notes on the rigs and payroll for the drivers.

Nick kept his drivers paid as long as possible but, in doing so, he got behind on his payroll taxes. Adding to his financial woes, he was being hassled by the IRS for over $60,000 in taxes they claimed he owed, plus interest and penalties. He was hoping a Johnson defeat would signal some type of impetus to change the tax code, and rid the country of the IRS once and for all.

The morning after the election, Nick poured himself a cup of coffee from his Thermos bottle, then drove the forty-five foot rig out of the truck stop parking lot onto the ramp to I-70 East. He tuned his satellite radio to one of his favorite talk show stations.

As he merged into traffic, and before he could get settled into the news and his coffee mug, his cell phone began to ring.

"Nick, are you okay? Where are you?" It was Caroline.

"I'm just getting back on the road, Caroline. I'm just east of Kansas City and I'll be home later this afternoon. How are you?" he asked.

"Honey, have you heard what's going on? I've been trying to call you all night!" She sounded panicked.

"Yeah, I know. We're stuck with Johnson again."

"No, no, Nick. Did you hear about Johnson being shot and then all the riots?"

"Shot?" Nick was stunned. "Johnson was killed? Are you serious? When?"

"No, he's alive. He wasn't assassinated, just wounded, but there are riots all over the country!" Caroline said.

"Wow!"

"Baby, you can't go through St. Louis. St. Louis is one of the worst. The National Guard has closed the downtown area. Roving gangs are destroying businesses and cars, and shooting randomly at people! You have to take another route."

"Okay... wow. Let me make some calls. I'll go around St. Louis. What's going on at home? Is everything okay there?" he asked.

"Yes, we're all fine for now. What should I do, Nick?"

Nick knew how fortunate he was to live in a small community on a few acres, but remembered the talk at Thanksgiving last year and on the Fourth of July with family members who predicted an Armageddon-type event, but not this kind of scenario.

Instead, it seemed his cousins in the banking industry were more concerned with a serious devaluation of the dollar and the chaos that could cause. He hadn't taken them seriously, but he and Caroline had made some half-hearted attempts to have a "plan."

"Caroline, call the kids. Have them get to the house NOW until this blows over. Jim and Donna can't go to work in St. Louis today. Call them NOW!" Nick yelled into the phone, holding it away from his ear and talking into it like it was a walkie-talkie or his CB radio.

"The local news said the bridges into downtown from the Illinois side are shut down. Apparently there were gangs coming over them from East St. Louis." Caroline now sounded like the calm one.

"Go to the store right now. Stock up on everything. I mean everything!"

"Nick, you're scaring me!" Caroline said, her calm demeanor starting to slip back into panic. "The last time I was this scared was the day Kennedy was shot. It wasn't the assassination; it was the fear I sensed from my parents and the older kids, grandparents, and other relatives. Nick, I was only six, and I still can't forget it." Her voice shook.

"I'm sorry. Honey, this will probably settle down soon. But let's not take any chances. Call me after you go to the store, okay?"

They agreed to check in often during the day to make sure Nick was traveling safely and for him to know the chaos in St. Louis hadn't spread to Lebanon.

He ended the call and immediately dialed his two brothers. While he was on the call with them, he reached behind the console and pulled out his Desert Eagle .45 caliber handgun. Keeping one hand on the steering wheel, he effortlessly inserted a clip into the gun and cocked it, chambering a round. He then set it next to his seat for easy access—just in case.

He decided to take Loop I-270 north of St. Louis to avoid going through or near the downtown area. He'd been listening to the satellite news reports, switching channels to hear updates and alternating listening to his CB radio about the scenes and experiences fellow truck drivers were seeing all over the country.

As he neared the I-70 interchange with I-270, traffic slowed to a crawl. Traffic coming westbound on I-70 from downtown St. Louis was heavy, even heavier than late afternoon rush hour traffic. As Nick slowed his truck, he noticed an unusual amount of cars and SUVs had luggage carriers and seemed to be loaded and packed similar to what someone might see in advance of holiday weekends.

He made his way onto I-270 headed east. As he glanced toward the downtown area, he couldn't believe what he saw. It appeared the entire downtown area of St. Louis was on fire. Heavy dark smoke billowed up, then settled over the city like an ominous fog.

Traffic slowed again to a crawl as Nick's rig approached the Chain of Rocks Bridge over the Mississippi River. Only one lane was open going east because a car was turned upside down and burning. How in the world had that happened? Interestingly, there were no police cars or emergency vehicles on the bridge. Nick couldn't see if anyone was in the vehicle, but nobody was stopping.

As the chatter on his CB radio increased, he heard that the scene downtown was so dire that all police, SWAT, fire and emergency services were deployed in that area. There was no one to respond to this scene. According to the radio, the vehicle had been attacked and overturned, though no one seemed to know who the attackers were.

Before Nick reached the end of the bridge, his cell phone rang. He pressed the "talk" button.

"Where are you?" Caroline asked.

"I'm just coming off the 270 bridge. Where are you?"

"I just left the store." She sounded defeated. "Nick, there was nothing left on the shelves."

"Are you serious?"

"I'm trying another store, but the scene in those stores is crazy."

"Where are the kids?"

"They're are on their way to the house."

"St. Louis is on fire," Nick told her.

"I know," Caroline told him. "I've been watching the news. That's happening everywhere."

"How much food do we have?" Nick asked. "How long do you think it will last?"

"We probably have enough food for a week, maybe two."

"After you get done with the store, make sure you go to a gas station and fill up. But, honey, be very careful. There's a pistol in the glove compartment. Make sure you can get to it and go ahead and load it. There's a clip next to it."

"Okay." She sounded scared, but he also detected strength in her voice.

"Tell the kids to fill their cars as well, and take all the gas cans and fill those, too. I don't know what we're in for but, with all these riots, you can be sure it will impact food and gas delivery. We don't want to be out of either."

"What do I do if there's no food at the next store?" Caroline asked.

"We may have to drive out to rural area stores," Nick said. "I should be home within an hour depending on traffic. Don't worry about food, but make sure you get gas. It's very important."

"I will as soon as I leave the store."

"Okay, keep your phone on and with you. Be very careful. If you see anything that doesn't look right, drive right by it and go home."

"Nick, I'm scared."

"I know, Caroline, and this could get worse before it gets better," Nick warned. "I wish we'd listened to others about stocking up on food."

"Nick, please, just get home. I'll feel better."

"I know. Be safe, Caroline," he said.

"You, too, my love."

Nick ended the call and tuned back to satellite radio to catch up on news reports about the continuing chaos in urban areas all around the country. The violence seemed to ebb and flow with no real logic.

Chapter 11

"As soon as liberty is complete it dies in anarchy."

~ *Will Durant, American Author, 1835*

Nick guided his rig south on I-255 to I-64 in Illinois about fifteen miles from downtown St. Louis. This interchange was only a few miles from East St. Louis, the origin of the gangs coming across the Mississippi River into downtown St. Louis.

As he exited to make the cloverleaf onto I-64 east, he noticed a pickup truck coming up on his left, half on the road and half off, headlights flashing. It looked like people were hanging on to the sides of the pickup bed.

He slowed down and, for a brief moment, the events of the day left his mind as he wondered what emergency would cause a driver to get to his left on the cloverleaf.

As the pickup truck pulled even with Nick's cab, he pulled to the right to allow room for it to pass him, even though the cloverleaf lane was meant for only one vehicle at a time.

"What kind of idiots are you people?" he muttered.

When the pickup got even and pulled all the way up onto the pavement, Nick looked over. In an instant, he snapped back to the reality of the situation.

The truck was full of angry blacks. Several were brandishing handguns and the rest had sticks, pipes and knives. Suddenly, two of the occupants in the back of the pickup began firing shots at the cab and the front left tire.

"Goddamit!" Nick exploded, anger and fear forcing the expletive from him.

A round shattered the driver's side window and continued its path to hit the front windshield. The impact-resistant glass spider-webbed, making visibility virtually impossible. Nick had no choice but to slow down even more. He would have to stop.

He guided the rig as far to the right as possible, keeping his head low and beneath the line of sight of the truck's occupants. More shots rang out and two rounds came through the door.

Nick had only an instant to make what was possibly the most important decision of his life. Should he keep the rig rolling, leaving him a sitting duck for the point-blank pot shots coming at him, or should he pull over and get out of the cab or retreat to the sleeper section of the cab?

He decided that, if he stopped, he was dead. The left front tire was almost flat, but he kept the rig rolling forward. He reached over and picked up the heavy Desert Eagle .45 caliber and put it on his lap.

More shots rang out just then, and he felt a sudden burning sensation in his left thigh. "Damn, I've been shot!" he yelled.

Another round of shots penetrated the truck door and one entered the same thigh about eight inches above the knee. He looked down and saw blood spurting from his leg. That was all he had time to think about other than driving. He was barely able to keep the rig rolling. He was pretty sure the left wheel was shredded; the sound of tread being hurled against the fenders was unmistakable.

His sense of survival turned into rage. He picked up the .45, one hand on the wheel and right foot firmly planted on the gas pedal. Keeping his head down, he stuck the gun through the blown-out driver's window and began shooting.

He fired off four rounds of the eight available to him in the clip, thinking he should save a few. It was the only clip he had. He would never have imagined any scenario where he would need all eight rounds.

As he shot out the window, he had no idea how close to the rig his attackers were. Even though his rig and the pickup were prob-ably going less than fifteen miles per hour, the shots were enough to cause the driver of the pickup to temporarily lose control. The pickup veered hard right. When the driver attempted to regain con-trol by hitting his brakes, the vehicle got hooked on the 18-wheeler's bumper right in front of the left rim that had nothing but rubber threads attached. The pickup slammed to a stop.

Three of the occupants of the pickup bed were thrown forward. One hit the pavement and rolled like a rag doll, finally stopping, life-less. The other two were catapulted forward over the pickup's cab into the grass along the pavement.

Nick's rig lurched forward. He had it in low gear under full pow-er. The rig tried to climb up on the pickup and the big truck pushed the smaller vehicle along the pavement with the left front wheel partly up on the bent frame of the pickup. Sparks began to fly, but Nick didn't relent.

The occupants of the pickup began unloading their guns into the cab, the radiator and the shattered windshield.

"What the hell is wrong with you people!" Nick yelled.

The unfolding drama happened so fast that Nick had no time to get on his radio or cell phone. He tried to keep the truck moving forward.

Just then, the rig's engine sputtered as steam from the punctured radiator poured out from under the hood. The big truck crawled to a halt. For a brief moment, it was quiet except for the hiss of steam spewing out from under the hood. Nick stayed down and wondered if his attackers had moved on.

No such luck. Two more shots hit the cab, coming through the windshield up into the roof. Nick grabbed his gun and retreated to the sleeper cab, crawling in between the seats. As he looked at his leg, he was shocked at how much blood was still spurting from it. It was puddled on the seat, the floor board, and in the area he'd just passed through to get to the sleeper.

He spotted his cell phone sitting on his console next to the gear shift. He knew he needed to get to it or the mic on his CB radio. As he leaned forward to reach for the cell phone, the driver's door was yanked open.

"Awwwww!" Nick screamed as he pulled trigger as fast as he could until he had just one round left.

A figure started to climb into the cab. Nick fired the one round left in his clip. The attacker collapsed limply.

Suddenly, the passenger window shattered. Nick crawled back into the corner farthest away from the door. Two attackers stuck their guns in through the window and began unloading their clips, shooting everywhere and every direction in the cab.

Three rounds caught Nick from the flurry of shots fired through the window. Two hit him in the chest; one hit his left biceps. Nick's thoughts instantly went to his family.

"Oh, God..." he breathed as he died alone and without help.

During this entire event, cars and trucks passed by but no one stopped. Calls to 911 were recorded, but dispatch for all local authorities were swamped. Nobody responded to the I-64/I-255 interchange for hours. Cars had to go around the two bodies on the pavement—the catapulted man from the pickup bed and the other the attacker Nick took out with his Desert Eagle.

One of the attackers climbed into the cab. He grabbed Nick's wallet and anything not bolted down. He emptied Nick's pillow case and threw his loot into it. He passed the keys to two other men waiting outside the cab, and they ran to the back of the rig to figure out which keys opened the trailer. When the attackers finally figured out which key opened the lock on the trailer, they used it to unlock the double doors. As the doors swung open, the six remaining attackers stared into an empty truck.

The next unlucky traveler that exited through the clover leaf was stopped at gun point, shot in the head execution-style, and his vehicle car-jacked.

As the attackers fled with Nick's possessions, Nick's phone began to ring. It was Caroline checking on his whereabouts, and to let him know they would need to go out to rural areas to shop for food.

Chapter 12

"The despair is there; now it's up to us to go in and rub raw the sores of discontent, galvanize them for radical social change."

~ Saul Alinsky, Radical Leftist Community Organizer

The day after the election and assassination attempt, the nation was completely polarized. Democratic leaders House Minority Leader Margaret Drummond, U.S. Congresswoman Eileen Burton-Ames, U.S. Senator Alicia Drew, Senate Majority Leader Duane Rafferty and many others saw their opportunity to tee off on the GOP, the Tea Party, white supremacists and the Second Amendment, preferably in the same breath but not necessarily in the same order.

Mayors, local politicians and black leaders in the cities hardest hit by the rioting pleaded with citizens to come together for a vigil for President Johnson's recovery. The mainstream media broadcasted the pleas for calm and promoted the vigils that were to begin less than twenty-four hours after the assassination attempt.

Attorney General Jamail Tibbs announced a news conference for 5:30 p.m. EST. The news outlets were given details on the would-be assassin that were sketchy at best, but the news conference was scheduled to bring the nation up to speed on the investigation.

Meanwhile, Tibbs' top aide scheduled an internal briefing for noon with only the top members of President Johnson's cabinet, Vice President Doolittle, the FBI, NSA and the CIA. Several administration officials cringed at the thought of Vice President Doolittle at such a high-level and secure meeting. He was known to have frequent episodes of repeating classified information and making faux pas on sensitive subjects. No member of the Joint Chiefs was invited.

Tibbs and Cliff Radford met privately before the noon meeting. "What do we know so far?" Radford asked.

"First of all, just so you know, I have ordered the FBI to be in charge of the investigation. The Secret Service, CIA and NSA will need to stand down for now," said Tibbs.

"That could cause some issues with those other agencies," Radford said.

"This investigation will stand on my orders and my orders alone. Now is not the time to be timid," Tibbs responded forcefully. "This is one hell of a scenario and a real opportunity for the president to advance his ideas. We just need to do some damage control and manage the crisis until he can recover enough to provide input and direction. I'm sure he will agree with me on this."

"Okay, so how do we respond to Congress? They'll want their own intelligence briefing on the situation."

"We'll keep our team updated. Screw the rest for now," Tibbs said sharply.

Tibbs left the meeting with Radford for another private meeting with Secret Service Agency Chief Matt Breckenridge, who had arrived in Chicago on a military aircraft within hours of the assassination attempt, along with the four Secret Service agents who were at Lincoln Park with the president. The attendance of the agents was no accident. They had proven to be very loyal to President Johnson and his administration. Also, although the Secret Service no longer reported to the Treasury Department, Treasury Secretary Gould was invited to the meeting but was instructed to leave any staff members behind.

To ensure ultimate security, Tibbs scheduled the second meeting to take place aboard Air Force One, which was parked at Chicago's Midway Airport.

"I want all personnel removed from the plane before the meeting," Tibbs ordered one of his aides, "and I want all electronic recording devices disabled."

"Yes, sir," the aide said.

When everyone was assembled in the plane's conference area, Tibbs moved to the head of the table. "Gentlemen, first let me state that this meeting is probably the highest national security event since the planning of D-Day. Under no circumstances will any information discussed here be disseminated in any written or verbal form, innuendo or opinion to anyone outside this room or to your staff. Any violation of this confidence will be considered the highest form of treason and my office will prosecute you to the fullest extent of the law. Is that completely and clearly understood?" Tibbs fixed the group with a glare that left no doubt in anyone's mind that he would do exactly what he promised. A chorus of "Yes, sir" sounded in the room.

"Thank you," Tibbs said. "Agent Patterson, what do you have so far?"

"Sir, the assassin's name is Rashid Safly-Allah. He is twenty-six and is from Dallas, Texas. He is the son of Iranian-born parents. His parents emigrated here after the Shah was deposed and received political asylum. Both parents are now deceased," Patterson told the group.

"Shit! He's Muslim?" asked Gould.

"Yes." Agent Patterson continued, "He has no living relatives we can identify, at least in the U.S. He had one sister, but she returned to Iran with her husband almost ten years ago."

"So are there ties to Al-Qaeda?" asked Tibbs. "The Taliban? Hamas?"

"We secured Safly-Allah's apartment in Dallas within two hours of the assassination attempt. As of now, the contents of his entire apartment, including furniture, clothes, computer, etc., were loaded into a pod by 0700 hours and are currently secure in a special hangar at Andrews Air Force Base. Special Forces are stationed at the hangar for security."

"Fine, but what do we know other than these details so far?"

"Well, sir, he was working on his Master's at SMU in Dallas," said

Patterson, reading from his iPad. "When we researched his emails, it was obvious that he was extremely dismayed and upset regarding Operation Python. His emails to other Muslim students and his entries on blogs are very clear. His sister and her family were killed in the assault on Natanz. We suspect that's what sent him over the edge. If he has ties to anyone outside the U.S. or any organized domestic terror cells, we have yet to find any during our preliminary investigation."

"How much does the FBI know at this point?" asked Tibbs.

"We have run the names connected to Safly-Allah through the FBI and CIA as separate actions. We don't think they've figured out the connection, at least not yet. All his contacts are from the Dallas area. If this guy was connected to any terrorist groups, we haven't found that connection yet," stated Patterson.

"You're not giving me a lot," Tibbs said.

Agent Patterson paused, then looked at Agent Clint Thomas. "Agent Thomas, please share what you have."

Agent Thomas, a thin, wiry man with a professional demeanor, stepped forward. "Sir, I have a document you will want to review." He pulled a document from his briefcase, handling it like it contained secret codes to a nuclear arsenal.

"Rashid Safly-Allah was a political science MBA student. He had completed a Master's thesis." Agent Thomas handed the document to Tibbs.

Tibbs read the title out loud. "Prejudice in the Tea Party Movement: Is there a Political Plank against Muslims?"

Agent Patterson leaned forward in his chair, drawing the rest of the meeting attendees with him. As he was about to speak, Gould interrupted.

"So, he was writing about how the Tea Party hates Muslims. So what? Why is that important?" Gould asked abruptly.

Agent Thomas took a deep breath. "Well, sir, the title is a little misleading. I read the thesis before you arrived. In the course of his research, Safly-Allah attended more than a dozen Tea Party events and even joined several Tea Party groups. His conclusions in the document end up being pro-Tea Party. He doesn't find rampant Muslim intolerance or prejudice to Muslims on a large scale in the Tea Party, according to his paper. And even better news is that his thesis has not been turned in to his professor."

Gould was the first one to have the pieces fall into place. "Holy shit!"

Tibbs, on the other hand, hadn't quite grasped the totality of the agent's statement. When it finally did, the puzzlement that contorted his face disappeared.

"Gentlemen, the assassination of President Johnson was attempted by a Tea Party member and sympathizer!" he beamed.

The Secret Service agents smiled broadly, waiting for the expected accolades for the extreme good fortune they'd laid at President Johnson's feet.

"But he's still a Muslim." Tibbs' frown reappeared. "That's a problem."

Agent Thomas said, "Well, he wasn't a practicing Muslim. He did not attend a local mosque for over three years; apparently he didn't like the local imam. Also, he was known as "Rash Sally" by his friends. His emails even used that name. That name really doesn't sound Muslim. Here are some photos." Agent Thomas handed a stack of photos to Tibbs and the others.

"He doesn't look Iranian or Arab," Radford said.

"Many Iranians are light-skinned and are technically considered Caucasians," added Agent Patterson.

"As unfortunate as the wounding of the president is, I can't imagine a better gift for him when he heals." By this time, Tibbs was beyond delighted. He turned to Breckenridge. "I want ANY close associates of this guy completely locked down. That means I want them out of contact with the public until we can control them and the media firestorm. Understood?"

"Okay, done," Breckenridge said.

Tibbs turned to the Secret Service agents. "You gentlemen have done an outstanding job. The president will be proud to call you his friends and protectors."

Agent Patterson tilted his head down. "Well, sir, this guy got to him on our watch. We owe him."

"Agent, one of yours lost his life in defense of the president. Nothing more needs to be said. The results of this investigation are outstanding, and the president will be ecstatic," Tibbs said.

He turned to the agents. "Gentlemen, you're dismissed, and remember, nothing said in this room today is to be repeated anywhere. Is that perfectly clear?"

"Yes, sir," they answered.

Tibbs waited until the agents left the room, closed the door tightly behind them, then sat down again. "And the rest of us are going to sit here and craft a statement for today's news conference."

It took a while to pull everything together. When they were all satisfied the statement said what it needed to and nothing else, Tibbs adjourned the meeting.

Chapter 13

"A system of licensing and registration is the perfect device to deny gun ownership to the bourgeoisie."

~*Vladimir Lenin*

The cafeteria of Children's Memorial Hospital was jam-packed with reporters, administration officials, police and Secret Service agents, as well as uniformed Marines.

United States Attorney General Tibbs threaded through the throng of people from behind the podium, coming through the kitchen area. He was flanked by Vice President Doolittle, Treasury Secretary Benjamin Gould, Democratic strategist Avery Smith, Chicago Mayor Davian Kyler and others. First Lady Maggie Johnson was expected to appear later.

"Ladies and gentlemen, I am happy to report to you that the president is steadily improving. We will not take any questions at this time; however, I would like to bring up Dr. Fagan."

Dr. Fagan approached the podium in green scrubs, his uncombed salt-and-pepper hair noticeably disheveled. He wore small round bi-focal glasses over weary blue eyes. "President Johnson is still in the Intensive Care Unit," Dr. Fagan said in a tired monotone. "The surgery to repair internal injuries was successful. We are officially listing him in "fair" condition; however, I would like to stress that we believe he's in no imminent danger from his wound. We have completely stabilized him, his vitals are fine and he is improving hourly. He is cognizant, alert and fully aware of his surroundings. He's still a little confused as to exactly what happened but, when he's awake, he's responsive.

"We do not anticipate the need for additional surgery, and we expect him to recover fully. Regarding his recovery period, there are too many factors to estimate that at this time, but let me repeat that the president is improving noticeably on an hour-by-hour basis." The doctor stepped away from the podium.

Tibbs strode to the podium, appearing in a freshly pressed suit and with a concerned scowl on his forehead.

"First and foremost, I would like to recognize brave Secret Service Agent Randy Miller, who bravely gave his life defending the president while also fatally wounding the would-be assassin. The condolences of an entire grateful nation go out to him and his family." Tibbs paused, almost as if to cry with each syllable.

"Several agencies of the federal government are involved in this investigation, including Justice, FBI, Secret Service, CIA, NSA and Homeland Security. These departments have been working in concert since this tragedy occurred."

Tibbs looked up at the crowd, then refocused on his notes. He knew the questions the entire nation wanted answered. Who was this would-be assassin. Was he a terrorist? Was he a white supremacist? Was he a lone wolf, or was there a greater conspiracy? Across the country, people who were still working stopped and gathered in front of televisions and streaming video on their computers. Times Square was broadcasting the news briefing live.

"At this time, the investigation is continuing. We are still in the process of locating the assassin's next of kin and conducting a thorough investigation. We are not prepared to identify the perpetrator to the public until our investigation is complete."

Tibbs continued from prepared notes. "What I can say at this point is that we have not linked the assassination attempt to any terror threat or international terrorist organization at this time, nor have we seen any early evidence of a conspiracy to commit this crime by organizations outside the United States. However, we do know the perpetrator was in his mid-twenties. *He was also a member of several Tea*

Party groups and was a Tea Party supporter." Tibbs said the last sentence emphatically.

At that juncture, the cafeteria erupted. Reporters literally charged out of the cafeteria with the news. Reporters attempting to advance past a rope providing a boundary for the media were held back by Marines.

Tibbs continued to try to speak, but the noise from flash bulbs, questions and shouts from the audience made the press conference impossible to continue. Tibbs folded up his prepared statements, slid them into his pocket and walked away. It was not completely clear to viewers if he was finished, but the news he'd delivered was huge.

The media feeding frenzy was on. Every news organization on TV flashed the report: **Tea Party member shot the president.**

Democrats of every shape, color, gender and geographic location began the onslaught on the GOP and the Tea Party, repeating the mantra that the "extreme right" had taken over the party. The GOP leadership was in a tailspin. Not only had they lost the main event—the presidential election and control of both houses of Congress—apparently one of their own had shot the president, and nobody could deny the possible racial implications.

Old-school Republican leaders throughout the country who had been defined by Tea Party groups as RINOs (Republicans in Name Only) took to the media to pile on those who had labeled them as part of the establishment. Members of established Tea Party organizations hunkered down, trying to understand how one of them could be involved in the attempted assassination of the president.

The Black Panthers and other organizations, emboldened by the lack of action regarding threats made against whites in various venues, including a rant on their own radio station, warned Tea Party members about violent reprisals.

Many experts were already predicting the end of the Republican Party. How could the party survive this?

Congressional Tea Party caucus members and their staffs were warned by capitol police to lay low and not attend to their daily duties at the nation's capitol building.

No national figures called for calm, and none suggested perhaps it would be best to wait until all the facts came out to react.

The United States of America was on the verge of a rolling boil.

Chapter 14

"If you tell a big enough lie and tell it frequently enough, it will be believed."

~ Adolf Hitler

There was no mistaking the air of tension in every public place, from restaurants, school events, airports, the workplace and even in church.

Chuck Dixon finished an important lunch meeting with some clients at his favorite Tex-Mex restaurant in downtown Houston. It had been a good meeting, and he was about to make the 25-mile journey back to his home in the suburbs to share the good news with Christy.

He'd parked his Ford pickup nose first against an older brick building at a parking lot two full city blocks from the restaurant. As he approached the lot, he saw a group of black youths next to his truck. Getting closer, he noticed they were beating the truck with tire irons and what appeared to be an ax handle without the metal head.

"Hey, what the hell are you doing to my truck?" Chuck yelled.

"Fuck you, Tea Party man! You tried to kill Johnson!" bellowed one of the four, waving the ax handle.

Confused at first, Chuck suddenly realized why they had scratched up the truck and broken the windows and tail lights. He had a pro-Tea Party bumper sticker on the sliding glass rear window with the Tea Party's adopted trademark, the yellow Gadsden Flag bearing the "Don't Tread On Me" legend.

"Get away from my truck!" he roared.

"Fuck you, Tea Party man! This is for Johnson!"

The largest of the men started running toward Chuck, holding the ax handle above his head. Another youth carrying a tire iron at his side ran to catch up with the big guy.

As they got within fifteen feet of Chuck, he reached behind him with his right hand and pulled a Smith & Wesson .38 from the leather holster concealed inside his belt loop. He'd gotten a concealed carry permit five years earlier. Now was the first time he'd ever pulled his weapon.

"You want some of this, Tea Party cracker?" the guy with the tire iron yelled.

"Stop right there or you're going to die today!" snapped Chuck.

The two young men stopped in their tracks, then threw the ax handle and tire iron at Chuck and ran. He kept his gun pointed at them until they vanished behind the old brick building.

As he lowered the weapon, Chuck noticed his hand was shaking. He didn't remember the gun shaking while it was pointed at the vandals.

He looked around to see if there were any witnesses. A nicely dressed woman with auburn hair appeared from behind a car two parking spots past where Chuck was standing.

"Ma'am, are you okay?" Chuck asked.

"Yes," she said, her voice trembling slightly. "I was getting my keys out of my purse to unlock my car when I saw them beating on that truck. I hid behind the cars so they wouldn't see me."

"That's good. They must not have seen you."

"I don't think they did. That was scary." She moved closer to him. "I've never seen anything like that. They were going to hurt you!" she said as tears rolled down her cheeks.

"I'm going to call the cops," Chuck said. "Do you mind being a witness?"

"No, not at all," she replied.

Chuck slowly sat down on a parking space curb. He was still shaking, but he managed to get his .38 back into the holster. After calling 9-1-1, Chuck called Christy.

When she answered, he said, "You won't believe what just happened." As he started to tell her about the damaged truck, Christy interrupted. "Chuck, I've told you I was worried about your bumper stickers! There are crazy people out there!"

"I know, I know. Geez, I never really thought those stickers were a problem. After yesterday, though, who knows?"

He was referring to the announcement the day before about the president's would-be assassin being a Tea Party member.

Just as he finished his call with Christy, a Houston police cruiser pulled up with lights on but no sirens. A black police officer and a Hispanic officer stepped out to speak to Chuck.

"Sir, do you have a weapon?" asked the Hispanic officer, keeping one hand on his own gun.

"Yes, I have a concealed handgun permit."

"Please identify where the weapon is and raise your hands."

"It's in my back belt loop in a holster," Chuck told him, raising his hands as ordered.

"Keep your hands up and turn around."

The black officer stepped behind Chuck and removed the handgun, then asked him to put his hands behind his back.

"Sir, I'm the one who called this in. That destroyed pickup over there is mine. Why are you cuffing me?"

"Until we sort this out, that's our procedure," the officer said curtly.

"My wallet is in my left rear pocket," Chuck told him. "It contains my driver's license and concealed handgun permit."

The officers frisked Chuck as two more squad cars pulled up. The black officer talked to the red-haired woman who witnessed the event while two other officers examined the truck. One picked up the thrown ax handle and tire iron.

"Mr. Dixon, did you feel it necessary to pull your weapon?"

"Absolutely!" Chuck blurted. "Two of them were coming at me with weapons. I probably would have shot them had they gotten five feet further."

"Really?" the officer said. "You would have shot kids?"

"I wouldn't call them kids. I would have called them a gang."

The officers put Chuck in the back of one of the squad cars as they talked to the witness at length. Several other people who saw what happened came out of buildings surrounding the parking lot and corroborated Chuck's story.

The black officer strolled back to the police car, opened the back door and helped Chuck get out of the backseat. It was a difficult maneuver for Chuck with his hands cuffed behind his back.

As the black officer was taking off the cuffs, he said, "I guess you really can't blame those kids. They saw those Tea Party stickers on your truck and figured you were part of the group that shot the president."

"Are you serious?" Chuck was astounded. "Those were thugs!"

"Why, because they were black?"

"No, because they destroyed my truck and were going to assault me."

"Well, that's your story..."

Chuck looked at the officer indignantly. "Are you nuts?"

"Sir, you better tone down your language to me."

"Fuck you, officer!"

Three officers nearby ran up as Chuck and the black officer stood nose to nose. The Hispanic officer moved Chuck away as two other officers restrained the black officer.

"Fuck him." Chuck sounded resigned. "I don't know what's happening to this country."

"That mother-fucker is going to jail," screamed the black officer. "You fuckin' crackers pulled that shit yesterday and you think blacks aren't going to respond?" He strained to get at Chuck, shouting at the top of his lungs. "We knew you crackers couldn't stand it if Johnson was re-elected. How did you expect them to react?"

"I want his name and badge number," Chuck said. His tone was filled with anger and disgust.

"Sir, we have your report," the other officer told him. "No charges are going to be pressed. It's best you calm down now or I'm going to handcuff you again. If you threaten that officer, you are going to jail."

"I never threatened him." Chuck leaned against his truck, his shoulders sagging.

The officer said softly, "Mr. Dixon, the situation is volatile everywhere. We are responding to calls like this all over the city. Thank God Johnson did not die or the situation would be ten times worse."

"I understand," Chuck said. "Just get him out of here so I can get my truck taken care of."

The officers finished taking pictures of the truck and got back in their squad cars. Chuck knew his assailants would never be arrested. How sad the country had been so split. He didn't see how such a thing could happen in his America.

Chapter 15

"'These are times that try men's souls. The summer soldier and the sunshine patriot will, in this crisis, shrink from the service of their country."

~ Thomas Payne

Government leaders pleaded for an end to the violence gripping major urban centers. Sixteen states called out the National Guard to help restore order.

Over the next two weeks, newscasts regularly updated viewers and listeners throughout the day on the president's condition. One video showed the president sitting up in bed, bandaged over his left shoulder and chest, showing thumbs up to the camera to indicate he was okay. NBC, which had taken the video four days after the assassination attempt, inexplicably did not publish it for almost two weeks.

Despite government leaders at all levels and from both parties continuously calling for an end to the violence, nothing had more effect than this video once it was released. It was almost as if the rioters could not believe President Johnson was alive until they saw it for themselves.

Fox News reported the violence had taken more than seven hundred lives. No mainstream news outlets reported near those numbers. The number included twenty-eight law enforcement officers and National Guard troops. Of those killed, the vast majority consisted of whites killed by blacks, or blacks killed during assaults on law enforcement and whites.

Because of the gridlock around major urban areas, entire downtown and business districts were completely shut down. Looting was rampant. Hundreds of thousands of people left the worst affected

cities en masse. Food and gasoline supplies in those cities were virtually non-existent. It was amazing how fast store shelves and gasoline
storage tanks went empty without resupply on a regular basis.

World-wide stock and commodity markets were rocked by the
assassination attempt and resulting violence. The Wednesday after
the election, the Dow Industrial Average took one of its worst set-
backs with a more than twelve hundred point drop in the first hour
of opening. All trades were automatically halted.

Oil futures, which had already jumped significantly the month
before following the Iranian military strike, were just beginning
to stabilize right before the assassination attempt. Oil now topped
$151.00 per barrel. Gasoline prices averaged $5.31 nationwide.

Gold, which traditionally moved higher with calamities, civil
wars, conflicts and uncertainty reached a record high and was trading in large volumes at more than $3,200 per ounce. Silver also
reached record prices, trading at more than $66.00 per ounce. The
U.S. dollar was trading at all-time lows against all foreign curren-
cies. America's currency was at its weakest point in modern history.

Food prices took the largest leap of all. In the sixteen states where
the most violence occurred, food prices soared—that was if you
could find food in those cities. The weakened dollar added to the
increase in food costs.

Even the geographic areas not directly affected by the riots were
strained to their limits due to the mass migration of people leaving
urban areas to distance themselves from the violence. Hotels, gasoline, and food supplies were strained in areas hundreds of miles from
the violence. Scenes of gridlocked freeways similar to the exodus of
more than one million in Houston from Hurricane Ike were com-
monplace all over the country.

Eclipsing the shortage of food, however, was a phenomenon that
started with President Johnson's first-term win. Gun and ammunition sales, which had enjoyed a boom since his first election, was
nothing compared to the run on guns and ammo in the immediate two

weeks following the assassination attempt and the resulting violence.

Gun retailers, pawn shops and firearms dealers were simply out of stock. America made a run on the bank for firearms and ammo— and there simply weren't enough in stock for the sudden massive demand.

Local newscasts broadcasted live from lines of people waiting outside gun retailers like Gander Mountain, Wal-Mart, Outdoor World, Cabela's and more. The bedlam America had seen before on TV for certain Christmas electronics, Nike tennis shoes and hot new toys was being played out again, this time for guns. Violence erupted in lines waiting to get inside and purchase weapons.

Several stores in various states, especially in the urban areas where most of the violence occurred, could not hold back the hordes of frantic shoppers and were overrun by mobs that ended up looting the stores for guns and anything else they could take.

Fresh off the defeat at the polls in the presidential election, the GOP leadership was lying low. The mainstream media blamed the GOP's failure to control the extreme right wing of the party for the attempt on the president's life.

On the other hand, the Democrats and the administration were not united in their call for peace and calm. Many of the traditional race-baiters on the fringe left of the Democratic Party incited and encouraged the violence. This included the typical rancor and dema-goguery that spewed from various congressmen and women, such as U.S. Congresswoman Eileen Burton-Ames and U.S. Congresswom-an Prudence Barkin, any time a black person was killed by a white.

The congressional members of the Tea Party Caucus especially stayed out of the public eye, scheduling their meetings and briefings in undisclosed locations. GOP establishment members in the House and Senate were in an "I told you so..." mode, blaming the election loss and ensuing violence on the most conservative base of the party. The GOP establishment, which had always been fearful and leery of this grassroots shift to the right, now saw their opportunity to bury it.

Days after the election, the Republican National Committee chairman resigned. The GOP was in free fall.

Public outrage at the violence continued to grow as talk shows and traditional conservative outlets called for the administration to have a more concerted effort in calling for peace and calm. State and local officials begged President Johnson to make a statement that would calm the violence, stabilize the markets and put America back on a recovery track.

Liberal TV hosts and the Democratic leadership claimed that local law enforcement tactics used to quell the violence in Southern cities (typically red states) overreached their mandate and were racially motivated in cities such as Atlanta, Dallas, Miami and New Orleans. The same news outlets showed the number of deaths in those cities higher per capita than places like Chicago, New York and Los Angeles, although local law enforcement officials in those cities backed off and essentially let the mobs destroy entire business districts with fires and looting.

The mainstream media called the violence a new "revolution." Not since 1860 had the United States been as polarized, fractured and in turmoil. None of the civil unrest in the 1960s compared.

America was on new and very troubled ground.

Chapter 16

"Power is not a means, it is an end. One does not establish a dictatorship in order to safeguard a revolution; one makes the revolution in order to establish the dictatorship."

~ George Orwell, English Socialist & Novelist

Ted Duncan called a White House news conference for a Tuesday morning three weeks after the election. Although Duncan was giving daily briefings to the press, this was the first major news conference since the one held by Attorney General Tibbs, Treasury Secretary Gould and Vice President Doolittle in the hospital where President Johnson was treated for his gunshot wound.

"I have a major announcement," said Duncan. He looked down at his prepared statement. "President Johnson will speak to the nation live from the Oval Office next Sunday night at 9:00 p.m. Eastern time. The president recognizes he is not the only person wounded by these events. Just as he has been healing from his wounds daily, he would like to help the country begin its healing process, too."

Duncan paused, then continued, "President Johnson asks the nation to put aside its differences and stop the violence. He reminds everyone we are all in this together.

"Although the president is not quite ready for the heavy schedule he was accustomed to, his love for his country dictates that he speak directly to the American public as soon as he is medically able," Duncan finished.

The general take in the mainstream media was to cast the president as a hero, rising up from his deathbed to heal a wounded nation.

Conservative media attacked the fact that the administration had not made any statement, even a press release, while the violence, riots and looting were taking place. For three full weeks, there was no direct call from the administration for a halt to the chaos, only sound bites delivered at impromptu interviews.

Several reporters challenged Duncan on the president's return to a "heavy schedule." It was widely known that President Johnson didn't begin his days until after 10:00 a.m. most mornings and that his last two years in office were primarily spent on the campaign trail fundraising, hosting celebrity musicians at White House parties, playing tennis or on lavish vacations with Maggie and the family.

Those questions were blasted by Duncan as irresponsible and disloyal to America. Duncan continued to echo the longstanding standard reply to members of the press corps who questioned the president's schedule in the past, comparing it favorably to other presidents.

The White House press corps in the East Room almost erupted into a mob scene as reporters and staff from the mainstream media castigated the questions and the reporters who asked them. The room broke into shouts, accusations and almost blows while everything was caught on video.

Democratic leaders in Congress, who had almost immediately called for a renewed effort to ban handguns after the assassination attempt on the president, ramped up the anti-gun rhetoric. The typical radical left in government, Hollywood, music industry and organized labor called for the *complete* outlawing of guns, period. There was an unashamed discussion in the media and Congress that the Second Amendment, like other amendments, articles and tenets in the Constitution, were outdated.

The left charged the Constitution was antiquated and not suited for modern America. Blacks felt the Constitution was a lie, as it treated everyone equal except slaves. Never in American history was the Constitution under attack in such a pernicious and public way.

News coverage of the president's first speech since election night was sure to get ratings that would top the highest-rated Super Bowl. After the Tuesday announcement, speculation reached a fever pitch. There had been very few photos or news feeds from the hospital, and the media and the world were anxious to see the newly re-elected president.

Talking heads from every news outlet globally speculated what the president might say. No advance copies of the speech were provided to the media until moments before the speech.

At 9:02 Eastern time, President Johnson appeared on TV from the Oval Office. He was in suit and tie, but showed no signs of the wound suffered just above his left clavicle. He looked tired and, to many, grayer than ever. Looking into the camera for nearly fifteen seconds, the president finally spoke.

"My fellow Americans, it is good to be back, sitting in this historic room at this historic desk.

"First, I would like to extend my heartfelt gratitude and those of Maggie and the girls for the outpouring of genuine concern over the events of election night. My family and I will be forever grateful for the sincere warmth of the prayers and get-well wishes by the American people.

"Again, I'd like to thank all Americans for their faith in me and my administration to advance our joint vision for America going forward. Even an assassin's bullet cannot and will not deter us from the path we set out on four years ago. Thank you for the overwhelming mandate you have given me and Congress to advance those ideals.

"Over the last two weeks, I have been reminded of a similar event in history that turned out a little different than this. Abraham Lincoln was close to bringing a divided country back together again before he was tragically taken from America. Sometimes, great ideas come with great sacrifice.

"My heart has been saddened over the last couple of weeks by the events that have occurred. I call on all Americans to put aside their differences and work to rebuild this great nation. America is hurting.

"America is greater than the division that separates us. Although it is very American to peacefully protest, there is nothing more un-American than to protest in violence.

"Now, let us turn to getting America back to work. We have a lot to do and we need America's help.

"In the coming days, I will enact tough regulations to stop the easy access to guns in this country. What happened on election night and the days following should never happen in a civilized society.

"I will also address actions of the states that have violated federal immigration policies, due to our misguided Supreme Court.

"And, most importantly, I will direct the newly elected Democratic majority in Congress to draft a new and fair tax code in the next sixty days. This tax code will require everyone to pay their fair share. It will be fairer to poor and working class Americans. It will require those that have enjoyed the fruits of America's bounty to pay a much fairer share of the tax burden.

"Again, Maggie and I extend our warmest thanks for all your support. Let's work to get America back on track, together.

"God Bless America."

The mainstream media was giddy over the president's speech, calling it one of the greatest in American history. The general consensus was that President Johnson had risen above the assassination attempt, barely mentioning it, and putting himself in the same light as Abraham Lincoln.

The next one hundred days of President Johnson's second term included a long sought-after laundry list of liberal socialist ideas, and now he had a Congress to do most of them, even if there wasn't a super majority in the House.

As expected, Fox News and other conservative media outlets saw an entirely different message in the speech and interpreted it as a predictor of an upcoming flurry of presidential executive orders. It was also apparent to the analysts that a renewed attack on the Second Amendment was coming.

Chapter 17

"Give me four years to teach the children and the seed I have sown will never be uprooted."

~ Vladimir Lenin

"Political Correctness is a doctrine fostered by a delusional illogical liberal minority & rabidly promoted by an unscrupulous liberal press which holds forth the proposition that it is entirely possible to pick up a turd by the clean end."

~ attributed to a Texas A&M student in 2006

Chuck Dixon's twelve-year-old son Colton came home from school in tears and walked into the house with a manila envelope.

"Mom, they won't let me put my ancestry poster in the Veterans Day display," cried Colton.

"What?" Christy said, reaching for the sealed envelope. She ripped it open and scanned the enclosed letter, then pressed her lips together in a tight line.

Every year, Tennison Middle School celebrated Veterans Day by having students create a poster with a relative or ancestor who served or was serving in the military during peacetime or times of war. There was a large grassy area in the front of the school, which was located on a busy thoroughfare. During the week of Veterans Day, over twelve hundred posters made by the students honoring their relatives who were veterans were placed in the grass on stakes.

The twenty-five year Veterans Day tradition at Tennison was a moving experience for all those who walked around the grassy lawn to view the sea of patriotic, appreciative and proud posters made by individual students. There were incredibly moving stories, pictures, pieces of clothing and memorabilia on the students' posters. During the week of the displays, traffic often stopped on the busy street because the parking lot could not hold the cars for people who wanted to participate.

Two years before, Chuck Dixon had taken his son to a non-political event sponsored by the Sons of Confederate Veterans. Members of the Dixon family fought on both sides of the Civil War, including two relatives who were in the same battle on opposite sides at the Battle of Fort Donelson, Kentucky. Chuck was proud of his heritage and wanted his kids to experience the same thing.

When Chuck got home from work that night, he couldn't believe what he heard.

"Dad, the assistant principal said the Confederates committed treason and didn't deserve to be honored on Veterans Day," Colton explained.

"What? Since when is fighting for your independence treason? If that logic were true, then Washington, Jefferson, Hamilton and Henry were traitors," Chuck told his son.

"I guess I have to make a different poster now."

"Nope," Chuck said emphatically, "we'll get to the bottom of this, son, I promise."

The next morning, Chuck drove Colton to school and parked in the teachers' parking lot, just like he tried to do every day when he was in high school. He marched in with Colton and headed straight to the principal's office.

After waiting for almost forty minutes, an assistant principal came and got them both. Colton motioned to his dad that this was not the person who told him the Confederates were treasonous.

Finally Chuck, Colton, the history department lead teacher, Assistant Principal Ms. Graham and Principal Mrs. Greeney were all seated.

Chuck got right down to business. "I understand you told Colton he can't display his poster because he made the poster on one of our

Confederate ancestors."

"Mr. Dixon, we have a couple of problems with the poster. Do we want to excuse Colton?" asked Ms. Graham.

"No," Chuck retorted, "I want him to hear this discussion."

"Mr. Dixon," Ms. Graham said stiffly, "we have a duty to be tolerant of all students, including those who may be offended by Colton's poster."

"How could they be offended?"

"The poster has a Confederate flag on it." Ms. Graham was adamant.

"I don't understand that."

"Well, sir, we don't allow hate symbols on our campuses."

"That's not a hate symbol," Chuck insisted. "That's the beloved flag of my ancestors."

"Sir, we know you feel that way, but others feel it has other meanings."

"Like what?"

"Well, it's offensive to African-Americans." Ms. Graham's face and neck reddened.

"So," Chuck said, "if a student came in wearing a Malcolm X or Cesar Chavez shirt, would you allow those?"

"Sir, the U.S. Navy just named a ship after Chavez."

"I don't see the relevance of that. Let's just get the real reason out here right now."

Principal Greeney had been quiet up until now. "Mr. Dixon," she said patiently, "it's no secret that many African-Americans consider this a hate symbol and associate it with the Ku Klux Klan and slavery."

Having anticipated this logic, Chuck reached into his briefcase and pulled out his iPad, which was already loaded to the KKK website.

"Here is the main website for the KKK. What flag do you see all over this page?" Chuck asked as he flipped the screen around to show a very colorful website with hundreds of American flags on it.

"Do you see one Confederate flag?" Chuck asked.

The teachers were dumbfounded and just stared at each other.

The principal leaned forward, resting her elbows on the desktop, and spoke in a very measured response. "Well, sir, that is also irrelevant. The district has determined the Confederate flag is inflammatory and may incite violence in the schools, so we cannot allow it."

"Okay, so if my son removes the Confederate flag on the poster, then he can display his poster?"

"No, sir. We do not recognize treasonous rebels on Veterans Day."

"Treasonous? So, in your mind, Robert E. Lee, Jefferson Davis, and Stonewall Jackson were all treasonous?" Chuck was incredulous.

"Absolutely," Principal Greeney said.

"So, if the definition of committing treason is to attempt to throw off a tyrannical government, wouldn't you say George Washington, Thomas Jefferson, Patrick Henry and all the founding fathers were also traitors?" Chuck continued to press his argument.

"Sir, I'm not going to get into an argument about history. My undergrad degree is in history. This is about district policy."

"Do you know Congress approved the same burial rights for Confederate veterans? Did you know they passed the same veterans' benefits for surviving Confederate veterans? Do you think they would do that for any person convicted of treason?" asked Chuck. "Do you know of ANY Confederate officer or enlisted man who was tried and convicted of treason? Did you, in your studies of history to get your undergrad degree, learn what the penalty for treason is?"

"Mr. Dixon, I'm not going to sit here and debate…"

"Mrs. Greeney, you have nothing to debate. Where did you get your undergrad degree in history?"

"Ohio State."

"Well," Chuck said a bit sarcastically, "that explains a lot, but it doesn't explain your ignorance on this issue."

"Mr. Dixon…" Mrs. Greeney tried again.

Chuck interrupted forcefully. "Mrs. Greeney, let me explain this to you in very clear terms. If you do not allow my son to display this poster, I will first contact the Southern Defense League, which legally pursues attacks on Southern heritage and not only will they sue the school and the district, but I will personally sue both of you for your intolerance and the anguish caused to my son."

"Mr. Dixon! There is no..."

"Ladies," Chuck said, standing up. "We are done. I'm sick and tired of people like you re-inventing history. You should be ashamed of yourselves. This is Texas, by God. We will have a temporary restraining order by Monday, and this poster you see right here will be on the school's front lawn."

"Mr. Dixon, there is no need to threaten anyone!" The principal was clearly alarmed.

"Mrs. Greeney, these are not idle threats. I promise you that there will be consequences if this school, this district or any of you subscribe to this intolerance of my son's Southern heritage. I, for one, am sick and tired of what teachers' unions have done to our educational system. One of the tenets of communism is to destroy national heroes. I bet you also teach these kids that Washington, Jefferson and Sam Houston abused slaves, and that the Civil War was fought over slavery."

"Mr. Dixon, you are welcome to voice your opinion over lesson plans and curriculum to the district," Mrs. Greeney said.

Placing his palms on the back of the chair he'd been sitting on, Chuck leaned forward. "Do either of you know who donated the land for this school? Is that history taught to these students?"

Mrs. Greeney and Ms. Graham cast quick, nervous glances at each other. They apparently didn't have any idea where Chuck was going with this question.

When neither teacher offered an answer, Chuck continued, "Johnny Tennison was the first son of Irish immigrants who settled in Texas. He was a self-made cattle rancher, mercantile shopkeeper, and banker. He was also instrumental in bringing the railroad to this area. Did you know any of this? Is it taught to the students?"

"No, Mr. Dixon, if what you are telling us, in fact, is true, the students should know about the man or family the school was named for," replied Mrs. Greeney.

Ms. Graham, who had largely been quiet for the last few moments, added, "Mr. Dixon, I'm not sure where you got that history lesson from, but the district has never shared that information."

"How long have you both taught here?"

After another long glance at each other, Mrs. Greeney replied, "I have been here nine years and I believe Ms. Graham about four?"

Ms. Graham nodded agreement.

"How long would either of you have had to teach here to begin to wonder who Tennison Middle School is named after?" Chuck asked.

"Mr. Dixon, many of the schools in the district are named after educators. That was my assumption. I've never heard any different, nor has the district published any information regarding the naming of the school."

"Well, maybe I should bring Mrs. Nessa Tennison over to meet the teachers and administrators who teach at the schools whose properties were originally donated by her grandfather. She is the granddaughter of Johnny Tennison, and she's ninety-four."

Seeing that the tension a few minutes earlier was easing somewhat, Mrs. Greeney responded, "Yes, we would love to know more about the history of the district and the schools."

"Outstanding! I'm sure Mrs. Tennison would love to share the pictures and mementos she has kept all these years of her Grandpa Johnny's service as a mounted cavalry soldier in Hill's Texas Brigade. That brigade was one of the most decorated units in the Confederacy," Chuck said. "You see, Miz Nessa—as we call her—has been to several of our Sons of Confederate Veterans' meetings and shared a cool tintype of Johnny Tennison holding a Confederate battle flag."

The two politically correct educators sat there, dumbfounded.

Chuck looked at his son. "Colton, I bet these ladies change their minds about your poster but, if they don't, there will be some very nice gentlemen from Mississippi with law degrees coming to visit them in court."

As Chuck turned to leave the small office, he said, "Ladies, you have just confirmed to me once again why this country is in so much trouble. Have a nice day."

Chapter 18

"The accumulation of all power, legislative, executive, and judiciary in the same hands... may justly be pronounced the very definition of tyranny."

~ *James Madison*

The second Thursday of every month at 7:00 p.m. was Chuck's night to go to his local Tea Party meeting. He was one of the original founders, and what started with six people had grown to over two hundred members. It was not unusual for at least half the members to show up at any given monthly meeting.

The group met alternately at one of the members' offices or at a local pancake house. The pancake house, a national chain, told the group that, because of the assassination attempt and the bad publicity surrounding the accused assassin and the Tea Party, it had to suspend the availability of the back room, but they could meet there one last time.

Chuck called the meeting to order at 7:16 p.m., noticing the meeting was one of the lowest attended since the beginning, with less than thirty in attendance.

The mood was somber, to say the least. The dual blow of the president's re-election, losing the U.S. House and failing to take the U.S. Senate was huge. Chuck put an electoral map on the wall to try to understand exactly what happened.

"In the red states, we actually gained five senators and, in the House, we gained twenty-seven seats," he said. "The election was turned in several swing states, including Ohio, Pennsylvania, North Carolina, Colorado and Florida." He pointed out locations on the map as he spoke.

"Blue states reinforced and even strengthened their hold on both Democratic Senate and House seats. The difference between red and blue is even more pronounced than ever. It's almost like we live in two different worlds. Their world believes in large government, welfare, high taxes and socialism. So, as all of you in this room know very well, we are two different worlds within the same country."

Stan Mumford, the co-chair, stepped up to the front of the room to assist Chuck with the presentation. He was almost bald, a sloppy dresser, and about one hundred pounds overweight. A respected businessman in the area, he had owned an independent insurance agency for the last twenty-five years.

"What we saw happen was a perfect storm," Mumford said. "First, since most of the states the Democrats carried are deeply in debt, with some even close to default, the message from conservatives in those states was all about cuts and austerity. Organized labor did a great job in those states, organizing their rank and file to continue the class warfare and class envy message carried by the president. In other words, they don't want to endure any sacrifices so the states can balance their budgets; let's just tax the rich and business owners."

Chuck added, "We saw this type of tactic used successfully in Europe as Greece, Spain and Italy struggled with their austerity measures. This is how organized protests, which turned to violence, occurred—and continue to occur in those countries."

"The 'September surprise' was obviously calculated. It was based on an action that should bother all of us. It was unconstitutional because the administration didn't consult Congress," Mumford continued.

Chuck sensed he was losing the crowd. He knew they really wanted to understand but, before he could bring it up, one of the ladies in the group did it for him.

"How do we recover from being blamed for the assassination

attempt?" asked Sylvia Brennan, a stylish middle-aged real estate agent who was always impeccably dressed, even in the most casual settings. "Do we know any more about this Tea Party guy that was responsible? I'm afraid we're going to have to meet in secret going forward, or we are in serious danger of government reprisals or worse. Perhaps the movement is dead."

"All we know is that he was associated with several Tea Party groups in the north Texas and Dallas areas. Poor Dallas; it's only been a few years since people stopped associating Dallas with the JFK assassination, and now this," said Mumford.

"I saw a video last night where a few of our fellow Tea Party compatriots in Dallas said this guy Sally seemed normal and a big supporter," Chuck commented.

"Unfortunately, the media and the left are continuing to paint us all as racists and now terrorists," Mumford went on.

"Yes, but we can't give up or give in." Chuck eyed the small group. "Let me assure you, the Tea Party is not dead. This is definitely a black eye, but I have kids and grandchildren and I'm not giving up because of one, or even two bad election cycles. I will keep fighting for them. I will keep fighting for my grandfather who landed at Utah Beach and earned a Bronze Star in Alsace-Lorraine, France during World War II." Chuck was defiant.

"Listen, folks," Mumford told them. "I expect reprisals. We should all expect reprisals. First, people will think the worst. I have a neighbor who is black but didn't know I was a Tea Party supporter. He went on and on about the racist Tea Party. I asked him if he had ever attended a Tea Party meeting or event. Of course, he hadn't. His opinion of the Tea Party was based on what he heard from uninformed friends, relatives and co-workers, not to mention how the mainstream media portrays us. We have to stay the course now more than ever."

"Should we be in fear for our lives, for our families?" Sylvia wondered.

Mumford looked at Chuck. He knew Chuck had not shared with the rest of the group what happened to him in downtown Houston just days before. Chuck shook his head slightly. "Just be careful," Mumford said. "Until the president was out of the hospital, it was extremely volatile. I wouldn't recommend Tea Party stickers on your cars and that kind of thing."

He glanced around the room, as if trying to gauge the feelings of the group. Then he continued. "With that being said, let's keep doing what's effective and that, more than anything, is winning people over one by one. Admittedly, this may be tough for a while until this assassination attempt is behind everyone." Mumford mumbled to himself as he vocalized what they were facing. "How am I going to recruit someone to the Tea Party after this?"

He was interrupted suddenly by someone in the back of the room. A young man with blond hair stood and said, "Hey, look at the TV!"

In the corner of the meeting room was a wall-mounted TV that had been muted. The TV was tuned to Fox News, which showed a bright blue-and-orange Breaking News banner common on Fox when a breaking story was first broadcast.

Chuck grabbed the remote and raised the volume as the Fox News commentator stated: "We have learned that the Justice Department has announced that the FBI, Homeland Security and the Bureau of Alcohol, Tobacco and Firearms have launched a major investigation of Tea Party groups across the country, focusing specifically on Tea Party organizations in Texas, Oklahoma, Arizona and South Carolina. The DOJ also announced a possible assassination conspiracy in the Tea Party with groups in Texas. Although no one claims there were more involved in Johnson's assassination attempt, the DOJ claimed there was enough evidence to expand the investigation beyond Rash Sally."

"Damn."

The entire group sat there in stunned silence.

"Look, this is what we expected," Chuck pleaded. "Don't panic. Most of you have been to every event we have ever had. None of you think like this maniac assassin. We have never had people in this group or at any event do anything or even say anything remotely racist or threatening. We have ALWAYS taken the high road. Remain calm. Pull your families close together. We WILL get through this!"

"Are they going to be investigating each one of us?" asked Sylvia, a concerned look on her face.

The rest of the group looked like they had just come from a funeral of someone they dearly loved. Some were in tears. There was a tangible fear now that they knew they were targets of the feds. A few, less than a half dozen, proudly stated, "Bring it on!"

Chuck adjourned the meeting, with a caution they should all be careful in the future. He and Mumford stayed behind, grabbed another coffee each and discussed what had just happened.

"We shouldn't underestimate how tough this might get for us, Chuck, but imagine how difficult this is going to make it for us to grow the cause," Mumford said.

"This smells to me. I don't trust Tibbs or Johnson. The whole thing doesn't make sense. Look how little information is coming out about this guy, except his relationship to local Tea Parties."

"Well, the attorney general seems determined not to put out too much information," Mumford said thoughtfully. "It makes me think they know more than they're letting on. I really think we may have lost the country for good," Mumford went on. "I just don't see how we can recover from this, do you?"

"God has a plan." Chuck tried to sound positive. "I sure wish He would reveal it, though. This is going to be rough for quite a while."

"At least four more years..." Mumford agreed.

Chapter 19

"I have a message from the Tea Party, a message that is loud and clear and does not mince words. We've come to take our government back."

~ Senator Rand Paul

Four dark blue unmarked panel vans pulled into a small strip center in Arlington, Texas near 5:00 p.m. Inside one of the storefronts, volunteers from the Arlington Tea Party were finishing up their day, getting ready to fight the rush-hour traffic home.

This Tea Party group had six full-time volunteers, four women and two men who were there almost daily. Three of the volunteers were over sixty years old. They were using their retirement to stay busy and devote time to what they thought was a worthwhile grassroots cause.

Three vans sped through the parking lot and parked in front, purposely blocking staff members' cars in their parking spaces. The fourth van pulled around behind the building near the back door. Just a few seconds behind them came two vans from the local NBC and ABC affiliates that parked approximately fifty yards away from the Tea Party office front. The station crews exited their vans with television cameras at the ready and appeared to be waiting for some kind of event to take place.

A woman came out of the Tea Party office and peered at the van parked directly behind her SUV. She started for her vehicle.

The back cargo doors of the vans swung open. SWAT police jumped out of the vans in full paramilitary gear—helmets, bulletproof vests and automatic weapons. Fully visible on the back of each were the bright yellow letters ATF.

The agents approached the Tea Party volunteer with guns drawn, screaming at her to get down on the ground. Two agents escorted her to the ground as the rest burst through the front door of the office, forcing the five other staff members to the floor. The squad's automatic weapons were pointed at them.

The agents struck two middle-age staffers, a man and woman, repeatedly with batons because they could not get to the floor fast enough to suit them. It was apparent the sudden commotion had confused them, and they didn't understand the multiple, sometimes conflicting commands being shouted at them.

There was a loud crack at the back of the office as agents violently forced the door off its hinges, charging in with guns drawn, yelling orders.

From the south side of the parking lot, at least ten police cars from various law enforcement agencies poured into the parking lot. As news cameras rolled, the ATF and local police led the staff members out of the office in handcuffs. The women were crying, and the men looked like they were in shock. The two that had been hit were bleeding, with blood running down over the man's ear from his head and the woman bleeding from the nose. They were hustled into one of the blue vans and escorted out of the parking lot by three police cars.

The news crews were allowed to videotape the agents as they removed computers, records, boxes and file cabinets, loading them into a Ryder rental truck that pulled into the parking lot after the van left the scene. More unmarked vehicles with federal government license plates arrived. Nearly fifty ATF and federal agents, along with a number of local police, were on the scene. The entire parking lot was barricaded, and employees and customers in adjoining retail stores were evacuated to a location two blocks away.

At the exact same time the Arlington raid was conducted, no less than six other raids took place at other local Tea Party offices in the Dallas Metro area and in Denton, Texas. In addition to these raids, ATF and FBI agents conducted raids at more than two dozen private homes, businesses, and offices of various Tea Party organizations in the area.

Dallas ATF Deputy Director Walt Griffey and the deputy director of the regional FBI office studied prepared written statements behind one of the blue vans. A small podium was pulled from one of the vans and TV teams assembled microphones onto it. By this time, at least six other local news outlets from Fort Worth, Dallas and national news organizations were on hand with cameras and lights ready to film.

Griffey, a tall angular man with a bold full mustache, gray hair and expensive suit, stepped to the podium with his statement, flanked by regional FBI Deputy Director Lee Cabot.

"Today, under the direction of the Justice Department, agents of the ATF, FBI, Homeland Security and local law enforcement officials raided the offices of various Tea Party organizations in the North Texas region with ties to would-be assassin, Rash Sally, who was responsible for the assassination attempt on President Johnson and for the death of a Secret Service agent," said Griffey. "Under the authority of the National Defense Authorization Act—the NDAA—we have confiscated all records, files and computers of Texas Tea Party organizations with ties to Rash Sally to further the investigation of any possible coordinated conspiracies to commit this act."

Griffey paused to let the seriousness of his remarks sink in. "Mr. Sally had known ties to this particular Tea Party office behind me, as well as others in the region. The Justice Department under U.S. Attorney General Jamail Tibbs is committed to a full investigation of the events surrounding the tragedy on election day. Rest assured, we will ultimately bring anyone who worked in concert with Rash Sally to justice. We'll now take a few questions."

A blonde woman, neatly dressed in a navy blue business suit, shouted, "Are the staff members who were taken away officially under arrest?"

"The staff members and the leaders of all these organizations are being questioned as we speak as to their relationship with Rash Sally."

"Are they incarcerated?" the blonde persisted. "Has anyone been charged?"

Griffey looked at her sternly. "At this time, nobody has been charged; however, that could change once the evidence we recovered today has been examined and we have conducted our investigation."

A tall man in a crumpled suit shoved to the front. "How many people have been taken into custody?"

"We cannot answer that question with any accuracy. It would have depended on who was on site at the premises we raided today."

"Do you have reason to believe there was a conspiracy within the Tea Party to assassinate the president?" another male reporter shouted.

"We cannot answer specific questions about the ongoing investigation, but let me just say we have credible evidence today's actions were necessary."

When the raid began, Heath Sagemount was three doors down at a wireless store. He saw the ATF agents bail out of the vans as the raid began. Running out of the store with his iPhone, he activated its camera. Heath, a journalism student at nearby SMU and an avid Libertarian, let his instincts kick in, filming most of the raid with his phone's video camera.

Now, with questions being taken, he stepped to the front, holding his iPhone high with video recorder running and shouted, "Did you have a search warrant?"

At first, Griffey ignored his question, but Heath continued to out-shout the horde of reporters, many of whom now had the same question.

"Did you have a search warrant?" Heath yelled again.

"We did not need a search warrant. The NDAA allows the federal government to act when there are suspected terrorists and terror cells in the United States."

"Has anyone been charged? Were they read their Miranda rights? I didn't see the people you arrested read their rights. Where are you taking them?" Heath insisted.

Fixing the young man with a baleful glare, Griffey shook his head dismissively. "Ladies and gentlemen, this is all we have time for today. The Justice Department will keep you apprised of the ongoing investigation. Thank you."

"Where are you taking them?" Heath repeated.

"Thank you." Griffey turned his back on the crowd and left to enter one of the vans.

As Heath continued to shout questions, two FBI agents came up and told him to leave or he would be arrested. One agent grabbed Heath, pinning his arms down. The other agent grabbed the iPhone and began deleting the videos from the phone.

From behind the line of reporters, Police Chief John Rodriguez of Arlington strode up to the ATF officials, obviously irritated. "What the hell are you boys doing?" he demanded.

"Sir, we have this under control," one official told him.

"I'll expect you and the rest of your team to meet me at my office," Rodriguez said angrily. "No one notified my department the ATF would be conducting these raids in my jurisdiction. And why are the Dallas police here? This is highly improper," he grumbled.

Chief Rodriguez, a staunch Republican, was particularly pissed off that the Dallas mayor and police chief, both card-carrying Democrats, were not only aware of the joint federal agency raids, but had prior knowledge well ahead of the raids.

"Chief Rodriguez," the ATF official said sharply, "someone from the bureau will be in touch with you shortly."

"You boys don't seem to know anything about common courtesy and common sense," Rodriguez told the ATF guy angrily. "You should have briefed local law enforcement before an effort like this was carried out." He turned and stomped back to his car. The ATF official shrugged.

As police, press and bystanders started to disperse, the ATF agent returned Heath's iPhone. As he walked to his car, Heath glanced at his phone and noticed the ATF agent hadn't erased every video. The agent erasing them must have gotten distracted and left two videos intact. Heath picked up the pace to his car, hoping the agents didn't come back to confiscate his phone.

When he was in his car, he drove two blocks, then pulled over to see what videos remained. As he watched the footage on the miniature screen, a huge grin crossed his face.

Chapter 20

"It is true that liberty is precious; so precious that it must be carefully rationed."

~ Vladimir Lenin

Chuck and Christy had just finished an early dinner when the phone rang. The Dixons had decided years ago to turn television off during dinner to give them a chance to talk about their day, and it was irritating to get telemarketer and political donation solicitation calls during this time. Chuck glanced at the phone sitting on the bar, seeing from the caller ID it was Mumford, so he picked up.

"Hello, Stan," he said.

"Damn, Chuck, did you see the raids today?"

Chuck hadn't heard any news since he left his office. Normally, he was busy switching stations between talk radio and news stations during his commute. Christy suggested that sometimes he just needed to listen to music so he could decompress. He knew she was concerned about the events of the last few weeks.

"No," Chuck said, "what are you talking about?"

"The feds hit several Tea Party offices in Dallas, arrested their staff and took everything—computers, files—everything!"

Chuck was shocked into silence, then he replied, more calmly than he felt, "Stan, we are all about to be targets of the feds. We need to get together tonight for an emergency meeting."

"Okay," Mumford said. "You call the executive committee; I'll call the membership directors. Let's meet at 9:00, but it has to be in a secure location."

"Yeah, I agree. Let's meet at my storage facility."

"Got it," Mumford agreed. "I'll see you there at 9:00."

"First meet me at the office. We need to pull out all donor files and membership files, and remove laptops and computers. You can bet they will come after all Tea Party organizations and, since ours is one of the largest and most organized, you can bet we're on the list."

"I agree," Mumford said. "I'll get Jeff and Michael and see if they can help us. We could get hit any time."

Shortly after 9:00 p.m., Chuck's storage facility was crowded with about twenty of his Tea Party faithful.

"I need a couple of volunteers," Chuck said.

He got the volunteers quickly. "Henry, can you go about a block up to the intersection and keep an eye out? Take your truck and your cell." He turned to the other volunteer. "Jack, you can stand behind the other building, out of sight but where you have a good view of the parking lot. Take your vehicle, too. Call Stan if you see anything even remotely suspicious. If someone shows up, scatter. We'll take care of everything in here."

The two men slipped out the door. Chuck knew they were good patriots, and they'd follow orders.

"Let's get this door closed," he said.

They closed the metal garage door behind the two lookouts.

"Okay," Chuck told the remaining members, "if we get one of those calls, we'll disperse and take the records with us."

An unspoken question hung in the air. Nobody asked how this would prevent the feds from absconding with information from these volunteers. There was a lot of whispering.

Chuck quieted the crowd. "Look, I know you're scared, and it'll be worse if you end up taking information home with you, but it should throw another obstacle in these bastards' path while they're trying to steal information. Folks, we are obviously under attack. We've taken steps to prevent that information from falling into the wrong hands by removing it from the office."

The group was silent, and Chuck thought they seemed less worried. He continued. "The most valuable information we have is our members' list. I suggest we find alternative methods of storing that information off site, maybe off-load it to a data center or some other solution."

He turned to the geek of the organization, a young, bright thirty-something computer guru who was head of a medium-sized management firm whose expertise the organization used for its technology and website. "Jeff, can you find a way to store this data virtually on Google or elsewhere, but not under the organizational name?"

"Yes, I have some ideas," Jeff said. "We've already begun wiping the laptops and computers. Most all the paper documents are now stored virtually, so we're going to shred all the paper stuff tonight."

Lisa Moreland, a young mother whose husband was in the Marines and stationed in Iraq, asked, "I don't understand. What do we have to hide? We haven't done anything..."

Mumford interrupted. "First of all, Lisa, my sources in Dallas told me that staffers arrested today were being held without charges at an undisclosed location. The authorities are showing up unannounced at members' homes and taking their computers." He walked to the front of the room, trying to keep a confident posture. "We don't want the feds grabbing you or ANY of our members and holding you without cause. If they get our membership list, they'll know who you are. When you get home tonight, please erase all organizational files on your own laptops and computers, including all emails sent and received from staff or fellow members."

"You have to understand, this is THE opportunity the Left has longed for to put a boot on the throat of its most effective opposition," Chuck told them calmly. "Don't underestimate what they might do. Really, does any one of THIS group not know what they're capable of now that this screwball has opened the door?" Chuck was referring to Rash Sally. "I don't say any of this to scare you. I just want us all to be as prepared as possible for any action that might be taken against us. The NDAA has given the feds and the president unlimited power in this type of situation, so go in with your eyes open."

Mumford piped up from the front of the room. "Here's a plan," he said. "Let's all reach out to state and congressional leaders who are pro-Tea Party, or at least sympathetic. We need to keep them informed about events, and get them aware of what an unfettered DOJ under Jamail Tibbs is doing."

* * *

That night, several Tea Party people secretly decided in their own minds and hearts that this was it. The risks were too great. Their families, businesses, jobs, retirement, and peace of mind dictated that they disengage from the group. They had been willing to fight the untrue stereotypes of racism and other charges associated with the movement, but fighting the feds, having their homes raided, and being on some type of "list" was too great a risk. Many were done.

Two days after the raids, several Texas state legislators and four U.S. congressmen held a press conference on the capitol steps in Austin.

Congressman Phil Cartwright, well-respected Republican Tea Party Caucus member, stepped to the microphones. "My fellow Texans and fellow Americans, the United States Justice Department is holding fellow citizens without due process. Staffers of various Tea Party groups in Texas were rounded up and have not had access to lawyers or their families. Their whereabouts are unknown, and the DOJ is refusing to provide that information.

"This is exactly why I and various elected officials standing behind me voted against the NDAA. The Constitution protects citizens from unlawful search and seizures but, in this case, no search warrants were associated with these raids. Staff members who have been detained have not been granted habeas corpus, due process, or any other protection afforded by the United States Constitution."

Congressman Cartwright turned toward the group lined up with him. He motioned to a clean-cut young man. When the man joined him at the microphones, the congressman said, "I would like to introduce you to an eyewitness of one of the Dallas raids by the ATF on a Tea Party office in Arlington. He watched as volunteers were arrested, assaulted, and detained by unnecessary force. This is Heath Sagemount, a journalism student at SMU. By now, many of you have likely seen the videos he's posted on YouTube that have gone viral."

Heath stepped close to the podium and spoke in a strong voice. "What I saw two days ago was the violent arrest of non-violent volunteers at a local Tea Party office.

"These folks could be your grandmothers, grandfathers or parents. As you will see if you watch my videos, these people were treated very badly. Two non-resisting volunteers were beaten into submission, and I never saw any of them read their Miranda rights."

Heath carefully measured his next words. "I saw one woman forced to the sidewalk by armed agents. Later, two of the arrested volumteers came out handcuffed and bleeding. These folks were not any threat to these heavily armed, armored officers. The video is now posted online. I call on any American to tell me that these beatings were justified," he finished, and was greeted with long moments of thunderous applause.

As the news conference wrapped up, the front door of the capitol swung open and a horde of reporters, capitol security officers and politicians surged forward. Texas Governor Brent Cooper was at the center of the group. He stood out in his signature dark suit and red tie, and appeared agitated.

There was momentary confusion, and then Texas State Senator Dane Conklin walked to the podium and announced, "Ladies and gentlemen, Governor Brent Cooper would like to make a statement."

The crowd that had started with about fifty people on the capitol steps had swelled to double that.

Governor Cooper was not on the list to speak. It was obviously a spontaneous and unrehearsed appearance. The governor had a reputation for challenging the federal government on multiple issues from healthcare to immigration and the EPA.

"I want to say a personal thank you for these brave leaders who have stepped up to challenge the Justice Department's handling of this investigation," the governor said. "I have just finished a personal meeting with the Arlington, Texas chief of police, whose jurisdiction includes the office in Arlington most of you witnessed on TV."

Standing next to Governor Cooper were the Arlington police chief and six elite Texas Rangers in cowboy hats, badges and holstered weapons.

"I have directed the Texas Rangers to conduct their own investigation into the conduct of federal agents who have rounded up Texas citizens without due process. Those citizens' civil rights have been violated. Texas will not stand for heavy-handed federal encroachment into its affairs."

Pointing his finger straight forward as if putting it in Attorney General Tibbs' face, a red-faced but confident Governor Cooper continued, "We hereby demand access to those who were arrested. We demand they be given access to the rights granted to every citizen under the Constitution, the right to a lawyer and the right to habeas corpus!"

Various mainstream media had conducted polls about the raids. On average, over 63 percent of Americans supported the raids because there appeared to be ties between Rash Sally and Tea Party groups in Texas. The majority of those, however, thought the agents had gone too far in beating two helpless volunteers. The criticism of the Justice Department was more prominent in traditional red states, especially in the South.

In Texas, there was growing outrage over how the volunteers were treated. The furious Texans were determined not to bow to this treatment, especially with their governor strongly opposed to the usurpation of Texas rights by the federal government.

Chapter 21

"Our main agenda is to have ALL guns banned. We must use whatever means possible. It doesn't matter if you have to distort facts or even lie. Our task of creating a socialist America can only succeed when those who would resist us have been totally disarmed."

~ Sarah Brady, formerly of Handgun Control, Inc.
renamed the Brady Campaign to End Gun Violence

Although weeks had passed since the election night violence, major urban areas were still dealing with continued sporadic violence, primarily on the West Coast, in the Rust Belt and Northeast. The Johnson administration continued to be mostly silent regarding the ongoing violence, despite pleas from local and state officials asking for federal assistance.

Food and gasoline supply deliveries had almost returned to normal; however, shortages of both continued in areas like Newark, New York, Los Angeles, Detroit and St. Louis. Because of the scarcity of food during the days after the crisis, people hoarded food and gasoline as soon as they became available, causing continued sporadic shortages.

Six weeks after President Johnson left his hospital bed, he issued the first executive order of his second term. The White House issued a press release that the president would make a prime time Monday night speech from the Oval Office regarding the order. News outlets speculated the executive order could be either healthcare- or economy-related.

In the meantime, the DOJ was the focus of most of the media coverage over the Tea Party raids and the pursuit of any assassination conspiracy. Attorney General Tibbs appeared on several Sunday morning news shows to discuss the investigation.

"We are continuing to pursue all leads," stated Tibbs in response to a question on an NBC news talk show.

"What do you say to the recent remarks from Texas Governor Brent Cooper and others in Texas that you are holding citizens without charges?" asked the show's host.

"Without commenting specifically on the facts of the investigation, there is no doubt Rash Sally had ties to the Tea Party. We are leaving no stone unturned regarding the investigation. This includes the DOJ, FBI, CIA, ATF and Homeland Security," replied Tibbs.

"Are you stating for the record that there are direct ties inside the Tea Party to some type of conspiracy to assassinate the president?"

"What I'm saying is that Rash Sally had direct ties to Tea Party organizations, especially in Texas. We are fully investigating whether he acted alone or if there was some type of conspiracy."

"Can we assume if there were raids conducted and Tea Party members arrested that there was enough evidence to support this type of law enforcement activity?"

"Under the NDAA, the federal government has the right to detain citizens it believes are tied to terrorist organizations."

"So do your department's actions indicate you believe the Tea Party is a terrorist organization?"

"Well, certainly the Tea Party is somewhat of a fragmented group with extreme factions showing racial and militant behavior," Tibbs replied. "It is certainly in the federal government's purview to act on behalf of our national security to detain those we believe are involved in terror activities."

"In light of recent Congressional hearings into some of the operations and oversight of your department, what do you say to the Arlington chief of police who claims no one from the DOJ, the

FBI or the ATF notified him of the raids, specifically the one in his jurisdiction?" the host asked.

"Our investigations indicated that the particular Tea Party in that area had a large membership and may have included some members who were in local law enforcement. The raid had to be conducted under extreme secrecy so as not to compromise the recovery of evidence or to put our agents in harm's way."

The news host sat up in his chair, getting even more attentive to Tibbs' answers. "Was law enforcement worried that Tea Party members would be armed?"

"Well, there is no doubt that, as a group, Tea Party members have a much higher rate of gun ownership than the American public as a whole. Given the seriousness of the assassination attempt, there is no doubt various agencies that participated took extra safety measures. I think Chief Rodriguez should understand the role the federal government plays in public safety and should completely understand the secrecy required was in everyone's best interests." Tibbs leaned back in his chair.

"We've all seen the videos. How do you explain the beatings of the Tea Party staff members? They don't appear to be a threat to the agents and those videos have sure riled up the group's fellow Texans."

"What the videos don't show is what happened inside the offices of that particular raid." A smug look flashed across Tibbs' face. "I can't comment on those particulars at this time, but I will say the agents felt threatened and acted accordingly. This is all part of the ongoing investigation. We will also evaluate the agents' handling of the situation."

The host nodded, then shot Tibbs another question. "Did the government find any weapons at this location or any other location? The videos on the Internet don't show your agents confiscating weapons."

The smug look vanished. Tibbs seemed to be getting a little irritated and fidgeted in his seat. He apparently hadn't expected this line of questioning from a network that was generally left-leaning.

"Again, I can't comment on specific details of the investigation, but I can say weapons were confiscated in the overall actions that were taken that day."

"So are you saying there were weapons at the offices where the raid took place in Arlington?"

Tibbs glanced down, then came back to the host. "Jim, I can't comment specifically where weapons were recovered but yes, these raids on groups associated with Rash Sally produced hundreds of weapons."

"Do you have any comments for Governor Brent Cooper and the others who have criticized your department and others in the federal government for the handling of these raids?"

"No, not really. It appears to be all politics. The federal government has full jurisdiction over these matters, so this seems like politics as usual from Governor Cooper. I would be more worried if I were him about Texas' image to the country." Tibbs spat the words. "Another potential assassin from Dallas? I'm sure the citizens of Texas wish the image of the JFK killing and now this would just go away."

"Thank you, Mr. Attorney General, for being on our show today."

"Thanks for having me. One more item I may add... the president's message tomorrow night relates to some of the topics we discussed today."

"I wish we had more time to discuss it," the host said, curiosity showing on his face. "We look forward to seeing you again soon. Good luck with your investigation. America wants to know all the details!"

Monday morning at 9:00 Eastern Time, the White House released the executive order as announced.

At first, news organizations in the mainstream media didn't pick up on the significance of the order. Mainly touted as a way to quell the ongoing urban violence and domestic terror activities, the order was hailed by most in the media as another tool in the fight against crime and terrorism, just like the Patriot Act and the National Defense Authorization Act.

Both Gallup and the Washington Times polling showed 53 percent of Americans wanted the federal government to take steps to end the violence that started on election night. The polls showed support of presidential authority to act to protect citizens against terror organizations at home, and it was clear the mainstream media had successfully painted the Tea Party as part of this group, especially since the would-be assassin was linked to them.

As the newly released executive order made its way through the daily news cycles, only Fox News and new media outlets began to pick up its significance.

Several members of Congress from Texas, South Carolina, Oklahoma and Alabama held an impromptu news conference questioning the constitutionality of the order. ABC was the only news outlet that mentioned their opposition, but did not show coverage of their comments on the order.

Chuck Dixon kept Fox News on at all times in his office, mostly muted. Throughout the day, he constantly monitored breaking news email alerts on his computer from Breibart.com, the Blaze, the Daily Caller and other new media sites. He saw the breaking news about the order on TV, but didn't unmute it in time to hear the details.

He got an email alert and had to read it twice. "Did I read that right? Are you serious?" he wondered, immediately dialing Stan on his cell phone.

"Stan, have you seen this new executive order?"

"No," Mumford said. "What's it say?"

"Johnson just eviscerated both due process and the Second Amendment with one executive order. I'm not kidding."

"Seriously? If that's true, that can never fly!" retorted Mumford.

"Stan, I've read this twice. Are you in your car?"

"Yes, read it to me."

Chuck read it to him slowly—three times.

"Chuck, I really don't know what to say here. Are the American people really going to put up with this? The whole assassination issue is Johnson's opportunity for the ultimate power grab. This is blatantly unconstitutional."

"We know it and there's no doubt many other people know it. But did the reality of what I read to you really, really sink in?"

"Well, I think so. They can restrict gun sales to anyone on their made-up list of terror organizations."

"Yes, but it goes much deeper!" Chuck was almost shouting. "It allows the administration to CONFISCATE, with no due process whatsoever, the firearms of citizens they FEEL pose a threat."

"Holy shit! Read that second section to me again."

Chuck read the entire second section again, this time slower but with emphasis on certain words he wanted Mumford to really grasp.

"We need to call an emergency executive committee meeting again," Stan said.

"Geez, Stan, I bet we are all candidates to have our phones tapped. We have to be very careful. In fact, we should rotate these meeting locations. Pick another place than where we met last time, but it has to be secure." He paused, almost breathless at his next thought. "Can you believe we have to assemble in secrecy?"

-Executive Order-

Domestic Anti-Terrorism Measures

- - - - - - -

ESTABLISHMENT OF NEW RESTRICTIONS ON ACCESS TO WEAPONS BY KNOWN DOMESTIC
TERRORIST ORGANIZATIONS

By the authority vested in me as President by the Constitution and the laws of the United States of America, and in order to promote the safe pursuit of Life and Liberty for United States Citizens, government employees, law enforcement and the military it is hereby ordered as follows:

Section 1 - Restrictions on Gun Sales to Domestic Terror Organization Members. New regulations regarding the sale of any firearm or ammunition for a firearm by a member of a known domestic terror organization as identified by the National Defense Authorization Act (NDAA). The Justice Department shall coordinate with Homeland Security, FBI, ATF, CIA, NSA (Intelligence Community) with state and local law enforcement officials to enforce such restrictions as follows:

    a) Nullify, ban or completely restrict the sale of any firearms and/or ammunition of any kind for a firearm, to any known members of domestic terror organizations as defined by the NDAA or which may be identified by the Justice Department from time to time.

Section 2 - Restrictions on Firearm Ownership to Domestic Terror Organization Members. New regulations regarding the Ownership of any firearm by a member of a known domestic terror organization as identified by the National Defense Authorization Act (NDAA). The Justice Department shall coordinate with Homeland Security, FBI, ATF, CIA, NSA (Intelligence Community) with state and local law enforcement officials to enforce such restrictions as follows

    a) Nullify, ban or completely restrict the ownership of any firearms and/or ammunition of any kind for a firearm to any known members of domestic terror organizations as defined by the NDAA or which may be identified by the Justice Department from time to time.

    b) Provide for the recovery of firearms and/or ammunition of any kind from a person or persons known to be a member of a domestic terror organization as identified by the NDAA or which may be determined by the Justice Department from time to time.

Section 3 – Establishment. The Justice Department will establish a special task force reporting directly to the Attorney General of the United States for the enforcement of this Executive Order.

Section 4 - General Provisions. This order shall be implemented consistent with applicable law and subject to the availability of appropriations.

    a) Nothing in this order shall be construed to impair or otherwise affect:
        (i)   authority granted by law, regulation, Executive Order, or Presidential Directive to an executive department, agency, or head thereof; or

This order is not intended to, and does not, create any right or benefit, substantive or procedural, enforceable at law or in equity by any party against the United States, its departments, agencies, or entities, its officers, employees, or agents, or any other person.

TYRELL JOHNSON

Chapter 22

"The tree of liberty must be refreshed from time to time with the blood of patriots and tyrants."

~ Thomas Jefferson

President Johnson made a short, pointed videotaped statement from the Oval Office. "My fellow Americans, events over the last several months have forced our nation to look at how we protect the American public, our elected officials and our military from domestic threats of terrorism.

"As we learned from 9/11, terrorism is not confined to some distant country. We must realize that terrorism and terrorists can and do operate within our borders and, as much as we would like to ignore this fact, it could be your neighbor right down the street.

"I have listened to law enforcement officials and the American public. They are tired of the old arguments of the past that have encouraged the rise of violence here at home. It is unacceptable for groups that present a clear and present danger to our country to be allowed to purchase, obtain and own firearms.

"I have signed an executive order, effective today, that prohibits those groups from obtaining and owning firearms. Make no mistake; this is NOT an attack on the Second Amendment. By definition, the types of groups and members of those groups that have been identified can be considered enemy combatants. In the same way we would limit enemy combatants' access to firearms and the ammunition of those firearms, we will do so under this executive order."

Pausing for effect and looking sternly into the camera, the president continued. "My most cherished responsibility is to protect every man, woman and child in America, and I will do so unashamedly."

The administration, buoyed by poll numbers showing the majority of Americans supported such actions, underestimated the ferocity of the opposition mounting from the typical places, and from some places not so typical, to oppose the administration.

Immediately, the president of the National Rifle Association conducted a press conference calling Johnson's executive order, "The most serious frontal attack on American liberty and the Second Amendment in the history of the United States Constitution."

Even the ACLU expressed concerns over the combination of the NDAA with the order. It was apparent that rage over the order was building within various caucuses of Congress. The Tea Party Caucus, which had largely gone silent since election night, was back in front of the cameras as a group, stating concerns about how the government might classify a terrorist organization, especially the Tea Party.

* * *

Chuck and Stan were wrapping up their Tea Party executive committee meeting at the lake house of one of the members. It was almost as if the cell phones of all twelve members of the executive committee started going off at once with a cacophony of ring tones and text messages.

Colton had sent a text to his dad. "Dad—get home right now. Police are here." Chuck dialed home, his wife's cell, and his son's cell and got no answer.

The rest of the small group was in a panic. It was clear homes of the executive committee members were being raided at the exact same moment.

Mumford was especially agitated. When he got a call from his wife, it was clear there was a scuffle before the phone went dead.

The executive committee members sped away from the lake house. Now their homes and families were under attack.

When Mumford got to his street, it was sealed off by the ATF and local law enforcement.

"I live down this street, and I want to get to my family right now," Mumford yelled at the ATF officer who came to his driver's side window.

"What is your name, sir?"

"Stan Mumford," Mumford replied, clearly irritated.

"Step out of the vehicle, Mr. Mumford."

"Why?" Mumford demanded.

"Just step out of the vehicle now," shouted the officer. Several others surrounded Mumford's F-250 truck, with weapons pointed towards the ground but clearly ready.

"Where are my wife and children?"

"Just get out of the vehicle," the officer repeated.

Mumford put his hands where the officers could see them, and the ATF officer opened the driver's door. Mumford stepped out.

As an officer put his hands on Mumford's arm as if to fold it behind his back for handcuffs, he pulled back violently.

"What the hell? You have no right to handcuff me. I am just trying to get to my home and my family."

"Mr. Mumford, put your hands behind your back now," screamed several officers at the same time. Just then, Mumford saw his wife and three children sitting in the back of a van on bench seats four homes down from the intersection.

"Why is my family in that goddamn van? What the hell is wrong with you people?"

Mumford noted that his wife and kids turned to see the commotion down the street, not knowing until then that Stan's arrival was causing the commotion.

Glancing at his house, Mumford saw agents carrying guns, files and computers out of the house into another waiting van. Mumford began walking toward his house as agents drew down on him, yelling at him to stop and put his hands behind his head.

"Are you freakin' kidding me?" Mumford roared. "Let me go see if my wife and kids are okay."

Mumford, who was six foot four and about 320 pounds, was wearing an untucked oversized Hawaiian button-down, short-sleeved shirt.

"Put your hands up and get on the ground!"

"I have a bad back," Mumford said, putting his hands up like a touchdown was just scored and then lowering them to about three-quarters of where he started. "You can handcuff me, but I want to see my family, please."

"Put your hands behind your back, now!" shouted one of the ATF agents. By now, seven agents had guns openly drawn on Mumford.

"Okay, okay, okay… Jesus!" Mumford whimpered.

He slowly put both hands behind his back so he could be cuffed. As he did, his right hand edged his shirt up over his belt, exposing the holster containing his Ruger .380 handgun. He tried to pull his shirt back over the weapon.

"He's going for his gun!" shouted the original ATF agent who got him out of his truck and was now positioned behind Mumford.

Shots rang out and for a few seconds, Mumford stood motionless with a look of disbelief on his face. Then he crumpled, his head and face smacking the concrete street with a sickening noise. Screams came from the van holding Mumford's family.

The agents shot Mumford six times. He was dead before he hit the ground. They began shouting orders and incoherent epithets at Mumford's motionless body, now lying in a spreading pool of blood.

* * *

The situation at Chuck's house mirrored Mumford's, and was apparently going down in the exact same manner all over Texas and several other states where Tea Party members had been targeted.

As Chuck pulled onto his street, he was pulled from his vehicle and handcuffed. Unlike Mumford, however, Chuck was allowed to talk to his wife and son before he was put in a separate van. He witnessed federal agents as they carried files, computers and guns from his home to waiting vans, where each item removed was apparently inventoried.

The lead ATF agent opened the rear door to the van holding Chuck. "I need the combination to your safe," said the agent.

"Where's your warrant? Let me see your search warrant!" Chuck was furious; none of the agents had offered him a warrant, and he damned sure wasn't going to give them the combination to his twenty-five gun safe.

"I don't need a warrant, Mr. Dixon. You're part of a terrorist organization, an enemy of the state. You are an enemy combatant who doesn't get the rights of a U.S. citizen. Now give me the goddamn combination!" The agent's voice rose angrily.

"Go fuck yourself," Chuck roared. "I want an attorney. Let my family go!"

"We'll just be here that much longer and your family will be held in detention for as long as it takes," yelled the agent. He slammed the rear cargo doors.

The agents huddled to discuss options regarding the safe. Chuck hoped his wife and son could read his lips as he tried to reassure them through the van windows they would be okay.

About thirty minutes passed before a heavily-armored SWAT vehicle with what appeared to be a gun turret showed up. The agents got together with SWAT officers on Chuck's front lawn.

As Chuck watched, the armored vehicle went over the curb right for his house. His memory flashed back to images of Waco, where tanks punched holes into the compound that eventually caught fire and so many died at the hands of some of these same agencies.

The armored vehicle punched several holes right into Chuck's study. It went back and forth, tearing down brick, mortar, windows and framing. He glanced over at his wife in the next van. She raised both hands over her face as if to block the carnage, but peeked through her fingers, unable to keep herself from watching as her home was destroyed.

To Chuck's horror, the vehicle's protruding arm ravaged the beautiful built-in cabinetry that he'd had a carpenter custom build to fit around the large safe. In a matter of two minutes, the entire cabinetry and wall around the safe were gone, and people on the street could see all the way through the house to the rear door. Pieces of the ceiling and load-bearing structural framing started to fall.

Two SWAT personnel in full riot gear entered the huge hole and wrapped a heavy link chain around the safe. They pulled the chain until there was no slack, then hooked it onto the armored vehicle.

The vehicle backed up. As it started to pull the safe through the rubble, the safe turned over on its side. The destructive vehicle continued to pull the safe all the way to the street, gouging the lawn and then the sidewalk. Within a few minutes, the long protrusion arm and ten agents positioned the safe on the lift-gate of a waiting Ryder rental truck. The lift-gate was activated, and the safe was raised and pushed inside for transport.

Fox affiliates in Dallas and Houston were the first news outlets to broadcast news about the raids. Local officials, including some law enforcement officials, blasted the federal government for conducting the raids only hours after the executive order was made public, for not keeping local law enforcement informed of operations in their jurisdictions, and for the nature of the raids.

In addition to Stan Mumford, two other Tea Party members were shot and killed. Two ATF agents were wounded in gunfire, one who died several hours later. The mainstream media pounced on this news as clear indicators that Tea Party members were heavily armed and dangerous.

At 10:10 p.m., Governor Cooper issued a statement:

"The federal government, particularly the Justice Department, has conducted unprecedented and unconstitutional acts tonight in the sovereign state of Texas. Not only were warrantless searches and seizures conducted on our citizenry, but three Texans lost their lives at the hands of government agents.

"Texas will not stand for this treasonous over-reach by the Executive Branch. I have reached out to both President Johnson and Attorney General Tibbs for an immediate explanation for the illegal operations conducted tonight. I have not had the courtesy of a return phone call or an explanation of federal government activities into the private affairs of Texans. This is not acceptable and the good people of Texas will NOT stand for it."

* * *

The DOJ conducted coordinated raids in other states— Arizona, Oklahoma, Alabama, South Carolina—on the same day as the raids in Texas. One Tea Party member in South Carolina was killed and a federal agent was shot and wounded in Arizona.

The administration, which had now identified the Tea Party and any faction, group or organization with pro-Tea Party ideologies as terrorist organizations under the NDAA, was now engaged in full-scale warfare against these groups. The Justice Department authorized wiretaps, surveillance, and confiscation of firearms, computers, and records. It even went so far as to freeze the personal and business bank accounts of Tea Party members.

Chapter 23

"The Constitution is not an instrument for the government to restrain the people; it is an instrument for the people to restrain the government—lest it come to dominate our lives and interests."

~ *Thomas Jefferson*

Steve Milford, a 38-year-old mid-level Justice Department attorney who commuted daily to the DOJ from Alexandria, Virginia, was becoming more and more concerned about his perception of the DOJ's trampling of individual citizens' rights and the apparent disrespect for the Constitution associated with the raids and the actions surrounding them.

Steve had grown up in the area that still clung to the region's proud heritage of Robert E. Lee, the Northern Army of Virginia, and the Confederate cause. On many weekends, Steve took his kids to see Confederate monuments in the area, teaching his children the true circumstances of the War of Northern Aggression, which was not what children were taught in most public and private schools.

Steve's favorite subject in law school was constitutional law, and he graduated with honors from Georgetown Law School. After a short stint as a deputy district attorney and then a criminal law attorney for a large firm, an offer from the DOJ was too good to pass up.

Most of Steve's recent case work for the DOJ involved the prosecution of drug cartel members brought to the United States under extradition, along with some case work involving jurisdictional case law against various Gitmo detainees. Steve found himself at odds with his superiors more often than not, and was concerned about the overall culture within the department.

Steve's discontent was heightened under Attorney General Tibbs, whom he wholeheartedly distrusted. Steve had always been critical of continuing scandals under Tibbs, and he knew his prospects for advancing in the department were almost non-existent with the re-election of Johnson. He was amazed Congress could not muster enough political heat for Tibbs to resign or to drive him from office.

As Steve sat in the first floor cafeteria of the Department of Justice building, reading a brief and wolfing down a turkey sandwich, one of his fellow co-workers and Georgetown alum Tim Spilner plopped down in the empty chair next to him.

"What's up?" Tim asked.

"Just trying to get through another brief," Steve replied around his bite of sandwich.

Steve had always known Tim as one of the most positive, glass half-full characters he'd ever met. Tim was definitely better connected in the DOJ than Steve, as evidenced by his recent assignment to the Rash Sally investigation. He was one of the very few DOJ attorneys assigned to the case and was involved in the investigation of the assassination attempt and conspiracy.

When Tim didn't say anything more, Steve glanced over at him. He could tell something was weighing on his friend.

"How's your day going?" Steve asked, trying to get Tim to open up.

After some short banter about their kids, wives, college football and Christmas plans, the subject of their conversation changed dramatically.

"So, Tim," Steve said, "what's with all the tension I'm feeling from you? How is the Rash Sally case coming?"

"Steve, you know I can't talk about it, not even to you."

"Well, you got a sweetheart assignment. I mean, hell, that's a career assignment. I knew you leaned left, but not that far left!" Steve laughed.

Tim looked down as if he wanted to say something but couldn't.

"So, not going too well?"

"All I can say is it's not going in the right direction."

"Well, you guys have essentially raided every Tea Party group in the South. Is there a conspiracy or not?" Steve asked, his voice lowered.

"Steve…"

Steve interrupted. "Hell, sorry. I can tell something is really bothering you. These raids are bullshit and you know it. Don't get yourself in trouble, but I have to admit you really have my curiosity piqued now."

Tim was tapping his foot nervously, still looking down and not at Steve while nibbling on a potato chip.

"I mean, shit, Tim, no due process on those guys? Really? No warrants? I know the administration and most of the public want answers and probably blood, but what the hell?"

Tim finally looked Steve in the eye. "All I can tell you right now is we have a major problem. If it blows up or comes out, guys like me will take the fall."

"Geez, must be serious. How can I help?"

"It's probably better you don't know anything. But I really have nobody to go to with this and it's eating me alive," Tim said in a hushed tone.

"Wow, man, sorry to hear that. Are you sure I can't help?"

As Steve asked Tim that question, he found himself questioning if he really wanted to get involved with something that could be career-ending.

"Okay, Steve. If you really want to help, meet me at that little Irish pub down on King Street in Alexandria tonight. Go upstairs and I'll meet you in a corner booth."

"Okay. Are you sure?"

"Yep. Are you sure you really want to know this? It will not be good for you, Steve," Tim said.

"Let me ask you this: Is it the right thing to do?" asked Steve.

Tim swallowed another sip of his Diet Coke, moved closer to Steve and whispered, "I don't know what's right any more. But, in the last few days, people have died, Steve, and everything I have seen and every bone in my body tells me these people died needlessly and they were innocent of any conspiracy."

"Holy shit!"

"Shhh…" Tim looked around to see if anyone had noticed.

"Okay, do you have evidence of this?"

Tim stammered and finally, after a long pause, with eyes closed, said, "Yes."

"Does DOJ leadership have the same information you do?"

"Yes, but I'm not sure how high it goes yet."

"Okay," Steve said, putting his hand on Tim's shoulder. "Let's stop right here and wait until this evening."

Steve headed back to his office. He tried to keep his mind on his job, but Tim's statement about innocent people dying in the last few days had him motivated to find out what Tim knew.

Chapter 24

"A government big enough to give you everything you want is a government big enough to take from you everything you have."

~ *Gerald Ford*

That evening, Steve was first to the quaint Irish pub on King Street. It had been built in the late 1700s, and Steve admired its old brick and exposed wooden beams as he climbed the stairs and found a corner booth with no other patrons around. As he sat there alone, he thought about getting up and leaving.

He knew how politics worked at the DOJ, and he figured the information he was about to receive could end his career, but he couldn't walk away. He had a bulldog mentality when it came to unanswered questions or getting to the truth on issues important to him. It became tougher every minute.

Tim was more than thirty minutes late. Finally, Steve saw him walk into the pub as he peered downstairs from his booth overlooking the bar. Tim spotted him and climbed the stairs.

"Hey, sorry I'm late," Tim said apologetically as he slid into the booth. "I parked about two blocks away, then just sat in the car thinking. What I'm about to do is very serious—for both of us. Do you understand?"

"I do, Tim."

"This could put your job, maybe even your life, in extreme danger. Are you sure you want me to tell you?"

"Tim, I'm here. Talk to me."

Tim rubbed the back of his neck, then said, "You know I admire your principles and beliefs, even when they're not politically correct. You're an Eagle Scout, for God's sake. I just trust you."

"Well, every bone in my body has been telling me to get up and go home." Steve laughed.

"You should listen to your instincts."

"I know, I know."

The bar maid stopped at their booth. "Hi, I'm Terri. Can I get you guys something?"

"You bet," Steve said. "I'll take bourbon and 7-Up. Tim?"

"Just a beer," Tim said, "Anything lite you have on tap."

"You got it." Terri set a couple of coasters on the table and went back to the bar.

Steve and Tim made small talk, not willing to get into a serious discussion until she got back with their drinks. Less than three minutes later, she came back and set the bourbon and 7-Up in front of Steve and a Miller Lite in front of Tim.

"Anything else, boys?"

"No, thanks," Steve told her.

Terri smiled, and left to wait on another group.

Tim took a long, deep sip from the mug and then fidgeted around on his side of the booth bench like he was trying to get comfortable for an uncomfortable conversation. "Okay," he said, "no turning back?"

"Nope, let's go," replied Steve.

Tim kind of slid down on the bench. "Well, I've been involved in several aspects of the Rash Sally investigation. I've seen documents that have come from Sally's apartment, from his computer, email and other sources."

"Okay. What has you concerned?"

"First, make no mistake, Steve. Rash Sally was a practicing Muslim."

"That doesn't fit the typical profile of a Tea Party backer, but I guess it's not impossible," said Steve.

"Actually, we found a lot of evidence critical of the Tea Party."

"Okay, now I'm confused."

"Well, so were we..." Tim said.

Steve interrupted. "But wait. What about the Master's thesis he was writing that was pro-Tea Party? What about his membership to several Tea Party groups and attendance at meetings and events?"

"Well, in reading all the evidence we collected, it appeared Mr. Sally was originally vehemently anti-Tea Party. His original Master's thesis was to be critical of the Tea Party, to infiltrate and expose the supposed anti-Muslim and racist beliefs of Tea Party members and their organizations."

"Tim, I'm not following..."

"It appears that, over a period of about eight months, as he spent more time with Tea Party groups, the more he related to them," Tim said. "He actually found himself liking them. Over time, the original thesis he was writing morphed from a critical piece to a thesis that was sympathetic and understanding of the Tea Party and their love for the Constitution."

"Let me get this straight, Tim. First, Sally was a Muslim, which nobody suggested or reported?"

"There is no doubt."

"Did he belong to a mosque?" Steve asked.

"Not actively, but it was apparent he still practiced his religion."

"Just so I'm clear," Steve interjected, "Sally was a Muslim student who basically wanted to infiltrate the Tea Party and write a negative thesis about them, and then ended up joining them?"

"Not exactly," Tim said. "He appreciated most of their values but not one hundred percent. His nearly final thesis was mostly favorable to the Tea Party, but his conclusion was that he didn't find any evidence of widespread racism or hatred toward Muslims as portrayed in the media."

"Well, they have only released positive excerpts about the Tea Party from his paper to the press. I can see why it's been spun this way. I mean, the administration was handed a perfect knife to eviscerate the Tea Party. I'm not hearing anything too earth-shattering, Tim."

"Sally was an Iranian."

"What?" Steve was stunned.

"In the preliminary evidence, we didn't see anything that indicated Sally was connected to any terrorist groups. A more in-depth examination found emails back and forth with suspected Iranian terror cells in the U.S., France and Middle East, mostly sent after Operation Python."

"Son of a bitch!"

"It turns out Rash Sally was incensed over Operation Python."

"Goddamn, Tim, are you telling me that Sally's motive had nothing to do with the Tea Party and everything to do with us bombing Iranian nuclear facilities?"

"Not only am I telling you his very loose association with the Tea Party groups was only for his Master's thesis," Tim said, "but those ties had absolutely nothing to do with the assassination attempt, at least from every piece of evidence I have seen."

Deep in thought, Steve raised his glass to take a drink and realized it was empty. Just as he set it down, Terri appeared and asked if they wanted another round. Steve was a little irritated by the interruption, but he told her they were fine. She moved away to the bar.

"So what evidence did you find that Sally was motivated by the strike on Iran?"

Tim shrugged. "We have hundreds of emails. Not only that, but Sally kept a personal journal. The journal had his personal extremist writings, including threats on the president that started the day after the raids."

"This is unbelievable."

"There's more," Tim said.

Steve leaned back on the bench, his mind racing. "Like what?"

"Sally's sister and her family lived in Natanz, Iran where one of the nuclear facilities was obliterated, and they were all killed in the bombings."

"Goddamit!" Steve tried to drink from his empty glass again.

Tim continued, "Now you know why I have a difficult time sitting on this."

"How many know what you know?"

"At my level, none," Tim said quietly.

Steve shook his head. "There's no way this doesn't go all the way to the top. Absolutely no way."

"Well, that's my belief, too, but I have no proof. This is beyond Watergate stuff." Tim's hands were shaking. "Couple this with the recent actions the DOJ and the administration have conducted against American citizens, and we're talking about impeachable criminal offenses."

"I know, I know," said Steve as he sat contemplating their next move.

"Steve, this is only going to get worse. DOJ is planning more actions against the Tea Party."

"How much of this evidence do you have access to?"

"Right now, none. I've only seen it and studied it with others. It is under very tight security."

"Where is that journal?" Steve asked as he nervously turned his empty glass around in a circle.

"I really can't say at this point. The journal is interesting. We had it for three full days while it was being translated from Arabic to English, and then it was suddenly gone. Every entry, copy and all the physical notes related to that journal are gone. We were all told never to mention it and to consider the journal nonexistent. Period."

"Wow!" Steve gasped. "Unbelievable!"

"Steve, all the notes from the investigation group are kept in laptops under security. I'm not using any of my own equipment. We are not allowed in the operations investigation room with anything and we can't leave the room with anything. We aren't frisked or searched, but nobody can leave with a document, laptop or anything else."

Steve was incredulous. "That means anything you say to anyone would be your word against the DOJ."

"I know that, but I have an angle I'm working on," Tim said. "I can't tell you what it is, but I know I have to have something to show or I'll be eaten alive if I come out with this information."

"You're planning on coming out with it?" Steve asked. "Damn, Tim, I can't tell you how much danger you could put yourself in. You're a good little soldier to them, which is why you're in that room. It would be the ultimate betrayal."

"Don't you think I know that? I can't sleep. I can barely eat or function."

"Who else knows?"

"Nobody." Tim sounded miserable, but somehow relieved. "And I do mean nobody. Not my wife. Not anyone."

"How many in the group have been exposed to this information?"

"Five, plus me. They have been very careful how information is disseminated to leadership. I don't know for sure who carries it forward, but there are two from our department and three from the FBI."

"How sure are you about this angle you are working?"

"Not sure at all," Tim said. "I'm not sure at all, but I'll keep you posted."

"Tim, I can't stress…"

"I know, I know. I'll be careful."

"Come on." Steve got up and dropped a tip on the table. "My treat."

"Thanks, Steve. You're a good friend."

Steve paid their bar tab on the way out. The two men separated at the exit, and Steve trotted over to his vehicle.

On the drive home, he was so deep in thought that he drove right past the last left turn to his house, going two blocks too far before realizing it. He tried to put himself in Tim's shoes. What would he do in the same situation? How could Tim produce evidence to be a whistleblower? As far as Steve could tell, Tim was sitting on a powder keg of unprecedented proportions.

Chapter 25

"He who allows oppression shares the crime."

~ *Desiderius Erasmus, 16th Century*
Catholic Priest and Scholar

After loading the safe into the Ryder rental truck, the federal agents turned to Chuck.

"Mr. Dixon, turn around and put your hands behind your back."

Christy began screaming at the agents. "What are you doing? Leave him alone! Why did you destroy our home? Leave him alone!"

"Ma'am, we are just taking your husband for questioning. You need to relax and settle down," retorted an agent.

"Honey, I'll be okay. Go to your mom's." Chuck couldn't think of anything else to say to his wife. All of this was happening in front of Colton, who was crying.

The agents shoved Chuck into a windowless blue van with metal benches in the back and iron shackles already welded to them. He was secured at the ankles, even though he was already handcuffed. Two agents jumped into the van as another agent outside closed both cargo doors.

"What are you doing with my wife and son?" Chuck demanded.

"We're not interested in them. They'll be released," said a tanned, muscled agent who looked out of place in his neatly pressed button-down shirt and black silk tie.

"Where is your warrant? What am I being arrested for?"

"We've already had that discussion, Mr. Dixon, yet here you are. I suggest you think seriously about cooperating with the agents who are going to question you on your anti-American activities."

"Are you kidding?" Chuck had never thought of himself as crazy, though these events might induce insanity in some people. "You think the Tea Party is anti-American?"

"Any group that produced Rash Sally surely isn't patriotic."

"I've never met the man in my life."

"It doesn't matter," the agent said, leaning back against the van interior. "You're part of a larger conspiracy."

"What?" Chuck squirmed around, trying to get comfortable in chains without much success. "Conspiracy to do what?"

"Dixon, you won't be asking the questions; we will. Now shut up and enjoy the ride."

"Go screw yourself."

The agent smiled grimly. "I'd say you're the one who is screwed right now."

Forty-five minutes later, the van pulled into Ellington Air Force Base just outside Houston and was directed by an armed guard into a large empty hangar. The giant doors closed as the van stopped inside. Someone from outside opened the cargo doors. Chuck was unshackled, and then he was hauled bodily from the van and portable leg shackles were placed around his ankles.

He noticed there were more than a dozen unmarked cars with U.S. government license plates in the hangar, as well as several marked Homeland Security.

He was manhandled into a small group of offices on the south side of the hangar. The offices were stark, empty except for metal chairs and tables.

The agents brought their prisoner to an empty room with a bare metal table and a metal chair. One agent led Chuck to the front of the chair, then shoved him down onto the seat. His hands were uncuffed and then recuffed in front of him so they could be attached to a hook fastened to the table, and his shackled legs were clamped to the chair.

For an hour and half, Chuck sat there alone, his ears trying to pick up sounds from outside the room. But he heard nothing at all, and guessed the room was soundproof.

Three men in dark suits burst into the room, accompanied by two uniformed ATF agents and several other men with audio and video recording devices. The technicians set up the video and voice recorders.

"Mr. Dixon, we are going to conduct an interview, so please hang with us for a few minutes," one of the suited men told him.

"I want to know why I am being held."

"Mr. Dixon, this will go a lot faster if you allow us to ask the questions."

"Bullshit. I want an attorney, and I want one now," Chuck said.

"Mr. Dixon, this is a matter of national security. As an enemy combatant, you are not entitled to rights you see on TV."

"Enemy combatant? Wow! You guys are something."

"Joe, is everything ready?" The suit in charge directed his question to the man operating the video equipment.

"Yes, ready when you are," Joe said.

The agent pulled a chair up and sat across from Chuck. "Mr. Dixon, my name is Agent Jackson with the FBI. We are here to ask you questions relating to your membership and activities of the Tea Party group you organized and helped found."

"Okay, let's get this over with. Then we can talk about how you are going repair my home," answered Chuck.

"Mr. Dixon, who are the other founding members of your Tea Party organization?"

"I don't have to answer that or any other questions without an attorney."

"Mr. Dixon, I'll ask you once more, and for the last time. Who helped you found your Tea Party organization?"

"I don't remember," Chuck said.

"Mr. Dixon," Jackson said in a clipped tone, "this will go a lot faster if you cooperate and your cooperation could help you if you are indicted or prosecuted."

"Prosecuted for what?" Chuck snorted.

"We will get to that. For now, I need those names."

"Not a chance."

"Mr. Dixon, have you ever traveled to the Dallas area and met with other Tea Party organizers and members from the North Richland Hills Tea Party? The Lone Star Tea Party Chapter? The Fort Worth Tea Party Patriots? The Dallas Tea Party Coalition? What about the Denton Tea Party Patriots?"

"Agent Jackson, is it? Yes, I have met some of them, but not all. Why?"

"Tell me when you first met them."

"Look," Chuck said, settling back as far as he could in the chair. "I'm not telling you anything more without an attorney present."

"Mr. Dixon, where are your membership files? Are they on your computer?" Jackson asked.

"No."

"Then where are they?"

"I want an attorney."

Agent Jackson was nothing if not persistent. "Mr. Dixon, who had access to your membership files?"

"I want an attorney." Chuck was adamant.

"Mr. Dixon, do you realize that, as an enemy combatant, we can hold you indefinitely. Are you familiar with contrition?"

"You bet I am, and it's unconstitutional."

One of the agents in the room who had remained silent until now looked at Chuck in a disgusted manner and said, "Save that for your Teabagger friends."

Jackson shot the guy a "don't interrupt me again" look. "Well, Mr. Dixon, you could experience that firsthand if you don't cooperate. It may be a very long time before you see your wife and your son."

"Screw you."

"How many times did you travel to Dallas to meet with these

other groups?" Jackson said.

"I want an attorney." Chuck had settled into defiance.

"Mr. Dixon, we have already looked at the two laptops we recovered from your house and your emails are erased. Why did you delete your entire email history?"

"I want an attorney."

"Does someone not guilty of anything typically erase his entire email history, Mr. Dixon?" Jackson persisted.

"Like I said, I want an attorney."

"Mr. Dixon, do you want to see your wife and son anytime soon?" Jackson got up and leaned on the table with both hands.

"Are you holding them, too?"

"No, we are not at this time," Jackson said. "How this all breaks down and moves forward, however, is up to you."

"Look," Chuck told him, "my organization is peaceful. There's no conspiracy in our group or the other Tea Party groups whatsoever. You're way off."

"Mr. Dixon, have you ever met Rash Sally?"

"The would-be assassin?" Chuck laughed. "Are you serious? Never."

"Did Mr. Sally ever contact you?"

"Holy shit, no."

"Could it be you forgot, Mr. Dixon? Could it be he attended one of your events or meetings?"

Chuck leaned forward again. "Some of our meetings had hundreds of people attend. Some of our large events had thousands. One of them in Houston alone was attended by over ten thousand people at Sam Houston Raceway. It's possible," he said emphatically, "but I never met him, nor do I know anyone who did."

"What about your compatriots in the Dallas area?" Jackson asked. "Did anyone ever speak of him when you met with or did joint meetings with those groups?"

"The first time I ever heard of that joker was on the news. I don't recall anyone mentioning him—ever."

Jackson slid into his chair again. "Would it surprise you that he was very active with numerous Tea Party groups?"

"Yes, it would. But you guys are the experts." Chuck made no attempt to hide his sarcasm. "Frankly, I'll be shocked if you find any true connection whatsoever. No real Tea Party group would ever advocate shooting a sitting president. None of us has ever advocated shooting anyone."

"Mr. Dixon," Jackson said, "we've already found connections."

"I doubt very seriously you found any legitimate Tea Party organization with conspiracy ideas."

"Yet you made sure your laptop was erased." Jackson looked like the cat that ate the canary.

"I never said the Tea Party wasn't suspicious of the federal government," Chuck exclaimed. "Look what you did to my house and how you terrorized my family."

"So I'll ask you again, Mr. Dixon, where are your membership files?"

"And I'll answer you again, Jackson. I want an attorney and I want to know exactly why you are holding me. What crime have I committed?"

"You are being held for investigation of conspiracy to murder the president of the United States."

Chuck looked at Jackson in disbelief. "And what evidence do you have that I have anything to do with a conspiracy like that?"

"We'll see once the forensics folks recover your email files from your computer," said Jackson, getting up and turning his back to Chuck. He stared down at the concrete floor, rubbing his chin. Chuck decided the agent was contemplating his next move.

After a few long minutes, Jackson turned around and stared at Chuck. "Is there anything you want to tell us before those files are recovered? If you cooperate now, it may help you later regarding an indictment. This is your last chance," he said calmly.

"Yes, there is."

Jackson and the others in the room adjusted their body language as if they believed they'd just broken their suspect. They looked at him expectantly. "Well," Jackson said, "what do you want to tell us?"

"Is your video recorder still on?" Chuck asked.

"Yes, it is," Jackson said, after he got a thumbs up from Joe. "Well, Mr. Dixon?"

Chuck leaned toward the microphone and spoke slowly and distinctly. "First, you invaded my home and damaged it without a search warrant. Second, you detained me and my family unlawfully. I was never read my Miranda rights. Third, I have not been granted access to an attorney. Now I want to know where my wife and son are and that they are okay."

Jackson looked like he was on the verge of an outburst, but he managed to get his emotions under control before he spoke again. "Mr. Dixon, that's cute, but I already told you that, as an enemy combatant under the National Defense Authorization Act, a suspected terrorist does not have those rights."

"Suspected terrorist?" Chuck mocked. "You guys are Keystone Cops!"

Jackson sighed and started over again. He tried for two more hours to get Chuck to say anything that would lead the agents to other Tea Party members, information about how they were organized, where they met and more questions about Rash Sally.

At a break in the intense interrogation, Jackson told his prisoner, "You're lucky. Your buddy Stan Mumford stupidly went for his sidearm, and we were forced to shoot him."

Chuck was incredulous. "You what? Stan would never try to shoot a bunch of your armed thugs. Where is he?"

Jackson had the good sense to at least look remorseful. "I'm sorry," he said. "Mr. Mumford was shot dead."

"Agent Jackson, I don't think you have a clue what that's going to cost you," Chuck said angrily.

"Is that a threat, Mr. Dixon?"

"Call it what you will," Chuck retorted. "Just remember you're in Texas."

Deep down, Chuck felt the whole series of events was surreal. How could this be happening in the United States of America?

Finally, weary of not getting anywhere, the agents moved Chuck to an adjoining room that had a small bathroom with a toilet, sink and small military-style bunk.

An agent brought in a bottle of water and gave it to Chuck. Before he pulled the door shut, the agent said, "Today was the easy day. I'm sure you've read what we do to terrorists in our interrogations in other countries." He laughed. "And we can't wait to see what was on your laptop. Believe me, your computer is being hacked, and these guys are good. They'll find everything you erased."

Chuck saw two more agents on either side of the door before it slammed shut. He heard the door being locked. He drank the small bottle of water, then went over and sat on the bed. Are they serious? he wondered. I guess I'm going to be water boarded tomorrow. I can't believe this crap is happening to me.

Chuck finally fell asleep about 2:00 a.m., with his last thoughts about where his wife and son were and if they were okay. Did they go home? Were they with relatives? Were they safe?

Chapter 26

"The power of the Executive to cast a man into prison without formulating any charge known to the law, and particularly to deny him the judgment of his peers, is in the highest degree odious and is the foundation of all totalitarian governments whether Nazi or Communist."

~ *Sir Winston Churchill*

At 6:15 a.m. two days later, six four-door sedans pulled into the main guarded entry of Ellington Air Force Base just south of Houston. The Great Seal of the State of Texas was prominently displayed on each car's front doors

The vehicles were at the guard shack for less than two minutes before the gate arm went up. The sedans entered and made a beeline to the hangar near the south runway where Chuck Dixon was being held by federal agents.

As the vehicles pulled up to a small door to the left of the giant hangar doors, two ATF agents appeared in full tactical gear, holding HK automatic weapons.

As the occupants of the sedans got out of the vehicles, one agent turned to the other and said laughingly, "Holy shit, it looks like John Wayne and his posse have shown up."

Texas Ranger "Pops" Younger, sixty-seven, a legend in the historic and elite independent law enforcement unit that reports directly to the governor of Texas, reached onto the front seat for his cowboy hat.

Eight Texas Rangers emerged from the vehicles, all with trademark cowboy hats, cowboy boots and holstered guns. Every one of them looked like they could have been peeled right off a 1960s Marlboro ad.

"Gentlemen, my name is Younger with the Texas Rangers. I have a search warrant in my hand issued by State Attorney General Jeff Weaver and Governor Brent Cooper of Texas, signed by a Texas circuit judge, allowing me access to this hangar to search for a missing Texas citizen named Chuck Dixon."

"Mr. Younger, I. . ."

Pops interrupted him. "It's Ranger Younger to you, son"

"Okay, Ranger Younger, this is a federal operation on federal property and your search warrant doesn't mean shit here."

"Son, the last time I looked, you were standing on Texas dirt."

"No, sir. This is a United States Air Force base. You will not be granted entry."

Just then, two more agents came out, also with HK automatic weapons. They were followed by lead agent Jackson.

Jackson planted his feet solidly on the ground. "Sir, my name is Agent Jackson with the FBI. I am in charge of this operation. You say you have a search warrant?" A look of curiosity flashed across his face. "How did you find out this operation was here at Ellington?"

Pops looked down and spit a small amount of tobacco on the tarmac. He adjusted his cowboy hat. "Well," he said in his Texas drawl, "Agent Jackson, I have a legal search warrant to examine this hangar. We have reason to believe you are holding a Texas citizen in this hangar unlawfully." He handed the warrant to Jackson.

Agent Jackson unfolded the search warrant and read it through. "Sir, what is your name?"

"Ranger Younger."

"Well, sir," Jackson stated, "this search warrant has no standing on federal property. You are on a United States Air Force base." A contemptuous smile formed on his face.

"Which is on Texas soil," replied Pops.

"Sir, we could sit here and argue all day long. If you'll wait, however, I need to call my superiors in Washington, D.C."

"Mr. Jackson," Pops drawled, "you go right ahead. I'll give you five minutes, then we are executing this warrant and searching this property."

Clearly agitated, smile wiped off his face, Agent Jackson replied, "We'll see."

Jackson opened the door and asked one of his fellow agents to come with him. As they walked into the hallway, Jackson said, "Call base security. Tell them we have an issue and dispatch them here. In the meantime, I'll call the director."

The scene outside the hangar door was getting more tense by the minute. Three Rangers left to walk around the hanger to station themselves near any rear entry point.

Jackson spent two full minutes on the phone with FBI Director Henry Woodhouse. As he hung up, he said, "No way in hell are they getting in here."

Jackson returned to the tarmac with a slight smirk on his face. He told the agent with him to stay just inside the closed door.

"Ranger Younger, I have been instructed by FBI Director Henry Woodhouse and the United States Justice Department that you have no jurisdiction on this base and you will be denied access to execute your search warrant."

"Agent Jackson, I am here under the direct order of the governor of Texas and I have a valid, legal search warrant issued by a Texas circuit judge."

"Like I said," Jackson said forcefully, "and I'm only going to say it one more time, you have no jurisdiction here and I have been ordered not to allow you to execute your warrant."

"Then, son, you and your fellow agents are violating Texas law."

Just then, the agent who had made the snide John Wayne remark couldn't help himself, "You redneck hicks need to leave. Screw you and screw Texas."

Suddenly, before the agents could act, Pops had his Colt .45 out of his holster and pressed against the neck of Jackson. Before any of the agents could pull their weapons up, all five of the remaining

Rangers had their guns drawn on the agents.

"Agent Jackson, I'm placing you and your agents under arrest for obstruction of justice, violating a court order and violating a direct executive order of the governor of Texas."

The agent who had been behind the door rushed out with his gun drawn and began to point it at Pops. Before he could get the gun raised to chest level, a shot rang out and the agent dropped where he stood. One of the Texas Rangers shot the agent when he drew his gun on Pops.

"Get down on the ground, NOW," yelled the Rangers. The agents immediately dropped to the ground. The Rangers picked up their weapons and began handcuffing them.

"Have you people lost your minds?" screamed Jackson.

As soon as the weapons were secure and the agents were handcuffed where they lay face first on the tarmac, the Rangers began attending to the agent who was shot. Although he was wearing a bullet-proof vest, the round hit above the vest on the shoulder.

The wounded agent cursed at the Rangers, specifically the one who shot him. Two Air Force security vehicles pulled up, and several military police rushed out. They seemed more shocked at what they were seeing than having any interest in picking sides. The Rangers instructed them to leave any weapons in their vehicles and they were told this was an operation under direct orders from Governor Cooper.

Several of them already knew a search warrant was being served from when the Rangers appeared at the gate, but there was no organized communication set up with the FBI and ATF agents to notify them. The airmen were obviously awed by the sight of the Texas Rangers: dress, mannerisms, ultra confidence and their air of invincibility were captivating.

Slowly the Rangers made their way into the hangar, guns drawn. As they approached the front door of the office complex, Pops positioned himself next to the entry door.

"My name is Pops Younger, Texas Ranger," he called out. "We are here under orders of the governor of Texas with a legal search warrant to search these premises for a Texas citizen you may be holding illegally."

The two remaining agents in the small office complex inside the hangar had heard the gunshot and barricaded themselves in the hallway leading to where Chuck was being held.

Agent Barrows, the senior of the two agents, shouted, "We heard a gunshot."

"One of your agents drew his weapon on us and was dealt with. Put your weapons down and come out with your hands in the air."

"I would like to see the warrant," Barrows said.

Pops slid the warrant under the door. "Here it is. I'll give you two minutes to read it."

Agent Barrows carefully approached, picked up the search warrant and read it. As he read, he tried to dial into headquarters to reach a supervisor with instruction on how he should proceed.

"Son, what is your name?" called Pops.

"Barrows."

"Agent Barrows, your time is up. Open this door and throw down your weapons," the Ranger said.

"I'm not sure I can do that," Barrows said. "I haven't been able to reach headquarters for instructions yet."

"Barrows, the Texas Rangers are outside your door with direct orders from the governor of Texas and have presented a valid and legal search warrant. You heard the gunshot. One of your fellow agents is wounded. We are not playing around here, waiting for you to call your operations center. Throw down your weapons and come out with your hands up or somebody is going to get hurt. Do you understand what I am telling you?"

There was a momentary silence. Barrows was apparently weighing his options. He heard the sound of an ambulance siren.

"Barrows, I cannot allow an ambulance to come into an active operations area. Your fellow agent is wounded and bleeding. I will not allow this ambulance to recover him unless you surrender, because it is unsafe," reasoned Pops, who was bluffing to avoid further bloodshed.

"We're coming out. There are two of us. Do not shoot."

"Open the door and slide your weapons toward me."

As the door slowly opened, two handguns slid into view, followed by two HK automatic rifles. The agents slowly walked out with their hands raised and were immediately cuffed.

"Are you guys really Texas Rangers?" asked Barrows' fellow agent.

Ranger Elliott, who at six-four looked like a giant sporting a large handlebar mustache and wearing a ten-gallon cowboy hat, said, "Hmmm, what gave it away, son? You federal guys are damn smart, that's for sure."

The Rangers went room by room, shouting Chuck's name. "Mr. Chuck Dixon, are you here? Mr. Dixon, are you here?"

Chuck could tell something had happened but he couldn't hear much but people yelling and a loud pop he thought might be a gunshot. Now he was sure. "I'm here!" he yelled. "I'm locked in a room!"

As the Rangers arrived at his door, they decided to go back to Agent Barrows for the key rather than destroy the door. Coming back with the key from Barrows, Pops opened the door.

"Mr. Dixon, my name is Pops Younger with the Texas Rangers and we have been ordered by the governor to find you and deliver you to him in Austin."

"Thanks much, fellas. What an ordeal this has been." Chuck stepped through the unlocked door. "You mean to tell me the governor knows I'm here and was detained?"

"Thank your wife, Mr. Dixon. After your home was raided, she went straight to the press and sought help from the governor's office. She is one smart cookie."

"So she's okay? My son...?"

"He's fine, too. They are in protective custody and safe in Austin."

"Thank God. Those guys had me in there for three days. I've barely eaten anything, was never formally charged and did not have access to an attorney."

Pops looked like he was pondering the situation as they watched EMTs load the wounded federal agent in the back of the ambulance. "This is getting out of control. The damn feds think they can do anything they want. I can sure tell you this. They may be able to get away with this in other states, but it sure as hell ain't happenin' in Texas."

Chapter 27

"The danger isn't that Big Brother may storm the castle gates. The danger is that Americans don't realize that he is already inside the castle walls."

~ *Wayne LaPierre, National Rifle Association*

News of the Texas Rangers' operation that extricated local Tea Party founder Chuck Dixon from federal custody infuriated Attorney General Jamail Tibbs. The fact that it was personally ordered by the governor of Texas made it worse.

"Who the hell does he think he is?" Tibbs asked ATF Director Barnaby Adamson.

"Obviously Texas and Governor Cooper think they can overstep federal authority whenever it suits them," retorted Adamson.

"Well, we'll just see about that."

* * *

Governor Cooper scheduled a news conference for 11:00 a.m. the next morning. News of the bold Texas Ranger operation to free a Texan being held by federal ATF agents was making national news. The fact that it resulted in a wounded federal agent was secondary.

Nobody could have guessed the sense of outrage by everyday Texans. Video was released to news agencies that were taken by a neighbor where the armored tank destroyed the Dixon home to get to their safe.

The crowd below the steps of the Texas capitol building had grown to over a thousand by 10:00 a.m. Satellite trucks from both domestic and foreign news organizations lined the blocks around the capitol grounds. Hundreds of reporters, photographers and cameramen were everywhere, but the most shocking element was the size and anger of the crowd, normal Texans who had traveled from all over the state in less than twenty-four hours to either voice their displeasure with the federal government's actions or to support Governor Cooper.

People held makeshift signs carrying messages such as "Get the Feds Out!" or "Don't Mess with Texas" and "I support our Texas Rangers!" People were genuinely upset, and the crowd was boisterous. Austin police and the Texas Department of Public Safety (DPS) dispatched extra units to the capitol grounds. Many in the crowd viewed the police with suspicion; however, the DPS officers wearing cowboy hats didn't receive the same suspicious looks and comments.

Texas Attorney General Weaver was introduced first. The crowd cheered when he came to the podium.

"Yesterday," Weaver said, "under orders from Governor Cooper, the Texas Rangers conducted an operation to free a Texas citizen from unlawful imprisonment by federal ATF agents at Ellington Air Force Base near Houston. Chuck Dixon, whose home was searched without a warrant, raided and destroyed and whose family was terrorized by these same agents, had been held without due process, was never read his rights, and was not provided access to an attorney. He was not provided any type of substantive meal for three days. As the attorney general, let me state emphatically that the governor, the Rangers and the people of this state were fully within our authority to conduct this operation. With that backdrop of events, I'd like to bring up Governor Cooper."

The crowd on the capitol lawn started cheering even louder, waving Lone Star flags, the Gadsden Flag, and others.

"Fellow Texans, ladies and gentlemen, and fellow Americans, three days ago, federal agents from the Bureau of Alcohol, Tobacco

and Firearms and the FBI, under the direction of United States
Attorney General Tibbs, conducted illegal searches and raids into
the homes of various Texans whose beliefs they feel are a political
threat to the Johnson administration.

"Chuck and Christy Dixon, and their son Colton, saw their
home destroyed by an armored tank. Their personal property was
confiscated by these same agents. Colton saw his father taken away
in handcuffs while he and his mother were held inside a van used
for prisoners.

"Mr. Dixon was held for three days at a secret location without
the due process afforded him by the Constitution of the United
States. Mrs. Dixon contacted our office and, when the facts about
this operation came to light I decided, as your governor, enough
is enough."

Applause rang out all around the capitol building. Governor
Cooper waited several minutes until the crowd quieted.

"These recent unprecedented attacks on sovereign Texans,
which include the loss of life during the unwarranted shooting of
Texan Stan Mumford in front of his wife and children, are unacceptable. As your governor, I won't stand for this and neither will
Texas!

"When we learned where Mr. Dixon was being held, I instructed the Texas Rangers to retrieve him from federal custody. The
Rangers did an outstanding job and, because of their brave actions,
Mr. Dixon has been reunited with his wife and son and will be
speaking to you here in a few minutes."

The crowd became so loud the governor again had to wait for
relative silence before he could continue.

"Let me state this for the record and for our friends in the attorney general's office, the Treasury Department, the Justice Department and the White House. You will no longer be able to conduct
these types of operations in Texas. They are unlawful, and we will
not stand for our citizens to be abused, arrested, terrorized and

subjugated with your unconstitutional actions. It's time this administration started to follow the Constitution, period."

The governor now had the crowd in a frenzy. Almost all major news media broke into regular programming. The scenes being shown across the networks and streamed live showed an angry but patriotic Texas crowd.

The governor again had to wait minutes to continue. Finally, he said, "It is unfortunate that a federal agent was injured during this operation; however, the fact of the matter is that the agent in question drew a weapon and pointed it with intent to use. The Rangers had no choice but to respond. Now let me take this opportunity to bring up the Texas Rangers who freed Chuck Dixon."

Now the crowd really went crazy. The sight of the iconic Texas Rangers stepping forward to surround Governor Cooper at the podium elevated the noise level to such an extent reporters couldn't be heard in their broadcasts. The cheering and flag waving went on for some time.

Governor Cooper and Attorney General Weaver went down the line to each Texas Ranger, shaking hands and offering congratulations. The crowd on the capitol grounds loved it.

Cooper moved back to the podium. "Now, fellow Texans, let me introduce you to Chuck Dixon. Chuck is a family man from the Houston area who owns his own business. Chuck, please come say a few words."

Chuck strolled to the stage flanked by Caroline and Colton. The crowd continued its loud approval. Reporters and cameramen edged closer to get photos of the family.

"Three days ago," Chuck said, "without any advance notice, ATF agents stormed my home and removed my wife and son. Caroline was able to get a phone call to me about what was happening.

"When I rushed home, I was immediately handcuffed, but not told why. The ATF agents herded my wife and son into a van and separated us. I continually asked them why they were there and I asked for a search warrant."

The crowd started a low grumble as Chuck continued, "They said they didn't need a search warrant for a terrorist. My involvement in founding a local chapter of the Tea Party was apparently enough for them. They removed computers, files, my guns and my safe. To remove the safe, which I had refused to unlock, they brought an armored vehicle in and tore my house down in front of my family."

Now the irate crowd began to boo, whistle and yell. Chuck held up his hands, palms down and signaled for quiet. The noise died down slightly.

"Thank you," Chuck said. "At that point, I was placed in another van, a hood was placed over my head, and I was taken to Ellington Air Force Base. At the time, I had no idea that's where I was and I was given no news on the condition or whereabouts of my family.

"I repeatedly asked what I was being held for, if I was being charged with something, and asked for an attorney. I was ignored. During questioning, it was obvious they wanted to know my relationship with Rash Sally, the president's would-be assassin. I have never met this man to my knowledge. He wasn't a member of our local Tea Party group.

"The agents demanded I provide them the names and addresses of each member of our local Tea Party chapter, and I refused. I did not want any others to experience the same terror my family faced.

"I finally learned from them that my friend Stan Mumford had been shot dead in front his family. I do not know the specifics, but I want to state for the record that Stan Mumford was an outstanding husband, father and businessman. Whatever the government may claim that would lend any credence whatsoever to his murder being justified is just a flat lie.

"During my captivity, I was given two peanut butter sandwiches, water, and two Cokes over three days. That's it."

Many in the crowd were yelling expletives at the ATF, the FBI, the federal government, Attorney General Tibbs and President Johnson.

"This is an attack on free speech," Chuck exclaimed. "I can't speak about the motives of Rash Sally. I can tell you, unequivocally, that our Tea Party organization is all about regaining fiscal sanity in this country and returning to the literal meaning of the Constitution.

"Right now, I wouldn't believe anything that comes out of this administration and, more specifically, the Justice Department."

Governor Cooper, Attorney General Weaver and other dignitaries, law enforcement, and elected officials joined Chuck at the podium. Weaver moved to the front.

"We will now open this up for a few questions."

Reporters began shouting questions. Pointing to a woman just below the capitol steps, Weaver nodded to her.

"This question is for you or Governor Cooper. What do you say to the federal government, particularly the Justice Department, who has claimed you overstepped your authority in this operation?"

The two men glanced at each other, as if to figure out who would answer the question. The governor took the microphone.

"A Texas citizen's family was terrorized and his home destroyed on Texas soil. He was kidnapped without cause, held without due process and wrongly imprisoned on Texas soil. It's well within our rights to conduct the action we took. You must also remember this is not the only incident of this type. The Justice Department has been conducting these types of raids all over the state in recent weeks. Next?"

"The president said this morning that this action by the Texas Rangers was unlawful," said a reporter from CNN.

"What the ATF did to this family and others like this is unlawful and it's not going to be allowed to happen ever again in this state," returned Cooper.

Another reporter yelled, "What if they try this again? What will you do? Essentially, they could deploy thousands of agents—even the military—to enforce what they believe is federal authority."

Cooper turned slightly to his left to indicate the small group of Texas Rangers and said, "Nothing to worry about. We've got these guys!"

The crowd loved it. They cheered and waved flags, shouting their disapproval of the actions of the federal government. It was apparent the crowd had grown since the press conference started. The entire grounds of the state capitol were full of proud and indignant Texans.

Chapter 28

"The patriot volunteer, fighting for country and his rights, makes the most reliable soldier on earth."

~ *General Stonewall Jackson,*
Confederate States of America

In a situation room in the West Wing of the White House, Tyrell Johnson, Jamail Tibbs, Benjamin Gould, Cliff Radford and other cabinet members watched the press conference in Austin on television.

"Damn, that looks like Chechnya or the Arab Spring!" one cabinet member remarked, referring to the thousands of people standing shoulder to shoulder with signs and Lone Star flags waving in the crowd, dotted with the occasional unmistakable yellow Gadsden flag of the Tea Party, and the famous "Come and Take It" Gonzales battle flag.

Several flat screen TVs in the situation room showed news coverage from various networks. On Fox News, commentators broadcast reactions from the governors of other states that had experienced similar raids on Tea Party activists in South Carolina, Oklahoma, Alabama and Arizona. Each of those governors denounced the actions of the Justice Department and voiced support of the Texas governor.

When they were asked if they would authorize the same type of actions to recover a citizen they felt was unlawfully detained by the federal government, almost all said they would. The Arizona governor noted that, although she didn't have an elite law enforcement unit such as the Texas Rangers, she knew a few local sheriffs who would jump at the chance for such an operation—referring to two sheriffs in particular who had already had run-ins with the president's attorney general.

"Mr. President, this sets a very bad precedent. We need to put this cowboy in his place and reaffirm the role of the federal government to him and to Texas. To let Texas set this precedent could have severe consequences on everything from the IRS to EPA regulation enforcement," stated Tibbs.

"Well, damn—they shot an ATF agent! I agree there has to be a response," said the president.

"Look, we've never been popular in that state. We need to halt this before it grows. Did you see the size of that crowd?" bemoaned Avery Smith.

"Jamail, what's our move here?" asked the president.

"First, the Texas Rangers involved in that operation should be arrested. Next, we should re-arrest Chuck Dixon."

"What are the national polls saying?" asked the president.

"We don't have any new data since this press conference but the popular notion overall is the governor acted improperly. Most American believe Texans are somewhat arrogant and went off half-cocked on this thing. Don't forget the majority of Americans believe the Tea Party is connected to Rash Sally—fully 63 percent of them," remarked Smith.

"Should we move before we have new polling data from this latest news conference?"

"Mr. President, the longer we wait, the weaker we appear. It will look like we backed off from the Texans. The country is with us on this. Nobody likes the brash arrogance of Texans who think they can trump federal law."

"What's your proposal?" Johnson asked.

"I propose we have our local agents in Dallas and Houston go to Austin and arrest the Texas Rangers involved in the operation, as well as this Tea Party guy, Dixon."

The president sat there for a long moment in silence, his chin in his hand.

"What is the backlash if you go into Austin and grab these guys?"

"Well, in Texas it will be pretty bad, but who gives a shit what Texas thinks? The rest of the country will be glad Texas is taught a lesson. What could have more impact than us going into Texas and grabbing the symbols of their Texas heritage?" Tibbs sounded smug.

"Do you think your staff can just drop into Texas and arrest a Texas Ranger?" asked Smith.

"Ha, you may need SEAL Team Six," laughed Johnson.

"Shit! To arrest some damn cowboys?" exclaimed Gould.

"Well, they did punk your ATF agents," Radford stated.

"With all due respect, Mr. President, if we just arrest the senior Texas Ranger who led this operation, it will have a significant impact," Tibbs said.

"That dude, Pops Younger? He's already a folk hero there," said the president.

"That's just it. He may be a folk hero in Texas but he interfered with a federal government operation as far as the rest of the country is concerned. It's now a matter of national security."

"What about Dixon?"

"He's easy enough to arrest again, just a regular schmoe, but word is they have him in protective custody."

"Were you able to recover anything from his computers? Any issues with the firearms you recovered?"

"Not so far, Mr. President," said Gould.

"But we aren't done with the forensics yet," Tibbs finished.

"Seriously? You guys have had those for days. Why is it taking so long?" questioned Smith.

"Don't worry, Avery, we'll come up with something," sneered Tibbs.

"Mr. President, I don't think you should be briefed on this operation. This is an operation that should be totally contained in Justice," Radford stated emphatically.

"Okay," Johnson agreed, "but don't let it escalate. If you're going to do this, it needs to be a smooth and successful operation."

"We'll put our best people on it. In a day or two, we will have this Texas Ranger and the Tea Party guy parading in front of the cameras in handcuffs."

"Are you going to issue arrest warrants this time?"

"Yes, that's likely," Tibbs said.

"Even though no arrest warrant was issued for this guy Dixon the first time?"

"Here's how it works, Mr. President. The Rangers violated federal law, so a federal warrant for them is easy enough. As far as the Tea Party guy, he can be counted as a fugitive under the terrorist provision of the NDAA. There's essentially no problem with either option."

"But we don't know where this Dixon guy is being held, right?" asked Radford.

"We'll find out," Tibbs said confidently. "We have plenty of friends in law enforcement in Texas. Now that the guy is something of a celebrity, he's harder to hide. When we publish that he's wanted by the FBI, local and state law enforcement will have their hands forced. They'll have to give him up."

The next day, members of the Texas GOP congressional delegation came to the floor of the House of Representatives, demanding a congressional investigation into the actions of the Justice Department and the Executive Branch's role in events that occurred in Texas and five other states. Most egregious, though, was the shooting of Stan Mumford, the destruction of the Dixon home and Dixon's three-day detainment without due process.

House Republicans had tangled extensively with the Justice Department over some of its cases and their cover-ups, holding the attorney general in contempt over relevant document production. The Executive Branch had claimed executive privilege in the case, effectively delaying the resolution of the contempt charge until after the election. Because of the actions of Rash Sally, the American public and most of Congress had their attention diverted elsewhere. Now, the Department of Justice was right back in the crosshairs.

"This is exactly why Congress originally opposed the National Defense Authorization Act. Once the administration determines you are their enemy, they can effectively target political groups whose ideologies and beliefs differ from theirs. This is no different than the old KGB in the former Soviet Union," claimed Congressman Cartwright, a regular critic of the administration and a long-time Tea Party favorite.

"It is downright despicable," Cartwright said forcefully, "that federal agents can go into a sovereign state and destroy a person's home, terrorize his family, and hold him without charges at an undisclosed location for three days. This is effectively rendition of an American citizen on American soil. It's unconstitutional. It's criminal. It must stop now. It has resulted in the unwarranted deaths of several of our fellow Texans. It's an outrage."

The war of words between Austin and Washington was just beginning to heat up. Later in the day, White House Press Secretary Ted Duncan held a news conference.

"The fact of the matter is that law enforcement from Texas violated federal law on federal property, including the shooting of an agent of the United States government," said Duncan at the news conference. "Let me state unequivocally that those responsible for this shooting and the release of a fugitive from justice will be dealt with accordingly. There is no room for state law enforcement officials to usurp federal law enforcement initiatives. We won't stand for it. In this country, we have something called the rule of law, and nobody is immune—including those in Texas who may think they are above federal law."

One of the beat reporters stood up. "Does this mean there could be arrests of those Texas Rangers involved in the release of Mr. Dixon? What about the Texas governor who ordered the operation?"

"The Justice Department will make that call. There are qualified professionals there who know the law and will act accordingly."

"Are you going to arrest the Texas governor?"

Duncan said pointedly, "As I said, I am not in a position to comment about an ongoing investigation. It is clear the state of Texas interfered in this investigation of a possible conspiracy associated with Rash Sally."

"Why didn't the administration notify Texas law enforcement before these raids? Why no search warrants?"

"Again, this is an ongoing investigation of significant importance concerning national security. Certain departments, including the FBI, NSA, Homeland Security, the CIA and the ATF cannot disclose every operation or mission to local law enforcement, as it may have significant public safety implications or jeopardize the mission itself."

The insistent beat reporter continued. "But, as a citizen, how would you expect someone to act if you raided his home without showing a search warrant? How would a person discern, for instance, an ATF agent from a common criminal?"

"Well," said a smiling Duncan, who looked like he had now cornered the beat reporter into a stupid question, "for one thing, your common criminal won't have a badge and normally won't have a jacket or shirt on that is emblazoned with a bright yellow A-T-F."

The rest of the room laughed. The beat reporter didn't give up so easily. "What if they don't show the badge? Can't someone buy a badge at a flea market? Couldn't I easily make an ATF-emblazoned jacket with yellow duct tape?"

"I'm not going to continue to play these scenarios with you." It was apparent Duncan's patience had run out. "The ATF and other federal agents adequately identify themselves. They are not common thugs or criminals and your statement, sir, comparing thugs and criminals to those brave men and women who are out protecting lives every day is regrettable."

"But, how can an unwarranted search and destruction of someone's home...?"

"Sir," an irate Duncan interrupted firmly, "we have already addressed these questions in prior press conferences. The ATF and FBI have full authority under the NDAA to perform necessary operations on suspected terrorists..."

The persistent reporter interrupted Duncan's interruption with one of his own. "How in the world can you classify the Dixon family as terrorists?"

"We are not privileged to the information the Department of Justice has in this investigation. The ATF was operating fully within..."

"Well, apparently the governor of Texas felt differently."

"The governor of Texas has a record of opposing this administration on everything from healthcare and the EPA to this issue. It is apparent this is a grandstanding event by Governor Cooper; however, this time he overstepped his authority, as the action he ordered was likely illegal and it interfered with a federal operation." Duncan glanced around the room and pointed to another reporter.

"What were the president's thoughts on the press conference in Austin, which essentially turned into a rally against Washington?" that reporter asked.

"The president didn't watch it and has no comment."

"What's the next step for the administration related to Chuck Dixon?"

"That's up to the DOJ; that's not a call the president makes."

"As the commander-in-chief and head of the Executive Branch, he has no input or direction for the DOJ on this matter?"

"The president has a capable attorney general and capable directors of the FBI and ATF. Anything related to that case will be dealt with by those departments," Duncan stated. "Remember, this is all related to the Rash Sally attempted assassination and is part of the overall investigation into any conspiracy he was involved in."

"Has President Johnson or Attorney General Tibbs talked to Governor Cooper?"

"Not that I know of, regarding the president. I don't know about the attorney general."

Another reporter piped up. "What do you say to the governor's claim that he made numerous calls to the DOJ and the administration before ordering the Texas Rangers to rescue Chuck Dixon?"

"Rescued? I think you meant to say kidnapped," laughed Duncan.

Nervous laughter came from some of the mainstream media in the room.

"What about the phone calls?" the previous reporter repeated.

"I don't have any knowledge of the governor reaching out to the White House or the Department of Justice," Duncan said.

"Does that mean the administration is contradicting his claim about numerous attempts to resolve the problem before ordering the raid on Ellington Air Force Base?"

Ted Duncan's body language had physically changed over the last few questions. The uneasiness caused by the recent questions and answers left many seasoned reporters wondering why the press secretary continued responding to the line of questioning.

"We've already covered this question and we are out of time," Duncan said abruptly. "Thank you all." He turned away from the microphones and headed to an exit on his right.

Questions peppered Duncan as he left. "Is the administration lying? Can you produce the phone logs from the White House to prove Governor Cooper didn't call? What about the Justice Department logs? Who's lying here?"

Chapter 29

"Freedom is never more than one generation away from extinction. We didn't pass it to our children in the bloodstream. It must be fought for, protected, and handed on for them to do the same, or one day we will spend our sunset years telling our children and our children's children what it was once like in the United States where men were Free."

~ Ronald Reagan

Tim Spilner knew in his heart that he didn't have much time to produce the evidence that could prevent further bloodshed and the trampling on the Constitution that had been initiated by the administration and his employer, the Justice Department.

Every few days, he gave Steve Milford an update, essentially telling him that he didn't have what he needed and that he was trying to find the right angle, time and opportunity to avail himself of the necessary evidence to try to stop what he saw as a grave crime on the American people. Tim knew Steve was beginning to wonder if he was having second thoughts, but he knew Steve knew better than anyone that further delays in exposing the truth could put more lives at risk.

Tim had tried several methods of nonchalantly carrying his laptop or smart phone into the investigation room, only to have the Marines who were guarding the room turn those devices away.

The investigation room looked like a war room out of the movies. It had more than six plasma screen monitors that were 65" wide on three walls. These monitors were tied to individual black laptops located at a large circular table, with each monitor displaying the same screen shot as the one on the investigators' assigned laptops. Each investigator had a password and login assigned to him or her for the same laptop they were to work from while in the room.

The investigators weren't allowed Internet access. If routine access was needed during the investigation, a CIA operative assigned to the room opened Internet access and monitored all activity. Each investigator was required to submit a request to a website or URL to get approval to go there. The sites were logged, including all keystrokes, time on the URL, and justification for it. The CIA monitor had the ability to flip a switch and immediately disconnect the Internet if he felt the search or URL chosen was not consistent with the investigation. There was absolutely no opportunity for Tim to take a specific file and send it out.

This lock-down on the Internet led to some heated exchanges between different departments. The CIA specialist was essentially the watchdog over the activities of the investigation team that was, on any given day, a combination of FBI, ATF, Homeland Security, Treasury and Justice Department personnel. There were never more than five investigators allowed in the room, monitored by a single CIA computer specialist.

On a late Thursday afternoon, the Arabic translator who worked for Homeland Security was back in the investigation room, translating more email conversations Sally had with people in London, Paris, Iran and Syria. The translator always occupied the computer to Tim's immediate left. Tim made a point to get to know the translator in the brief time he was there. The translator, Mitesh Patil, was an Indian-born naturalized citizen with degrees in various languages including Arabic, Russian and Chinese. Homeland Security had recruited him straight out of college after 9/11.

Patil was not a covert agent of any kind. He was a translator the government used to monitor suspected terror chatter in the U.S. and abroad. Patil was also frequently used to interpret foreign government documents acquired in the course of CIA covert operations. The translator probably had the highest intelligence clearance of anyone on the team because of the sensitive nature of highly classified documents and conversations.

Tim began studying the routine used in the investigation room in earnest after his initial meeting with Steve. There were some days when traffic in and out was heavy, and some days that were very light. The CIA agent who monitored computer activity sat on a riser that overlooked the table. Either one of two CIA agents were at the riser on any given day. These two characters were not friendly whatsoever, never made any small talk, and none of the investigators appreciated that the CIA was looking over their shoulders at every point of the investigation and on every click of their mouse.

Tim didn't know every person who came into the investigation room. Although he knew which department they might be from, he didn't always know their specific role in the investigation, what they were looking for or who in their chain of command was aware of the important elements taking shape regarding Sally. There was no doubt a sense of inter-agency competition, which Tim thought was more distrust than anything. This distrust was heightened by the presence of the CIA.

Tim still did not have a plan. The key pieces of evidence were the journal and emails, but the Rash Sally journal itself was the Holy Grail.

As they sat next to each other reviewing their own documents in the investigation room, Tim and Patil rarely spoke to each other. Tim decided to strike up a conversation.

"I'm running a cross check on the latest Tea Party list. Do you have an updated list of the Tea Party contacts Sally had from his email or journal?"

Patil looked up slowly, apparently shocked that Tim brought up the journal when they were expressly instructed not to discuss it. Others in the room were too busy to recognize what Tim had just asked. Tim pulled his chair close to Patil so he could look at his laptop screen.

Patil began going through the files he had access to on his laptop.

Tim watched every key stroke to see where any important documents might be stored on the translator's laptop.

"I'm looking for a Pearson, David Pearson," said Tim, and he watched as Patil cross-referenced the names Tim had pulled out of the emails, careful to watch how everything was stored. Tim knew he had no such name on his own list.

"No, sir, nothing on my list matches that name."

"Can you check again?"

"Sure." Patil began the process again.

"Does this have the names on it that may have been in Sally's journal?" Tim asked softly.

"Mr. Spilner…"

"Mr. Patil, everyone in this room knows that document exists. I can't do my job if I don't get cooperation. Do you want me going to the attorney general to complain about lack of cooperation from Homeland Security?" asked Tim in a forceful but hushed tone.

"Well, I…"

"Mr. Patil, we are all on the same side, sir. Pull your data up and let's have a look please."

Two other agents in the room stopped what they were working on and lifted their heads up to glare at the two. One was FBI; the other was ATF.

"Gentlemen, do you have an issue?" asked Tim.

Both shook their heads no and returned to their tasks. The CIA staffer on the riser was almost asleep. Nobody in the room was accessing the Internet or requesting access to files other than those made available on the laptops and servers that were connected to the laptops. His job, for the most part, was to stay awake.

Patil began going through different files and then Tim saw it.

"Wait, stop a minute. Is that the journal?"

"That is the translation copy to English."

"Transfer that to my drive."

"What?"

"Do you have a problem with that? We are in a secure room. That document is not going anywhere."

"I cannot copy this to your drive, sir. I'm not authorized."

"Mr. CIA, there is a file on Mr. Patil's drive that I need. Is there a restriction you are aware of where files cannot be exchanged within the investigation group in this room?"

The CIA supervisor rubbed his chin for a few seconds, then said, "Nothing specifically is called out as restricted to one department; however, there are codes within the drives that let us know when someone has transferred or downloaded any document. If his computer or the shared drives allow him to drop and save to your folder on the investigation shared drive, then I'm sure it's okay. If it doesn't allow it, I will get an alarm on my computer."

"Transfer it," said Tim forcefully to Patil.

"You're sure this is okay?" Patil asked the CIA supervisor.

"We'll know in a few seconds," said the CIA supervisor. He refocused his attention to his computer screen to see if any type of alarm came on.

"Here it goes.... Done. It went through."

"Must be okay then," said the CIA supervisor as he went back to working on what he was doing. Since nobody could see his screen at any time, for all they knew he could be playing solitaire.

"There it is. It's on my drive. Thanks, Patil. I'll look through this myself."

"You heard him. I got permission from CIA to offload a copy to your folder on the investigation shared drive. If shit hits the fan, it's not my fault."

Tim's heart was beating so fast he was worried other people in the investigation room would hear it. He took two deep breaths and then dove into Rash Sally's journal. For the next six hours, Tim pored over the document. He was afraid of what he was going to find. Worse yet, he felt an overwhelming sense of responsibility with the knowledge he was gaining.

When he was done, he excused himself from the investigation room and went to the men's restroom, walking confidently past the Marines posted at the investigation room door and sixty feet down the hall to the bathroom. He went into a stall, sat on the toilet and cried.

After reading Sally's journal, there was absolutely no doubt in Tim's mind about three things.

First, Sally had intended to expose the Tea Party but, in doing research for his Master's thesis, actually came to respect the Tea Party for its stance on the Constitution and conservative fiscal beliefs.

Second, there was no doubt Sally was incensed over Operation Python on his ancestral Iranian homeland and the death of his sister and her family.

Third, there was no doubt these two facts were known by the leadership of the Department of Justice and beyond. The implications were seismic. The administration had seized an opportunity to obliterate a political opponent and, in the meantime, American citizens had been killed.

Chapter 30

"The truth is that all men having power ought to be mistrusted.

~ James Madison

For the next two days, Tim focused on a plan to get Rash Sally's journal text out of the investigation room. He knew he couldn't bring anything in or take anything out. Every time he entered the room, he was scanned with a hand wand metal detector, but he did notice one thing—the wand was never waved near his head.

Tim's first thought was to bring a memory stick with a USB connection into the room and simply plug it in and download the file. There were two problems with that plan: how to get the USB device past the Marines, and then how to download it without anyone knowing. He knew the CIA supervisor would see him download the file if he was paying attention, but Tim had no idea if there was some type of alert or alarm that would go off when it started or finished. The first thing he was going to do was to transfer a copy of the file that resided on the investigation room server under the shared files to the laptop he worked on. If this didn't bring up any alarms, then he figured it would be safe to download the file to a USB device, provided he could get the device into the room and back out again undetected.

The next morning, Tim went to the investigation room carrying a paper clip in his shirt pocket underneath his suit to see if it would set off the electronic wand. As the Marine waved the metal detector over his body, he noticed again that they never waved it near his head, but the detector did pick up the paper clip.

As soon as Tim got into the investigation room, he noticed there were three others in the room plus the CIA supervisor. The room had never been a model of friendliness; however, everyone involved knew they were on a mission and seemed to get along, even though there was an air of mistrust between the government branches. Tim purposely made small talk to see if he could distract others or the CIA supervisor.

As Tim left for lunch, he decided today was the day. His plan was to sneak a USB memory device into the room by putting it in his mouth. Since the Marines never waved the wand near his head, he hoped it wouldn't go off. Tim had no plan if it was discovered. He could swallow it, but it would still likely set it off, even in his stomach. How would he explain that? If he put the device between his teeth and gum in his upper jaw, it wouldn't be sitting in saliva and shouldn't be affected.

During his lunch hour, Tim went to two different office supply stores before he found a USB device small enough that had a plastic coating on it, in case he needed to swallow it.

During the past two weeks, he had put his personal finances in order, including his will. He wasn't taking any chances. He had hinted to his wife and his father that he was involved in the Sally investigation but had not told them anything of substance, nor did he tell them the risks he faced being a whistleblower of a government cover-up that would make Watergate pale in comparison.

Tim took the plastic-coated USB device and stuck it between his cheek and gum by his upper right molars. His heart pounded as he walked down the hall toward the two Marines in front of the investigation room. As he approached, he started making small talk with the guards as he had done over the last couple of weeks. The young Marine had the wand. Tim hoped he wasn't sweating.

"Hey, guys, have you been outside today? It's cold."

"Yeah, it was cold coming in today," said the youngest Marine.

Tim hoped he wasn't slurring the words with the device in his mouth.

"They're saying snow," remarked Tim as the young Marine started waving the electronic wand up each leg, then his waist.

"Yeah, I think they're saying we could get two inches tonight."

The Marine was just going through the motions. Over the length of the investigation, this particular duty had to have been boring. They had no idea what was going on in the investigation room, only that pretty much the same people came and went and that nobody was allowed to take anything in or out.

The Marine, as Tim suspected, never waved the wand much higher than his waist. The ruse worked. He was inside the investigation room with a USB device. Now came another tricky part of the plan. Surely people would see him plug the USB device into the side of the laptop. Even if they didn't, Tim couldn't be sure the CIA supervisor wouldn't get alerted to a device being plugged in or if files were being transferred.

Tim coughed with his hand over his mouth, forcing the device into his hand. He calmly slid his hand under the table and dropped the device next to his crotch. The device had a flip top lid that Tim could open with one hand when it was time to plug it in.

Tim sat there for hours, nervously working on his laptop and waiting for everyone else to go home for the night. The CIA supervisors were usually on two six-hour shifts from 6:00 a.m. until noon, then the second shift until 6:00 p.m. or when everyone was ready to go home. Tim waited for the perfect opportunity as people left or just before the CIA supervisor began shutting everything down.

At 5:45, Tim and the CIA supervisor were the only ones left in the room. The CIA supervisor asked Tim how much longer he needed.

"I should be done in about fifteen minutes."

"Okay, I'll shut everything down about six, but I can't wait that long to go to the head."

"Go ahead and go."

"All right. I'll be right back," said the CIA supervisor as he scurried to log off his computer and get out the door. Tim couldn't believe his good fortune.

There were cameras in all four corners of the room, but Tim could not miss this opportunity. He slowly slid the USB device from his crotch under some papers and plugged it in. It took ten very long seconds for the laptop to recognize the device. Tim immediately started copying files from the shared server directly to the USB device through his laptop. He waited for some kind of bell or alarm to go off. None did. If the CIA supervisor was alerted, he wasn't at his desk to see it.

Tim's main focus was the journal. It took nearly a minute to download it. Tim also loaded his files and copies of the emails to and from Sally onto the device. Tim slipped the device out and stuck it back in his mouth, just in case he was scanned on the way out the door. He had only been scanned leaving the room twice, but the chance existed. Most of his actions were not deliberate and he tried to hide what he was doing as much as possible. Then he immediately powered his laptop off.

The CIA supervisor came back in right after the laptop shut down. Tim was standing up putting on his suit coat.

"Wow, already done?"

"I didn't want to keep you. It can wait until tomorrow."

Tim started to walk toward the door.

"Wait a second. Why is your laptop off?"

The protocol established for the investigation room was that nobody was allowed to turn on or off any computer device. They could only log on or log off with their login credentials.

"Oh, shit, I'm sorry. Bad habit. Do you want me to log back on?"

"No, it's all right. You know the rules next time?"

"Yeah, just a bad habit. I do it at my office every day and at home. Just a habit."

"Well, I'll have to power it back up because we pull reports off each laptop daily. I kick these on and run the reports so they go to CIA and Justice for review every morning," the CIA guy said.

"Do you need me to stay?" said Tim, trying to keep the device in his mouth and talk normally.

"Nah, go ahead. It will only take me a few minutes. Have a great evening."

"You, too." Tim knocked on the door to be let out. The young Marine opened the door, but didn't have the wand in his hand.

"See you, guys. Stay warm."

"You, too," said the Marine.

Tim kept the device in his mouth until he got out of the building. He was worried the device had gotten too wet. When he got in his car, he blew into the device violently and shook it to get any remaining saliva out of it.

He had done it. As long as the saliva did not affect the device, he simply needed to plug it into a computer to copy the files.

As he drove home, panic started to set in. He had no idea about the reports that went from the computers to the CIA and Justice every day. Did they do it at night or during the day? He knew enough to know that his superiors would know exactly what he'd done by tomorrow morning, if not sooner.

Tim knew he now had to tell his wife because they needed to leave immediately. He wondered how he was going to explain it all to her. On a normal mid-December evening, he was going to come home and tell his wife they needed to pack up and leave immediately because they could be in danger. They had dinner planned with his in-laws tonight. He could break the news over dinner that they might be leaving town for an extended period.

Tim badly wanted to call Steve, but he knew he couldn't do it from his cell phone. On his way home, he pulled into three gas stations before he found one that still had a payphone. Apparently cell phones had put a big dent in the payphone business, making them scarce. He couldn't remember the last time he'd used one.

"Hello?"

"Hello, is Steve home?"

"Yes, who's this?"

Tim paused for a minute and then lied to Steve's wife, "This is Walter from the department."

"Okay, he's in the garage. I'll get him."

Tim felt like it took forever for Steve to answer.

"Hello?" Steve said when he picked up the phone.

"Steve, this is Tim."

"Tim? Oh, okay. I wondered who the hell Walter was."

"Steve, I don't have much time. I'm calling from a payphone. I just want you to know I got the evidence I needed."

"Wow, really? How? Well, never mind that. What the hell are you going to do now?"

"I have to leave town tonight."

"Damn, Tim, is there anything I can do?"

"Not yet, but I will tell you the shit is going to hit the fan. My guess is they will know by tomorrow morning what I copied. I'm leaving town, but I'll be in touch." Tim took a deep breath. "You can bet you'll be interrogated because you're my friend."

"Tim, please, put your evidence in a safe place," Steve pleaded. "They can't do anything to you if you have it in a secret location. What about your wife?"

"She doesn't know anything. She's going to be frightened and very upset." Tim's voice trembled. "Can you imagine?"

"Okay, Tim. Listen, you will be a hero for this but it's going to be very, very rough. It may even be dangerous."

"I know, I know... I'll be back in touch in a few days. Let's cut this short in case they pull your phone records and see a call was made from this payphone to your house."

"Tim," Steve said, "God's speed."

"Thanks, Steve." Tim hung up the phone, a sense of deep foreboding welling up inside him. It was done. He had likely killed his career and his life. Not only his, but his wife's as well.

Chapter 31

"One riot, one Ranger."

> *~ Texas Ranger Captain "Bill" McDonald, 1896*
> *Answering the Dallas mayor's question where his*
> *reinforcements were to quell a local riot over a prize fight.*

Chuck Dixon sat on a couch outside the governor's office in Austin waiting to meet with Cooper, the Texas Rangers, Lieutenant Governor Gene Foster and various congressional and state legislators.

After the ATF raided Chuck's residence, they hit his business the next day and took all the computers. His terrified employees were sent home. The IRS levied his bank accounts. His operations manager could not pay any bills or run payroll.

The negative publicity Chuck received in the mainstream media for allegedly being tied to Rash Sally chased many of his customers away. What was a vibrant going concern a couple of weeks ago was now a business with no way to operate. Still, most of his employees still showed up every day with no promise of being paid. His employees knew him well, and many of them were also involved in the Tea Party movement. They didn't believe a word of the government's claims of Chuck being a co-conspirator with Rash Sally.

Chuck had just gotten off the phone with his operations manager, who had given him the latest update on the state of his business, when Pops Younger appeared in the hallway.

"Hey, Chuck, the governor is ready to see you."

"Okay, Pops, thanks."

Chuck entered the governor's office. The room was packed with men in suits and men wearing cowboy hats. Cooper stood up to greet him. Chuck stuck out his hand to shake but the governor hugged him.

"Let's all have a seat. We have a lot to discuss," said Cooper.

Jeff Weaver spoke up. "Gentlemen, we are likely to have some type of constitutional crisis as a result of our operation to free Chuck. I have received a call from Deputy Attorney General Justin Coleman in Washington and he is demanding we turn over Chuck and the Rangers involved in the Ellington operation."

"So, Tibbs himself didn't call you?" one of the congressmen in attendance asked sarcastically.

"Of course not. He's too goddamn arrogant," replied Weaver. "After consulting with the governor, we called them back and provided our answer."

Chuck was worried. Something told him he could be back in federal custody in no time.

"We told them to go pound sand!" Weaver said.

The room erupted in applause and yells. "Additionally," Weaver continued, "we have filed for search warrants this morning with a state district judge to search all FBI, ATF and Homeland Security offices for all documents and emails related to the raids on Texas citizens involved with the Tea Party. We believe their actions are unwarranted and do not fit within the terrorist definition of the NDAA."

The people in the room got more excited with each bit of news coming from Weaver.

"We have also just filed charges for those in connection with the deaths of the three Texans who died at the hands of these federal agents."

Chuck Dixon was visibly moved. "Thank God. Stan Mumford did not deserve to die. He was my friend."

"Yes, Chuck," Governor Cooper said, "we know. And he won't be forgotten. We are committed to bringing those responsible to justice right here in Texas. We're currently conducting searches to find the names of all those involved. And, let me assure you, if this is like other Justice Department operations that have proven to be unconstitutional or illegal—which we believe they are—we will not rest until they are brought to justice."

Cooper stood and walked around his huge desk to lean against it.

"Pops, can you update us on what you are doing with Chuck and his family?"

"Sure, Governor," Pops said. "Right now we have Chuck's family at an undisclosed location. We believe it's possible that the DOJ could send a team to snatch Chuck back. For that reason, his location will be kept secret on a need-to-know basis."

"Governor, I do ask that I am able to communicate to my employees who are still dependent on me," Chuck said.

"Of course, Chuck," Cooper said, "we'll find a way for you to continue to communicate with your staff so as not to put you in jeopardy. For those that don't know or aren't aware, the feds took all the computers out of Chuck's business and had the IRS levy his bank accounts. Right now, his employees cannot get paid and are there out of sheer loyalty to Chuck."

"Damn," said several people at the same time.

"We are raising the ante with the actions taken this morning that we feel are absolutely necessary," Cooper said. "We fully expect the administration to try to punish Texas. That means withholding matching federal funds for everything from schools to highway projects. This may take many months to resolve, and I expect Texas is not going to be popular with most of the country. But we have many friends in Congress and elsewhere who will support us."

The closed door of the governor's office flew open and a Texas Ranger came in with a piece of paper he handed to Pops. Pops read the paper, then asked Weaver and Governor Cooper to sidebar in another room.

The rest of the participants made small talk, anxiously waiting for the three to come back in.

When they returned, Weaver held the paper. He took a deep breath, then said, "Gentlemen, it appears our esteemed colleagues in the DOJ have beaten us to the next steps. They have issued federal warrants for all members of the Rangers team that rescued Chuck at Ellington. They have also issued a fugitive arrest warrant for Chuck."

Chuck sat there in disbelief. "Wow. One minute I'm a family man and independent businessman, and a couple of weeks later I have no home, barely have a business and now I'm a fugitive from justice?"

"Chuck, we will work through this," Cooper said. "They are not only messing with you, but they're messing with Texas. I will do everything within my power to get this straightened out. It's in our best interests. This administration has been stomping on the Constitution since it came into power, and now they've got four more years to trash it. I won't stand for it. Texas won't stand for it. And it's not only us. I am in daily contact with the governors of Arizona, Oklahoma, South Carolina, Alabama, Georgia and Louisiana. Enough is enough."

Turning to his brain trust and Pops, the governor said, "Okay, folks, we know our next moves. Everyone is getting an assignment or two from this meeting. Let's get through the list. I ask that everyone in this room keep our mission public, but our strategies confidential."

During the next six hours, the team assembled in the governor's office was assigned certain tasks. The State legislators were to brief their colleagues and report in town hall meetings with their constituents. All agreed to update their newsletters, staff and websites with information related to the public relations war that was about to begin between Texas, other like-minded states, and Washington.

The same was true of the congressional members who attended. There were eleven congressmen in the meeting, including two Democrats. The congressional delegation was to take their fight to the House and Senate floor. Only one of the two senators from Texas attended the meeting. The missing senator wasn't invited. Although he was a Republican, the governor's office didn't trust him and he hadn't been an ardent supporter of the Tea Party.

The next day, a press release was issued from the governor's office:

"Yesterday, the Texas attorney general obtained arrest warrants from a Texas district judge for the federal agents who were involved in the unwarranted searches, destruction of private property, trespassing, and theft of private property of certain citizens of Texas. In addition to these charges, we have referred the three unfortunate deaths at the hands of federal agents to a grand jury, where we expect them to recommend indictment of the federal agents involved.

"We have also learned that the Justice Department has issued arrest warrants for the Texas Rangers involved in the rescue of Chuck Dixon from an illegal kidnapping and unlawful imprisonment. This is a political stunt by the Justice Department and we fully expect these Texas Rangers to be fully vindicated."

* * *

Jamail Tibbs was livid. "Who the fuck do these cowboys think they are? Issuing arrest warrants for federal agents? They need to be taught a very strong lesson."

Tibbs was speaking to Deputy Attorney General Coleman, FBI Director Woodhouse, ATF Director Adamson, and Homeland Security Director Sarah McDermott at a meeting in Washington, DC.

Adamson, the ATF director who took over after the demotion of the prior ATF director in the gun-walking fiasco, spoke. "I have been in touch with our field offices in Texas, and there is definitely some hesitation from those local agents acting on the arrest warrants for this guy Pops Younger and the other Rangers. Apparently, Younger is somewhat of a law enforcement legend in Texas. They believe it would be a public relations nightmare, not to mention the fact they may meet resistance."

Tibbs was still fuming, "Are you serious? You have agents in your department who will not exercise a federal arrest warrant? Will they not follow orders?"

"Mr. Attorney General, you're talking about arresting Texas icons. Hell, you might as well go piss on the Alamo. This will be hugely unpopular."

"Unpopular where, in Texas? Who gives a damn? These jokers violated federal law."

Tibbs turned to his staff members. "What are the polling numbers telling us?"

A thirty-something assistant with an Ivy League MBA and wearing a three-piece suit stood up and said, "The Texas Rangers have a very high approval rating; however, when asked about the raid at Ellington, the majority—51 percent—believe it was a violation of law. The ATF, on the other hand, only has a 42 percent favorable rating. When asked if the federal government should arrest the Rangers involved, 49 percent said yes."

"What did the polling say about Chuck Dixon?"

"In latest polls, 59 percent said he should be arrested, but only if he was connected to Rash Sally."

"What is the latest we have regarding that subject?"

Adamson stood up and stopped the conversation, "Jamail, let's discuss this offline. I'm not prepared to discuss specifics of the investigation here."

"Okay, let's take that up directly after this meeting. Now, what I want to know is, what steps are we going to deploy to arrest these fugitives?"

"Jamail, do we expect to just walk into Austin and march down to the Texas Department of Public Safety and arrest these guys?" Adamson asked.

"Why not? What's your plan?" Tibbs looked at Adamson inquiringly.

"I think we give them the opportunity to turn themselves in."

"Well, that's fine, but I want a ton of publicity when they do. I want cameras everywhere and I want them in handcuffs doing the perp walk."

Adamson stood up. "I'll call Jeff Weaver and give him that opportunity. I can't imagine they want to see any Texas Rangers get handcuffed."

Tibbs retorted, "Actually, that's *exactly* what I want to see, and I want the country to see it."

Adamson looked worried and a little disappointed with Tibbs' response.

Tibbs continued, "Let's give them the opportunity to report to the FBI office in Austin, then they get handcuffed and transported to a federal facility for processing. But the offer is off the table in forty-eight hours. Do you understand?"

"Yes, sir."

"I also want the staff coordinating with media. Now, can everyone else leave the room so we can discuss the Tea Party guy Dixon? I want ATF, FBI and Homeland Security directors here only."

The rest of the room took about three minutes to clear out.

"Adamson, what do we know about Dixon's whereabouts?"

"Not much. We think they have him and his family in some type of protective custody. I do know the IRS has locked down his accounts, but he is still communicating with his office staff."

"Let Texas know we want Dixon, too. We'll give him the same opportunity to turn himself in as the Rangers."

Chapter 32

"No arsenal… is so formidable as the will and moral courage of free men and women."

~ *Ronald Reagan*

Texas beat Tibbs to the punch. The next day, units of the Texas Rangers arrived at the ATF and FBI offices in Houston, Dallas, San Antonio and Austin at exactly 8:30 a.m.

In Houston, Pops Younger came with a twelve-man unit to the ATF office in the Bob Casey Federal Building. The Rangers carried eight arrest warrants for ATF agents based in the Houston office.

The Rangers walked straight into the federal building and up to the security entrance, where three U.S. Marshals operated the walk-through metal detector. Pops flipped out the search warrants on the table in front of the scanning machine.

"We are here to serve arrest warrants. You will need to allow us through this entrance with no encumbrance."

The U.S. Marshal in charge at the entrance knew exactly why they were there, but couldn't believe it.

"Sir, I'm sorry, but this is a federal facility. You will not be allowed to enter with your weapons."

"Son, I'm here to serve arrest warrants on eight men who are more than likely armed. I am not about to give up our weapons."

"Then you may not proceed, sir."

The U.S. Marshal standing directly behind the man in charge picked up his two-way radio. Before he could push the button, Pops drew his Colt .45 and put it right in his face.

"I would strongly advise you to put that radio down, sir."

The Marshals were stunned.

"Sir, you have drawn your weapon on a U.S. Marshal inside a federal courthouse."

"Yes, I guess I have. My guess is this nice man was going to radio up to the sixth floor and announce our presence to the ATF office."

"You have no right to…"

"Shut the hell up and move back away from this table. Rangers, take their weapons. Smith and Turner, man this station. The rest of us are going to the sixth floor. Keep your radios on. We'll keep you advised of the situation. If these men resist, shoot them."

The U.S. Marshals moved back and sat down in chairs. The Rangers took their weapons but did not keep weapons drawn on them. The Marshals sat there, looking defeated. One of the Rangers took over at the table for people still coming in and going through the metal detector to their court appearances or for other business. Nobody realized what was happening, but the Ranger got some extended looks as some of the attorneys who frequented the courthouse were not used to seeing a Texas Ranger manning the security checkpoint.

Pops and the rest of the Rangers got off the elevator at the sixth floor and took a right turn, went around the corner and came to a glass window marked in gold lettering: Bureau of Alcohol, Tobacco and Firearms – Houston Division.

Pops threw open the door to the reception area where a young lady was sitting at the front desk.

"Ma'am, we are here to see whoever is in charge and we need to see him or her right away. Hicks, Lawson, Stanford, go cover any other exits on this floor."

"Duty Manager Agent Hansen is here. I'll get him right now."

"You do that."

In less than fifteen seconds, Agent Hansen was confronting seven Texas Rangers standing in the ATF office entrance.

"Can I help you gentlemen?"

"Yes, sir, you can. We are here under orders from Governor Cooper, and we have arrest warrants for these eight individuals that I am told are based out of this office."

"Arrest warrants?"

"I'm sure your good friends in Washington have informed you about these warrants?"

"Well, we knew about them but didn't think you would actually try to serve them."

"Why the hell not? They are signed by a Texas judge. Look at them."

"Sir, you can't come in here like this and simply arrest my agents...."

"Agent Hansen, you have about three seconds to produce these eight agents or you will be arrested for interfering with a law enforcement officer in the line of duty, obstruction of justice and harboring fugitives."

"Are you serious? You can't get away with this!"

As the confrontation got louder, a couple of ATF agents strolled to the front to see what the disturbance was about. Both agents had weapons attached to their belts.

"Men, I'm going to ask you to raise your arms so that my Rangers can remove your weapons."

One of agents started to back up slowly.

"Sir, any one of these boys can draw from his holster and put a bullet through your eye before you blink. I highly suggest you stop where you are."

Both agents raised their hands in utter disbelief, looking at Agent Hansen for some type of explanation as the Rangers removed their weapons. The Rangers had the agents so flustered that they had raised their hands without the Rangers having pulled a single handgun out of their holsters.

"Gentlemen, can we please have your names?"

"Martinez."

"Schneider."

"Boys, are they on the list?"

One of the Rangers scanned the names on the arrest documents. "Yep, both of them."

"Gentlemen, on behalf of the State of Texas, you are hereby under arrest for trespassing, destruction of property, conspiracy, attempted murder and unlawful imprisonment. Bill, read them their rights."

The Rangers handcuffed the agents and escorted them quickly out into the hallway.

"Now, Miss, can you tell me if the rest of the agents on this list are on duty and in the office today?"

"Yes, sir, three of them are here today."

"Can you please call them up here one by one and tell them there is someone here to see them?"

"Yes, sir."

Agent Hansen took a step toward Pops. Two Rangers stepped in between them, hands on weapons.

"Do you guys really think you are going to get away with this? You are going to have every federal agency come down on you like you have never seen before."

"You mean like Waco?" said Pops, referring to the botched raid of the Branch Davidians that killed innocent women and children in a badly managed standoff with the ATF. "Or do you mean like Ruby Ridge? Sure, you invite all your friends from Washington to come on down. Make sure your big boss Tibbs joins 'em."

As the ATF agents came to the front, they were arrested, handcuffed and read their rights. It was an understatement to say the agents were caught off guard, arrested in their own offices in a federal building.

"What was your name again, sir, so I can report to my superiors?" Hansen asked.

"Pops Younger, Texas Ranger. Now you have a nice day."

The Ranger contingent and their prisoners made their way to the elevators and down to the first floor. The prisoners were marched right out the front door of the federal building where two passenger vans with the State Seal of Texas on both doors waited.

The sight of twelve Texas Rangers on the sidewalk loading handcuffed prisoners stopped people in the streets as they watched. Neither the governor's office nor the Rangers called the press.

That day, the Texas Rangers made a sweep of FBI and ATF offices in four Texas cities, arresting seventeen of the twenty-six agents who had arrest warrants out for them.

When Pops Younger got back to Austin that evening, he was greeted with the news that Jeff Weaver had also requested arrest warrants for those who knew about and approved the Tea Party operations, including the directors and deputy directors of the ATF, FBI, Homeland Security and the attorney general himself, Jamail Tibbs.

Pops read the warrants and said out loud, "Well, boys, this is about to get real interesting...."

Chapter 33

"If you tell a lie big enough and keep repeating it, people will eventually come to believe it. The lie can be maintained only for such time as the State can shield the people from the political, economic and/or military consequences of the lie. It thus becomes vitally important for the State to use all of its powers to repress dissent, for the truth is the mortal enemy of the lie, and thus by extension, the truth is the greatest enemy of the State."

~ Joseph Goebbels, Reich Minister of Propaganda
Nazi Germany

Smoke was still rolling from the engine of the black BMW as it sat smashed against a brick retaining wall near a small apartment complex in Georgetown. The BMW hit so hard it toppled the top half of the wall and sent bricks crashing down onto the windshield and roof, caving it in so the top was only six inches from the tops of the doors. The vehicle struck the wall with such impact that the rear end of the car must have raised six feet or more, as it burst the rear tires from the weight of the car striking the ground.

EMTs and fire department rescue personnel frantically tried to get to the two occupants, but the doors wouldn't open. The frame of the car had been bent so badly that they needed the Jaws of Life™ to open the door. Another emergency vehicle with the device was within four minutes of the single car accident.

"We can't get to the vitals of the driver, but the woman passenger is gone," said a resolute EMT.

The fire department rescue personnel and two police officers were using crowbars to pry the roof from the door so at least the EMTs could get vital signs of the driver and possibly start an IV or administer oxygen until the Jaws device arrived.

"We've got enough room now!" screamed a fireman to the EMTs.

The EMTs rushed to that side of car and one reached in to feel for a pulse on the driver's neck.

"No pulse, damn! Where's the Jaws?" the EMT yelled.

Four rescue workers who had just arrived with the Jaws scurried to the driver's side of the car and started to feverishly cut through metal. Other firefighters sprayed foam over most of the car in case any fuel was leaking.

The Jaws made a horrid noise as it clipped through the roof columns, throwing sparks ten to fifteen feet in front of any direction the operators pointed it. Their best bet was to cut what used to be the columns and try to peel the roof back because it would take too long to cut through the thicker doors.

By now, a sizable crowd had gathered and police were required to stop traffic on four streets and hold the growing crowd back. Finally, after a full eight minutes, the rescuers could peel back the roof enough to administer to the driver and the woman passenger. Despite working frantically on both occupants, the EMTs were not able to revive either. Firefighters draped a blue tarp over each of them.

"Damn, we lost them both, but I don't think it mattered. I think they were pretty much dead on impact. We never got a pulse on either and that car is horrific," the lead EMT told a police officer.

"That car had to be going sixty or seventy miles per hour. Why in hell would anyone be driving that fast on a residential side street?" wondered the cop.

"I don't see any skid marks so there was no attempt to brake," added a second cop.

"Makes no sense. The couple inside looks middle-aged." He paused to look at a van that pulled up to the scene. "The accident investigators are here. I guess they'll make sense of it all."

It took a full thirty-five minutes for the county coroner's team to show up to do their investigation and recover the bodies.

By this time, there were more than ten law enforcement vehicles onsite, along with one plain sedan with U.S. government license plates. Two men in suits from that vehicle approached the two county coroner employees just after they shut the rear doors of the hearse. One of the men flipped out his wallet, showing his badge.

"Gentlemen, I'm from the FBI and these fatalities are a matter of national security. I am accompanying you to the coroner's office with the bodies."

"Sure, just follow us," said the first coroner worker.

"No, I'm riding with the bodies."

"We aren't allowed to…"

"Sir, this is a matter of national security. You don't have a choice." The FBI agent pulled back his suit coat to display his holstered gun.

"Okay, but I have to radio in."

"No, you will not radio anything. You are not taking these bodies to your regular county coroner. We will provide instructions along the way. Let's go."

"Well, okay," shrugged the driver.

* * *

Steve Milford's cell phone rang at close to 11:00 p.m. while he was brushing his teeth and getting ready for bed.

"Honey, your phone is ringing," called his wife from the bedroom.

"I wonder who that is this time of night." Steve strolled into the bedroom with a toothbrush still hanging out of the side of his mouth.

"Hello?"

"Steve, this is Calvin from Justice. Sorry to call you so late."

"No problem, Cal. What's up?"

"Steve, Tim Spilner was killed this evening with his wife in an automobile accident."

Silence…

"Cal, say that again. I'm sorry."

"Tim and his wife were killed in an auto accident tonight in Georgetown."

"What? How? In Georgetown?"

"Apparently they crashed into a retaining wall at a very high speed."

"Wait a minute… wait. Wow. That is unbelievable."

"It happened right after seven tonight. They were meeting her parents for dinner in Georgetown but never made it to the restaurant."

Steve's heart sank. He had known Tim a long time through college and at the DOJ. The immediate shock of the news obscured thoughts of any possible connections to the project Tim had been working on and the confidential information he had shared with Steve.

"Honey, what's wrong?" asked Steve's wife. She'd come to stand next to him while he was on the phone with Cal.

Covering the phone, Steve said, "Tim Spilner and his wife were killed tonight in an auto accident."

"Oh, my God."

"Cal, do you have any information other than that? His family? Anything?"

"No, word is just spreading through the department and I wasn't sure if you had heard."

"Do you know if his dad knows?" asked Steve. He knew Tim's mother had died of cancer five years ago.

"Not sure but, if they were meeting her parents, I'm sure he knows by now. The accident happened just four blocks from the restaurant where they were supposed to meet."

"Why in hell would they be driving that fast in that neighborhood? It's very hard to drive over fifteen miles an hour anywhere in Georgetown."

"Who knows, Steve, but I heard they needed the Jaws of Life™ to get them out."

"What? Geez. How could that happen in that residential area?

The streets are too narrow for that kind of speed."

"No clue, Steve, but much of what I have heard is second hand so it may not be correct information."

"Damn, Cal. Thanks for calling me. Let's touch base in the morning."

As Steve ended the call, he sat on the edge of the bed, and his wife put her arms around him.

"Well, at least they didn't leave any kids behind," Steve said, referring to the fact Tim and his wife had no children.

"What a shame. Such nice people," said his wife.

"I'll call his dad tomorrow to see if there's anything I can do."

Steve and his wife continued to console each other as the knot in Steve's stomach began to grow. At first, he was shocked and saddened by the loss of his friend. Then, with every passing minute, he began to have the sickening feeling that this was too much of a coincidence with Tim trying to find a way to become a whistleblower about the Rash Sally investigation and the DOJ's attacks on the Tea Party faithful.

Chapter 34

"Most people, sometime in their lives, stumble across truth. Most jump up, brush themselves off, and hurry on about their business as if nothing had happened."

~Winston Churchill

The next morning, the news was all over the DOJ. The deputy director put out a statement of regret internally to the department. It was a sad day for many of the folks at the department because Tim was very well liked.

Steve was not looking forward to calling Tim's dad. It had probably been two years since he had been around Ed Spilner, but he knew he needed to do it. Finally, shortly after noon, Steve got the courage to call.

"Mr. Spilner, this is Steve Milford. Are you doing okay?"

"Oh, hello, Steve. Well, I'm still in shock but I have other family with me, and we are doing the best we can under the circumstances."

"Mr. Spilner, Tim was such a special guy. He was loved by everyone at the department and he was always a glass half-full type of guy. His wife was gracious and they were just a class act. I am so, so sorry for your loss."

"Thank you, Steve," said Tim's father, and it was apparent he could barely speak without choking up.

"Mr. Spilner, I know you are with the rest of your family right now so I won't keep you. Seriously, though, is there anything I can do for you, anything at all?"

"No, thanks, Steve. I have his brother and sister here, nieces, nephews and such, so I think we're okay for now. The Department of Justice sent some guys over to Tim's house to make sure it was secure and they have their belongings from the accident they're going to bring to me tomorrow."

"Someone from the department was at Tim's house?"

"Yes, very nice people."

"Well, okay, Mr. Spilner. Again, Tim was a great friend. I am so sorry."

"Thank you, Steve. Goodbye."

Whatever Steve's worries were about the information Tim possessed were now confirmed. What the hell were DOJ personnel doing at Tim's house the very next morning after he was killed? Why would they have his personal effects from the crashed vehicle?

"This is surreal," he told himself.

At 2:15 p.m. that same day, three men appeared at the desk of Steve's administrative assistant. She led them directly into Steve's office.

"Mr. Milford. I am Agent Anderson with the FBI and this is Agent Michaels and Agent Tomlinson. I am sure you heard about the tragedy of Tim Spilner and his wife?"

"Yes, Tim was a friend of mine. Very sad and extremely tragic. What can I do for you gentlemen?"

"This is standard protocol after a tragic event like this, but we just want to visit with family and friends and find out Tim's general state of mind leading up to the accident."

"State of mind? What do you mean?"

"When was the last time you spoke to Tim?" Agent Anderson asked.

"I talk to Tim several times a week."

"So when did you speak with him last?"

Steve fought to conceal his panic. He'd talked to Tim yesterday when he called from the payphone indicating he had the evidence he was seeking. Steve had a split second to decide how to proceed. The first thought that came into his mind was that, if they suspected

Tim was up to something, it was possible Steve's home phone was tapped.

"I talked to him yesterday at the office."

"What was the conversation about?"

"Work-related. I asked him how his project was going, the weather and the fact he had dinner plans last night."

"What did he say about his project? You are well aware he is part of the Rash Sally investigation."

"Yes, I am, but he never talks about it."

"But you said you talked about his project."

"Just in general terms, and only because I asked him."

"Why would you ask him about a project you know he can't discuss?"

"Seriously, gentlemen, this was a general conversation. My question was more about the hours he must be putting in, because I haven't talked to him as much as usual."

The agents sat there silent for a few moments, and Steve felt they had their bullshit detectors on full force, scanning his entire body for signs of deceitfulness.

"Did Tim ever share any specifics or any concerns he might have had about the investigation?" Agent Anderson asked, breaking the uncomfortable silence.

"Concerns? Why would he have concerns?"

"Mr. Milford, just please answer the question."

"No, he didn't share any specific information or concerns," said Steve, doing his best to act in a way so as not to create suspicion.

"Did he call you last night?"

"I stated I talked to him here at work yesterday."

"But not last night?"

"I thought the car accident was last night," Steve said, managing to look puzzled.

"Mr. Milford, did he seem at any point depressed, stressed out or not himself in any way?"

"Tim? No. Did you guys know him?"

"No, unfortunately, we did not know him personally."

"Tim was one of the most optimistic people you have ever met." Steve had no trouble with the truth on this answer.

"And was he his normal self the last time you spoke?"

"Sure."

"Mr. Milford, do you see any reason why he would have crashed his vehicle into a brick retaining wall?"

"I'm not sure what you're asking."

"Well, sir, accident investigators have reported there were no skid marks and the vehicle was likely going sixty mph when it hit the wall on a small residential side street."

"Are you inferring that Tim killed himself?"

"We are trying to understand his mindset at the time, sir."

"Well, if you are inferring that Tim somehow committed suicide and took his wife with him, then you obviously didn't know him," Steve said bluntly.

"We aren't inferring anything, Mr. Milford. This is part of why we are asking these questions."

"Do you provide this type of post-mortem investigation for every Department of Justice employee who passes away or is in a car accident? I've never heard of anything like this before."

"Routine stuff, Mr. Milford. Also, as you are surely aware, Mr. Spilner had top secret clearance. These types of post-mortem interviews are a normal process for folks with that type of clearance."

"I would suggest that you gentlemen look for another cause of the accident if you are telling me there was no attempt to avoid this collision. It would not make any sense to me why he would be traveling that fast and not hit his brakes to avoid that wall. Was someone possibly chasing him?"

"Why would anyone be chasing him, Mr. Milford?" inquired Agent Tomlinson innocently, looking at Steve as if he was looking through him.

"Who knows? Trying to carjack him, rob him?"

"Carjack him in Georgetown?" asked Agent Tomlinson, as if this couldn't happen in a high-income prestigious Washington, D.C. suburb.

"I'm sure you guys will figure it out."

"Yes, we will," said Agent Anderson confidently.

Everyone sat silent for a few uneasy moments while Agent Michaels flipped through a small notepad. He closed the notepad. "Mr. Milford, is that all you wish to tell us?" he asked.

"I'm confused, gentlemen. What else do you want to know?"

"Do you know anything about Mr. Spilner that we did not cover in this interview?"

"I'm sorry, as I'm not clear what else besides the questions you have asked you want to know. Why does this sound like an interrogation?"

"Mr. Milford, we are not trying to offend you. We are just trying to understand Mr. Spilner's unfortunate death."

"Then, no, there's nothing I can add that you probably don't already know, like the fact we went to the same college together and stuff like that."

"Yes, we are aware of that. We are more focused right now on the last few months, as you can imagine."

"Okay, then I can't think of anything to add."

The three men rose in unison.

"Thank you, Mr. Milford. We may reach out to you with other questions." Agent Anderson pulled a card out of his billfold. "In the meantime, please keep my business card." He handed it to Steve.

"No problem. Nice meeting you, gentlemen."

After the agents left, Steve sat for a few minutes trying to grasp what just happened. He tried to contain his panic, as he felt like the agents somehow knew Tim had called him last evening. If Steve's home phone was tapped, he was toast. That explained why Tim had called from a payphone and didn't want to be on that call for any amount of time—to protect Steve.

Three days later, Steve attended a large funeral for Tim and his wife. As far as funerals went, he estimated over three hundred were at the service. He wanted to grieve the loss of his friend, but he was distracted. He found himself looking for signs from anyone at the funeral that might know something about the evidence or what Tim was about to do. Nobody gave him any hints. Steve thought there was an outside chance that Tim had somehow shared his predicament with his dad but, if he had, Steve could not detect it—even when throwing out hints that might get Tim's dad to call him aside and talk privately.

Was Steve now the only one in the world who knew what Tim knew? What in the hell did Tim do with the evidence? If Tim had it, surely the DOJ had it back by now. They obviously scoured his home and his car. Steve only had hearsay from Tim. He hadn't seen anything personally, but he still felt like the agents suspected him of something.

Worse, what the hell caused the accident? The death of Tim on the very day he told Steve he had evidence to blow the whistle was too much of a coincidence. Did this mean Steve and his family were also in danger?

Chapter 35

"Texas has yet to learn submission to any oppression, come from what source it may."

~ *Sam Houston, Texas Hero of The Battle of San Jacinto and First President of the Republic of Texas*

A Federal Express overnight delivery came to Attorney General Weaver's office the same day the FBI agents were interviewing Steve Milford in Washington, D.C. The package was marked "Urgent" as well as "Highly Personal & Confidential." Because Weaver was out of the office on business in other areas of the state, the package remained unopened on his desk for several days.

* * *

Meanwhile, Steve was consumed by what the FBI and DOJ might know about his conversations with Tim. Was his phone tapped? Where in the hell did Tim's evidence go? Did Steve put himself and his family in danger by speaking to Tim about this in the first place? Hell, they may have even tailed him and observed their meeting at the Irish pub in Alexandria.

Steve surmised that what happened to Tim happened so quickly after he got the information out of the room that he likely did not have any time to safeguard it.

Steve's thoughts kept going to the accident. None of it made sense. Why in the world would Tim be driving that fast? Clearly someone was after him. That was the only thing that made any sense to Steve. Tim and even Steve himself had hinted he could be in danger. Was this what Tim was referring to? The information

Tim had discovered could topple the United States presidency.

Steve was at home working on his notebook computer, simultaneously answering emails from the office and watching the news. He had also heard there was a nice tribute to Tim on Facebook, so he logged in and read what everyone had put on his wall. It had been so long since Steve had been on Facebook that he had to try to remember his personal email password to login. After he finished reading the tributes on Tim's Facebook page, mostly by friends and co-workers, he decided to log in to his personal email, which he rarely checked.

Because Steve got so many emails at work, he rarely gave out his personal email and sometimes went months without checking it. He dreaded it most of the time because of the volume of junk emails he received, probably because he used a free email site.

When he opened his email account, it showed over two hundred unread messages.

"Ugh..." he thought.

He started deleting emails, watching to see if there were any worth reading or keeping. When he had completely deleted the first twenty-five, there it was....

Four emails from Tim Spilner's personal email address!

Tim had marked the emails *confidential*. They had all arrived within minutes of each other. Steve looked at the date. It was the date Tim was killed. It read:

"Steve — Here are the files from the investigation of Rash Sally that includes Sally's original journal in pdf, a transcribed journal (Arabic to English), a copy of the different Master's thesis' as they evolved, and a file containing several hundred of Sally's emails. I am sending these in four emails to make sure the attachments are not too large to get through."

Steve could hardly believe what he was seeing. The email went on:

"My apologies in advance for sending these to you and possibly putting your career in jeopardy or maybe putting you in danger. I am only sending these to you in the event I am somehow prevented from making them public.

Please keep this information safe. In a day or two, they will become common knowledge. Wish me luck! If for some reason this information does not get out, please do what you think is right. Your friend Tim."

Steve was stunned. He began scanning the documents. After only thirty minutes of reviewing a small portion of the documents, he was in shock.

"Am I the only one he sent these too? Please, God, tell me Tim sent these to news outlets all over the country or somebody besides me." It had been days since Tim was killed, and there was no outward evidence that Steve had seen or heard that this information had been made public.

* * *

Sixteen hundred miles away in Austin, Jeff Weaver finally came back to his office after a couple of days on the road in Dallas and Houston. He planned to quickly go through his mail, answer a few emails, then get home by 8:00 p.m.

As he thumbed through the small stack of mail, he noticed a Federal Express envelope marked confidential and addressed to him personally. He opened it. Out came a letter on Department of Justice letterhead and a small USB memory stick.

The letter read:

Dear Texas State Attorney,

My name is Tim Spilner. I am an attorney in the U.S. Justice Department who has been working on the task force in the investigation of Rashid Safly-Allah. I have been exposed to information that would unequivocally exonerate the Tea Party from any conspiracy to assassinate the president. Safly-Allah actually attempted the assassination because he was sympathetic to Iran, largely because he is Iranian and his sister and her family were killed in Operation Python.

In fact, Justice has had this information from the very begin-

ning of the investigation. I have only recently become fully aware of the information I have included in this package. I feel partly responsible for the constitutional violations that have occurred to citizens in your state and elsewhere, but I am especially remorseful about the associated and unnecessary loss of life. Please know the decisions about this information and who had access were made at much higher levels than mine. Also, not every person involved in the investigation is entirely responsible for what happened.

Although the files provided are complete, there is no associated evidence included or was it made available to me who knew what and when, but I can assure you this information was known at the highest levels, including the attorney general and possibly even the president. Therefore, I ask that you act on this information at once as I am in fear of my family's safety and of everyone I have contact with. There is only one other person with this same information. Below is my contact information. If for some reason you cannot reach me in a reasonable amount of time, please contact Steve Milford below. I will be happy to share what I know beyond these files. Sincerely — Tim Spilner

Weaver sat there and read the letter three times. He then plugged in the memory stick. Forty-five minutes later, he called his entire staff in for an emergency meeting. After that phone call, he called Pops Younger.

"Pops, we have been given a gift of unspeakable proportions. I hate to call you this late at night, but you are going to want to see this and you aren't going to want to wait until tomorrow morning."

The next phone call was to Governor Cooper.

"Governor, I am so sorry to interrupt your evening but what I have to tell you is gigantically unbelievable."

"Okay, Jeff, what's up?"

"I have been sent files by a whistleblower in the Department of Justice, actually an attorney involved in the Sally conspiracy investigation. From what I am seeing here, there is a major cover-up of

Sally's actual intent, his involvement with the Tea Party and motives for the assassination attempt. The DOJ is criminally hiding these facts and has used them to terrorize our citizens."

"I'll be right there. Where's your team?"

"They're already on their way."

"Have you called the Rangers?" Cooper asked.

"Yes, Pops is on his way here, too."

"Geez, this is huge. Do you think it's for real?"

"From what I am seeing, Governor, it's surreal. This is criminal. This is going to take down the entire Executive Branch. This makes Watergate look like nothing."

"Who else knows?"

"According to this guy's letter, only one other person at the DOJ."

"Get them both to Austin."

"My thoughts exactly, Governor. I am going to contact both of them as soon as my team arrives. This information is so sensitive I'm worried about their safety."

"Get Pops on it."

"Yes, sir. See you in a few."

The team in Austin pulled all the documents off the memory stick and began dividing tasks among individuals so the entire treasure trove of documents could be reviewed and documented. After consulting with Pops, Weaver decided to call Tim Spilner personally. He dialed the number provided in the letter.

"Hello?"

"Mr. Spilner?"

"Yes, this is Ed Spilner."

"Ed Spilner? I'm sorry for calling so late, but I'm trying to reach Tim Spilner."

"Who's this?" Mr. Spilner asked.

"This is Jeff Weaver, the Texas attorney general."

"I'm sorry, Mr. Weaver, my son Tim passed away several days ago in an auto accident."

"Oh, my gosh. I'm so sorry. He had given me this number to call him."

"We had his funeral last Thursday."

"Sir, if I may ask, what was the date of the car accident?"

"A week ago Monday."

Weaver looked at the Federal Express package. That was the date the package was sent.

"Again, Mr. Spilner, I am so sorry for your loss. Please give my condolences to your family."

"Thank you, sir. Is there anything I can do for you?"

"No, Mr. Spilner. I'm sorry to intrude on you and your family at such a time. I may touch base with you again in a couple of days."

Weaver figured if Mr. Spilner knew anything about what his son knew and who he sent the information to, he would have brought it up after Weaver identified himself. He also realized that it would likely be painful for Mr. Spilner for Weaver to release any news about what his son had sent him without letting him know first. He told his staff to make sure they knew nothing was to be released without briefing Mr. Spilner.

Weaver moved into the next room where Governor Cooper, Pops and several other Rangers were poring over documents printed out by Weaver's staff.

"Ladies and gentlemen, listen up. I just learned Tim Spilner, the DOJ employee who sent us this information, was killed in an auto accident on the very same day he shipped this to me."

Several gasps came from the group in the room. Weaver turned to one of his staff members.

"Laura, please find out what you can about this car accident. I'm sure it was reported somewhere. Let's see what we can find out."

"Yes, sir."

Pops and Weaver exchanged glances. They didn't have to say a word. It was just too coincidental. Tim Spilner died in an auto accident the same day the information was shipped FedEx to Weaver.

In less than five minutes, Laura ran back into the room.

"Tim Spilner and his wife were killed in a one-car accident on a residential street in Georgetown, D.C. The report said he hit a brick retaining wall at high speed."

The room was deathly silent for almost twenty seconds, then Pops spoke up.

"I'll see if my boys can get a copy of the accident report."

At 2:00 a.m., the governor walked back into the main room where the staff was making copies, binding and printing. "Folks, it's late. Wrap up what you are doing. Everything needs to stay right where it is. Jeff or Pops, do you want to say anything?"

"I sincerely appreciate everyone coming in on short notice," Weaver said. "Obviously, I don't have to tell you how important it is not to mention anything about this to anyone, including your spouses. I promise we are not going to sit on this information, but we need a day or two to process it. This information is historic, but it could also put every person in this room in danger until it is released."

One of the younger members of the staff, a young female attorney, asked, "Can you tell us who knows we have this information now?"

"No, we can't know for sure, but we believe Mr. Spilner got this information out very shortly before his death. According to his letter, only one other person knows it exists and we plan to contact him first thing in the morning."

Chapter 36

"The individual is handicapped by coming face to face with a conspiracy so monstrous he cannot believe it exists."

~ J. Edgar Hoover, former head of the FBI

The next morning at 6:15 a.m., Steve Milford's cell phone began vibrating. He turned off the volume every night before bed but left the phone on his nightstand. He was already awake, because he had trouble sleeping since Tim's accident.

"Hello?"

"Is this Steve Milford?"

"Yes, who's this?"

"Mr. Milford, we were given your phone number by Tim Spilner."

Steve immediately got out of bed and started walking toward the kitchen.

"So who is this?"

"My name is Jeff Weaver. I am the Texas attorney general."

"How do I know this is you for sure?"

"I can give you my phone number here in Austin and you can call back and go through the capitol switchboard to verify the number."

"You said Tim gave you my number?"

"Yes, Steve. Can I call you Steve?" Weaver asked.

"Sure."

"Steve, I received a package directly from Tim Spilner that contained a thumb drive with certain information. Are you familiar with this particular information?"

"Yes, I am."

"Are you aware that only you and I received this information?"

"No, not for sure," Steve responded.

"Are you aware if anyone else has this particular information?"

"No, I'm not," Steve replied.

"Steve, what do you know about Tim's accident?"

"Not much, but I can tell you he was worried about his safety. Did you know it happened on the same day he emailed me this information?"

"No, but I'm not surprised," Weaver told Steve. "He sent us the information on the same day as his accident as well. Steve, I'm not trying to frighten you, but I really believe you could be in serious danger. This information is extremely explosive. I would like to send the governor's jet to pick up you and your family immediately. Can you do that?"

"Uh, sure, I guess."

"Steve, I need to ask you. Who else knows? Who have you told?"

Steve didn't have to give that question much thought. "Absolutely not a soul. Not even my wife."

"Well, I'll let you figure out how to tell your wife you need to leave D.C. immediately. We fueled the jet last night and it left Austin at 5:30 a.m. Can you be at the private terminal at Reagan airport by 8:30?"

"Sure, I think so. Wow. I can't believe this is happening." Steve was stunned at the turn of events.

"Steve, Tim must have trusted you. You and I both think his car accident was suspicious. We haven't gotten a copy of the accident report but, from what we have read, it doesn't add up."

"No, it doesn't."

"Then you know how serious this could be?" Weaver asked.

"Of course. I've been worried sick about it for days. The FBI has already interviewed me. I'm sure they'll be back."

"Okay," Weaver said. "I'll have one of my staff call you back with details for the terminal and your flight. Do not tell a soul outside your immediate family. The rest of your family and friends can find out once you're in Austin safely."

* * *

The DOJ announced a press conference scheduled for 9:00 a.m. Eastern time for U.S. Attorney General Jamail Tibbs to make a special announcement. The talking heads with the media speculated on Tibbs' next actions since the Texas Rangers had thoroughly embarrassed the ATF and FBI. Polling data showed the country was shifting its opinions on the Rangers' role in freeing Chuck Dixon.

At 9:00 a.m., Tibbs walked up to the podium flanked by FBI Director Woodhouse and ATF Director Adamson, along with three congressional Democrats from Texas.

"I will read a statement, but will not take any questions at this time. Today, the Department of Justice is issuing arrest warrants for various officials in the State of Texas associated with the shooting of a federal agent, aiding and abetting a federal fugitive, obstruction of justice, attempted capital murder, trespassing and other charges in relation to the incident at Ellington Air Force Base outside of Houston, Texas. Both the Department of Justice and the administration are highly disturbed that Governor Cooper of Texas would take it upon himself to order the Texas Rangers to conduct illegal operations on federal property and against federal agents that ultimately led to the shooting of an ATF officer.

"These actions are unprecedented and all those involved will be held accountable, including Governor Cooper."

The news organizations were now wildly anticipating the sight of federal agents arresting a sitting governor. Even more dramatic was the thought that the highly professional Texas Rangers could face charges. The news cycles, which had shortened dramatically with the advent of the Internet, 24-hour news channels and new media, were in overdrive about this developing story.

Pops was back at his office at the Texas Department of Public Safety by 6:30 a.m., despite the late night before. Out of the elite corps of one hundred fifty-five Texas Rangers, Pops had assembled his top twenty-five Rangers for a 9:30 a.m. briefing. This elite crew was going to receive assignments for continued special protection of Chuck Dixon's family as well as the expected arrival of Steve Milford's family.

Chapter 37

"The true danger is when liberty is nibbled away, for expedience, and by parts... the only thing necessary for evil to triumph is for good men to do nothing."

~ *Edmund Burke, Irish Statesman,*
considered the founder of modern conservatism

At 10:10 a.m., more than thirty U.S. government vehicles pulled into the sprawling Texas Department of Public Safety (DPS) headquarters campus just north of downtown Austin. At the same time, two military helicopters landed at the front entrance to the main headquarters building, and another two landed at an elementary school field located directly behind the DPS complex.

Immediately, troops in full combat readiness gear with automatic weapons blocked all entrances and exits to DPS headquarters, while dozens took up positions behind buildings, walls, vehicles and trees. A group of men in suits broke from a small tight circle and proceeded to the front entrance. Federal agents walked into the headquarters building and announced themselves.

"My name is FBI Agent Masterson," an agent told the receptionist. "We are here to serve federal arrest warrants for these gentlemen. We will need these folks assembled at once." He motioned to one of the other agents, who provided the receptionist a list of over two dozen Texas Rangers.

The receptionist called the DPS commissioner's office. Less than a minute later, the commissioner and two associates, along with three DPS troopers, came downstairs to meet the agents.

"Gentlemen, what can we do for you?"

"Commissioner, I am Agent Masterson of the FBI. We are here

to serve arrest warrants for Texas Rangers involved in the unlawful operations at Ellington Air Force Base and the Bob Casey Federal Courthouse in Houston, attempted murder, obstruction of justice, trespassing and other operations against the federal government in other Texas locations."

"Okay, I see what you are up to. This is tit for tat, huh?" the commissioner said.

"We are under direct orders from United States Attorney General Jamail Tibbs. Make no mistake, Commissioner; these men are going to be brought into custody this morning. If you or any of your staff assist them or resist, they will also be arrested."

"I see military personnel outside," the commissioner pointed out. "What are military personnel doing involved in what is essentially an FBI operation?"

"Sir, I'm not here to debate the three branches of government with you. I'm here to do a job and we damn sure aim to get it done."

The commissioner turned to one of his staff members. "Call the governor immediately and tell him what is happening here."

"Sir, you can call God himself, but right now you need to produce the men on this list."

Right in the middle of Pop's briefing, a DPS trooper barged into the room and yelled, "The feds are here to arrest the Rangers, Pops!"

Pops stood. "Gentlemen, report to the DPS warehouse immediately. Stop at the armory first and grab a rifle, and make sure you have your sidearm."

Pops was referring to a warehouse on the property where many DPS vehicles were maintained, repaired and housed. At the time of the meeting, less than half of the one hundred fifty-five Texas Rangers were on site at the DPS campus.

At the entrance to the main headquarters building, FBI Agent Masterson was becoming impatient.

"Commissioner, you can either have these men assemble peacefully, or my men will go to every cubicle, office and closet and find them."

"Agent Masterson, your threat puts all my staff and the employees of the DPS at risk. I am asking you to allow us the necessary time to respond to your request. Because the Rangers report directly to the governor, I will have to speak to him personally."

"Okay, you've got fifteen minutes," said Agent Masterson reluctantly as he directed the other agents to coordinate with the troops and ATF outside. Masterson was taking this mission personally; he felt the ATF and FBI had been embarrassed by the Texas Rangers—a bunch of what he perceived as "cowboys"—waltzing right into the Ellington Air Force Base hangar and retrieving Chuck Dixon.

***

At the state capitol building in downtown Austin, a similar contingent of FBI, ATF, and fifty U.S. Army Rangers entered the capitol grounds headed for the governor's office. Two military helicopters landed in nearby parking lots.

Fox News broadcast Breaking News:

"Imminent Constitutional Crisis: Federal government takes on the State of Texas over Tea Party raids, issues federal arrest warrant for governor of Texas."

Capitol police were overwhelmed. At any one time, there might be twenty-five police officers on the grounds. ATF and FBI agents made the capitol police turn over their weapons. They were disarmed so quickly that no radio transmission or phone call could be made to the governor's office to inform him of the situation.

Inside the capitol, ten Texas Rangers were assigned to duty for the governor and lieutenant governor's security.

The DOJ had notified media outlets friendly to the administration about the federal agents marching right into the Texas state capitol building and slapping handcuffs on the governor. According to those with knowledge in the administration, this would make great drama, boost the administration's overall perception of being in charge, set

the federal government as the centralized authority for law and order, and would finally squelch the states' rights movement gaining
traction throughout various Southern and Western states challenging voter identification and immigration enforcement laws. It was
also in retaliation for the Texas Rangers' arrest of the ATF and FBI
agents in Houston and Dallas.

Chapter 38

"A vote is like a rifle; its usefulness depends upon the character of the user."

~ *Theodore Roosevelt*

Despite capitol police not being able to communicate to the capitol building, the Texas Rangers on duty there were ready and fully aware of what was taking place. Rangers had called the capitol immediately upon the appearance of federal agents at DPS headquarters. Ranger Capitol Duty Manager Truman Mallory spoke directly to Pops.

"The governor is not to be arrested under any circumstances. Do you understand?" Pops said.

"Yes, sir, no federal agent is arresting our governor," replied Ranger Mallory.

Two Texas Rangers met the FBI agents climbing the steps outside the capitol building. Before the agents got half-way up the steps, both Rangers drew their 30-30 Winchesters like they were from a saddle holster on a horse.

"Stop right there. Do not climb another step. You are on state property. I advise you right now to turn around and leave the capitol grounds."

Lead FBI Agent Hixson stopped, pulled back his suit coat to expose a shoulder holster where he carried a .38 revolver.

"Gentlemen, I have more than fifty Army Rangers here as well as a full contingent of FBI and ATF personnel. We have an arrest warrant for Governor Brent Cooper and Lieutenant Governor Gene Foster. Now, we can make this easy or we can make this hard. Regardless, those two gentlemen are going to be escorted from the capitol premises."

"Sir, let me see your arrest warrants."

One of the FBI agents moved forward with two folded documents.

"Stop right there, sir. Put your sidearm on the ground before taking another step."

"Are you serious?"

Ranger Mallory cocked the 30-30. The FBI agent complied, then approached the Ranger. "Here you go."

Ranger Mallory flipped through the several pages of each warrant, looking for the judge's signature.

"Sir, your arrest warrants aren't valid in Texas."

"Those are federal warrants, cowboy. They are good anywhere."

"Mister, these warrants are signed by a judge in D.C. They aren't valid here," spat Mallory as he tossed the documents back to Agent Hixson.

"Well, we have a problem then. I have a job to do here and I understand you have a job to do as well." Agent Hixson turned around and motioned affirmatively to the Army Rangers who were standing behind them.

They all started to climb the tall, steep steps to the capitol building's double front doors. Both Texas Rangers raised their rifles. "Stop!" they ordered.

Suddenly a gunshot rang out, striking the pink granite façade over the door where the Rangers stood. An ATF agent standing behind one of the Confederate monuments on the front lawn less than fifty yards from the steps had taken a shot with a high-powered rifle, missing the Rangers by inches.

Two shots rang out from the second story windows, striking the base of the monument where the shooter fired. The agents at the capitol steps hit the ground to take cover.

Now shots rang out from all across the lawn, striking the windows and granite of the capitol. While hundreds of shots struck the capitol building, TV camera crews broadcast the onslaught to the world. The Texas capitol was under siege by federal government troops and agents. No more shots came from inside the capitol, leading to speculation that some Rangers had been hit.

The Rangers moved the governor and his staff to a secret bunker below the capitol. Similar to the U.S. capitol, there was an escape route and hiding place known only to top state officials.

Word spread quickly to the DPS headquarters that the capitol building was under siege and the Texas Rangers were taking fire. Pops had his Rangers take up defensive positions in the maintenance warehouse where they were joined by thirty DPS state troopers.

Texas is the only state that maintains a state militia under the governor's direct command. This Texas State Guard is typically used in natural disasters like hurricanes and works in conjunction with the National Guard in the same capacity. The governor put out the call to the Texas State Guard.

"The Texas capitol is under siege by federal troops. Immediate interdiction and assistance required."

ATF troops stationed on the capitol grounds began to use tear gun cannons to launch tear gas into the capitol. Each one that made it through a window was unceremoniously tossed back out within a few seconds. Still, no more shots had been fired from the capitol building.

The FBI got on the capitol police frequency and asked someone to provide the radio directly to the governor. Governor Cooper was brought from the underground shelter to communicate with the FBI.

"This is Governor Cooper."

"Sir, this is FBI Agent Hixson. We are here to serve a federal warrant on you and the lieutenant governor. This is already out of control. Your Texas Rangers have pointed their weapons at me and my men."

"My understanding, Hixson, is that one of your agents shot at the Rangers."

"Yes, sir, they did—after the Rangers pointed their weapons at them."

"Mr. Hixson, I am telling you right now to pull back the federal troops you have on the lawn of the Texas capitol. The citizens of Texas will not stand for this federal encroachment and bullying tactic."

"Sir, if you do not allow us to enter and take you into custody, there will be bloodshed today and it will be on your hands."

"Your Department of Justice and this administration have violated the U.S. Constitution. You will not be allowed to enter the capitol building. Do you understand?" the governor retorted.

"Sir, with all due respect, I have highly qualified agents and Special Forces personnel surrounding the capitol and the blocks around it. Besides the advantage in weapons and training, we outnumber the capitol police, troopers and Texas Rangers in the building."

"Give me a moment to speak to my staff here."

"If it will avoid bloodshed, please do. But my patience and the patience of the administration has limits, sir."

The governor huddled with his staff, the Rangers and Lieutenant Governor Foster for a few minutes. Then he got back on the phone with Agent Hixson.

"Agent Hixson?"

"Yes, sir?"

"You will not be allowed to enter; however, I will make myself available to you at another location, provided we have access to the media here in the capitol building for fifteen minutes to make a statement."

"I don't think I can get clearance for that, Governor Cooper. Let me call D.C. and I'll get right back to you."

Agent Hixson was on the phone with FBI Director Woodhouse, ATF Director Adamson and Attorney General Tibbs, who were all set up in a situation room watching news coverage and feeds coming in from their staffs.

"In fifteen minutes, if you get the wrong answer, I want you to invoke the plan already laid out. Do you think you have the special escape routes covered if the Rangers try to get them out?" Tibbs asked.

"I believe so, sir, but our intelligence about the escape routes is dated. As noted in our last briefing, some of these tunnels were re-directed after 9/11 and after the capitol renovation."

"Are you prepared to embark on the plan to arrest the governor as outlined in your briefing?" repeated Tibbs.

"Yes, sir, but sir, just so you know, these Rangers are a proud bunch. They are also holed up with no telling how many DPS troopers. After all, this is Texas and they've been known to fight to the last man. We don't want another Alamo here, but I can't assure you this will be easy or that there won't be casualties on both sides."

"I want you to announce on loud speakers to the DPS troopers in the building and on radio that anyone who wants to leave can do so and avoid federal charges. I'm sure most of these folks don't want federal charges pending against them, so you may be able to peel off most if not all of them by giving them a chance to exit prior to the extraction of the governor."

"Yes, sir, I'll give them and anyone else that opportunity. If the situation changes before we begin extraction, I'll let you know."

"I want that son of a bitch in handcuffs and I want a very long walk to the helicopter so that every TV camera there sees what happens when a state violates federal authority."

"Well, sir, I think every camera crew within five hundred miles is here. I had to deploy additional troops to hold them back and keep them at a safe distance, but many are shooting video from the roof-tops of downtown buildings. It's a freakin' circus," said Agent Hixson, who was having a hard time understanding why Justice would have tipped off TV networks ahead of the operation.

For all his grandstanding and his personal vendetta against Governor Cooper, Tibbs had diverted needed personnel from the operation and Agent Hixson felt it put innocents and his agents in danger needlessly for Tibbs' personal pride. When he hung up the phone, Agent Hixson knew deep down this was not going to turn out well, even if he did apprehend the governor.

"Sir, we have the governor's people back on the radio," said a fellow agent."

Hixson took the radio. "This is Agent Hixson."

"We are trying to get the governor back on the radio. He's on the phone; give us a second."

"I want everyone on this frequency to know that I am giving the last warning," Hixson said. "I have just gotten off the phone with United States Attorney General Jamail Tibbs. He is giving all personnel, but especially the DPS state troopers who are in the capitol building, an opportunity to come out without weapons. Anybody that comes out without weapons will not be charged. For those of you still in there, you are violating the law you swore to uphold. I will give you five minutes. After those five minutes, you will be charged with anyone else we have to arrest."

"This is Governor Cooper."

"Sir, what is your decision?" Hixson asked.

"Agent Hixson, you have no authority here..."

Suddenly, Hixson was interrupted by Captain Fowler, who was leading the U.S. Army Rangers.

"Hold on, Governor, I'll be right back to you. What is it, Captain?"

"Sir, look at the rooftops."

On nearly every rooftop within sight, uniformed personnel could be seen with automatic weapons pointed at the agents and the U.S. Army Rangers.

"Sir, are those ours?" Fowler blurted as helicopters approached.

"Apaches? That wasn't in the plans..."

Agent Hixson was back on the phone talking with FBI Director Woodhouse.

"Sir, do we have birds of any kind in the air?"

"Air support? No, only the extraction choppers. Why would we need air support to extract a governor who is protected by some damn cowboys? You outnumber them twenty to one. What is it you're seeing?"

Agent Hixson was interrupted again.

"Agent Hixson, we ran the tail numbers," one of his agents told him. "Those are Air Wing of the Texas Militia Apaches out of San Antonio."

"Are they armed? Are they allowed to be armed?"

"They sure appear to be. They wouldn't be at tree top level locked onto to us if they weren't."

"Shit, are you kidding me?" Hixson went back to the phone. "Mr. Director, we have three Apaches staring down our throats..."

A sound so loud it shook the ground drowned out his phone conversation. Four F-16 fighters barely above rooftop height buzzed the capitol building.

"Goddamn, are those ours?" Hixson asked.

"What was that?" asked Woodhouse.

"Captain, what were those?" Hixson asked.

"Sir, those were F-16s and their tails had the Lone Star Flag on them. It's more Air Wing of the Texas Militia."

"Goddamn it, sir, did we plan on this contingency?" Hixson was very close to yelling at Woodhouse. "The governor now has fully armed air support. What the hell do I do now?"

"Execute the extraction, Hixson."

"Come again, sir. I don't think I heard you correctly."

"Agent Hixson, execute the extraction."

"Sir, did you hear what I just said about the Apaches and F-16s? Also, I didn't tell you there are Texas State Guard troops poised on every building for blocks. We are eventually going to be outnumbered here, and possibly outgunned."

"Agent Hixson, the air support units will not fire on the capitol grounds. They are there to intimidate only. There is no guarantee those birds are even armed. They are not going to blow up the capitol building. Now go get the damn governor."

Hixson jumped back on the two-way radio.

"Governor, are you there?"

"Yes, this is Governor Cooper. I assume by now you have some company out there?"

"Yes, sir, we do, but I have very clear orders, sir. I need you to give yourself up; otherwise, people are going to die here today."

Chapter 39

"You may have to fight a battle more than once to win it."

~ *Margaret Thatcher*

All news stations were breaking with live feeds. The scene at the capitol was surreal. F-16 fighters continued to buzz the downtown area, and Apache helicopters hovered near the capitol grounds. The chaos caused a traffic jam of unprecedented proportions and traffic came to a standstill on every street downtown. Highway I-35, which ran north and south through downtown, was completely closed. Live coverage showed hundreds of Texas State Guard volunteers abandoning their vehicles and running along streets to the capitol carrying gear and weapons. Most of the militia were mustering at the University of Texas Darrell K. Royal football stadium, about ten blocks from the capitol. The Texas State Guard had gotten the call, and the response was overwhelming. The Travis Rifles were coming in from all over Travis and adjoining counties.

Austin police had no advance notice of the federal operation until right before it started and were reduced to bystanders. All they could do was keep crowds and news crews back and try to deal with the traffic logjam that enveloped the entire downtown area. The police chief, who reported to the staunchly Democratic mayor, was instructed to stand down and let the feds conduct their operation despite growing sentiment against the feds for this action from the rank-and-file police officers. Democrat or Republican, Texans were extremely offended with the federal government's actions.

* * *

Pops and his Rangers, along with the DPS troopers, remained stationed in a defensive position in the maintenance warehouse. Troopers and Rangers were armed with 30-30 Winchesters and each one had a handgun, mostly .357s, .38s and .45s.

Agent Masterson tired of waiting and gave the order to search the building. FBI and ATF agents started combing the building, backed up by U.S. Army Rangers. Agent Masterson's radio was non-stop as each cubicle, office and floor was cleared. Employees and staff of the DPS were rounded up and escorted to the cafeteria. Each employee had to produce ID to prove his or her identification.

Masterson's radio went into high gear.

"Agent Masterson, this is Captain Wickham. Did we order air support for this operation?"

"No," Masterson said. "Why?"

"We've just been buzzed by two F-16s and an Apache chopper is hovering one hundred yards behind us. I haven't been able to communicate with them yet."

"Apache? F-16s? That wasn't in our plan, but maybe Defense ordered extra air support. Keep trying to establish communications."

Like Agent Hixson, Agent Masterson had zero clue that Texas maintained an arsenal of aircraft under the Air Wing of the Texas Militia.

"Sir, our spotters indicate there are uniformed troops gathering at two sites within three blocks of the entrance to the DPS compound," Wickham continued. "Did we order additional troops? Who are they?"

"Shit, I don't know. Let me call the director and see what's going on." Masterson was indignant. "Why do we only find this stuff out when we are already under way? Goddamit!"

His radio started up again. "Sir, Rangers have been spotted in what looks like a maintenance building."

"How many?" Masterson barked.

"We've seen at least three, but there are also DPS officers in there."

"Surround the building and demand their surrender. I'll be there shortly."

Agent Masterson was more than a little irritated. He couldn't understand why additional troops and air cover were not part of the operational plan for the arrest of the Rangers.

"Sir, I have Director Woodhouse on the phone." An agent handed him the phone.

"What is your situation on the ground there, Agent Masterson?" asked Woodhouse.

"Sir, we are doing a sweep of the main headquarters building right now. So far, no Rangers."

"No Rangers? What the hell do you mean, no Rangers?"

"Sir, we haven't identified any yet. We have several buildings yet to clear."

"What the hell! Were they tipped off?"

"I don't know, sir. I need to know what the plan is for the additional troops assembling three blocks to the north. Also, when did the plan include air cover, and why do we need it?"

"Additional troops? What do you mean?"

"Our local intelligence states several hundred troops are assembling a few blocks from here. We are not in communication with them. What is their operational function?"

"Agent, those are likely Texas State Guard."

"Texas State Guard? What the hell is that? That was never covered in our strategy assessment. What about the F-16s and the Apache?"

"Air Wing of the Texas Militia."

"What?! Texas has F-16s and Apache helicopters?"

"Agent Masterson, our intelligence tells us they are trying to intimidate federal operations. These aircraft are never armed."

"What about the militia? They are definitely armed."

"Agent, conduct your operation as quickly as you can and get those Rangers extracted. Do you understand me?"

"Yes, sir," Masterson said. "What do we do if we are engaged by this militia?"

"If you are fired upon, instruct your team to return fire. The object is to get out of there before this ragtag bunch of vigilantes shows up. Understand?"

"Yes, sir."

"Report back after all buildings are swept."

Masterson handed the phone back to his fellow agent.

"Did I hear you say Texas State Guard?" he asked Masterson. "Air Wing of the Texas Militia?"

"Yes, but supposedly the air cover is for show; they aren't armed."

"Are we betting on that?"

"Agent, I was on the phone personally with Director Woodhouse. If he says they aren't armed, they aren't armed. Do you understand?"

"Yes, sir. What about the militia? They're armed."

"That is an unproven group of volunteers," Masterson said. "Let's get this compound swept and get out of here with our arrests."

The agents went building by building, methodically moving DPS employees to central locations to check IDs and keep them out of the operation. For the most part, the agents were apologetic; however, numerous DPS employees were calling them names like the "Gestapo" and "KGB" for conducting a paramilitary operation like this in a state office. The agents hadn't found a single Ranger.

"You know," Masterson said, almost to himself, "it's not like Texas Rangers are hard to spot. They're like no other law enforcement officer in the world. When you see one, it's impossible not to know who they are. Wouldn't you agree?" he asked the agent standing next to him. The agent noded.

"Sir, we have one last building, a maintenance building where we know some Rangers are hiding."

"Hiding?" Masterson laughed. "I doubt they are hiding, Agent. They are likely taking up positions."

"Positions?" The man was aghast. "Do you think they'll resist?"

"Agent, we are in Texas. The feds and Texas aren't on very friendly terms. I don't think we should expect them to just walk out."

All four sides of the building were surrounded. Agent Masterson got on the loud speaker.

"This is FBI Agent Masterson. We know there are Texas Rangers and state troopers in the building. Lay down your weapons and come out with your hands up."

As soon as he said that, one of Masterson's agents whispered in his ear, "The capitol is reporting gunfire."

"Shit. I guarantee you those guys in that building know exactly what is going on in downtown Austin. Is that all they said? Who's firing?"

"A little confusing, but apparently shots are coming from inside the capitol at our guys."

"Okay, if they will do that there you can bet your ass they'll do it here."

"There's one! He just came out," an agent shouted.

"Holy cow, that's Pops himself."

Pops Younger came out the side door of the maintenance building with his hands up, unarmed.

"Gentlemen, I would like to speak with Agent Masterson."

Agent Masterson and two fellow FBI agents started forward.

"Boys," Pops said quietly, "you need to lose your weapons. Right now, some of the best marksmen in the world have your foreheads in their gun sights. We can talk, but don't move any further with your weapons."

One of the agents with Masterson said, "Sir, you are threatening a federal agent."

"Boy, I'm not threatening. I'm telling you that, unless you want a 30-30 tattoo on your forehead, drop your sidearm now."

"Do what the man says." Masterson removed his weapon and glanced at the other two agents as they stopped and removed their handguns. He signaled to another agent to come up to retrieve the weapons. The three again started walking toward Pops, who was standing approximately twenty-five feet from the side door.

As Masterson got closer, he found himself impressed with the

Ranger. Here's an old school law enforcement legend right out of Texas folklore, he thought, yet he was there to arrest him.

"Mr. Younger," he said, "I'm sure you are aware we have an arrest warrant for you and numerous other rangers. Now, I know this is embarrassing..."

Pops interrupted. "Embarrassing for who, boy? You feds made all this stink when you took it upon yourselves to arrest Texans without cause, terrorizing their homes and businesses, kidnapping one and even killing a few. If I were you, I would be embarrassed to be associated with any federal department that tramples the Constitution in that manner. I would also be embarrassed by the fact that you are going home today empty-handed. You will not be arresting any Texas Rangers today, tomorrow or ever."

Masterson felt like he just got reamed by the headmaster and he was some schoolboy taking his lessons.

"Mr. Younger, I respect the hell out of you," he said. "We all do. But you know you will have your day in court, as will your Rangers. What I'm asking you to do is to surrender. We don't want this to get out of hand."

"Agent Masterson, let me ask you a question. Did Chuck Dixon have his day in court? No, he was hauled off to some jet hangar and illegally detained without any due process. What about that guy Stan Mumford? Shot dead right in front of his family."

"Mr. Younger, I'm not here to debate you. We all have a job to do. I'm here to do mine and I hope you respect that."

Pops ignored that. "Where are your warrants? If they are signed by a Texas court from a Texas judge, I will abide by them."

One of the agents fumbled in his suit coat and produced two warrants, including the one for Pops. He looked down at the ground when he handed them to Pops, knowing he was also going to be reprimanded by the headmaster.

Pops flipped through the papers, then said, "Shit, boys, these are signed by some damn judge in the District of Columbia! Do you want me to tell you what you can do with these warrants?"

"Mr. Younger, I am out of options here," Masterson said. "I have a job to do. Now, you are either going to instruct your folks in that building to lay their weapons down and come out, or everyone is going to jail."

"Agent Masterson, we have what we call here in Texas a Mexican stand-off. Now the last time something like this happened, one hundred and eighty-seven brave Texans fought the Mexican army to the last man. But they took a couple of thousand with them. You don't want to go there, son."

Masterson, frazzled and irritated, instructed his agents to return to their positions. The three walked away without saying a word.

Pops stood there for a second, looked at the ground, then shook his head and deftly repositioned his Stetson before spitting some smokeless tobacco he had between his lip and gums on the ground, leaving a small piece of tobacco on his bushy handlebar mustache. He turned and went back into the maintenance building.

Masterson was beyond frustration. How was it he always ended up with the intractable ones? "We have no choice," he said. He motioned to Captain Wickham. "Bring up the tear gas canisters."

* * *

At the capitol, ATF, FBI and U.S. Army Rangers advanced on the multiple entrances to the capitol, stopping fifty feet from the building. Making their way to the front of the assault lines were specialists with tear gas cannons that looked like small bazookas. The operators and two support troops for each cannon readied their weapons and awaited word to launch the tear gas grenades.

"Governor, this is your last opportunity. We are prepared to enter the capitol building. If there is blood spilled, it will be on your hands," said Hixson.

Just as Hixson finished his sentence, a deafening noise shook the capitol lawn. Two Apache helicopters had positioned themselves near the capitol building, hovering approximately one hundred feet above the trees and building, looking as if they were prepared to fire on the assault lines that surrounded the capitol.

Chapter 40

"A people that values its privileges above its principles soon loses both."

~ *Dwight D. Eisenhower*

The news media was going crazy as this unfolding drama broke on televisions across America and on the Internet worldwide. Would the feds fire tear gas? If they did, would the Apaches fire on federal agents and the U.S. military? Would a battle ensue between Texas and the United States?

"Agent Hixson," Governor Cooper said, "I want you to patch me through to your FBI director or the attorney general. Do you understand if you fire upon the capitol, my instructions will be to fire back?"

"Sir, are those Apaches and F-16s armed?"

"Agent Hixson, in Texas we don't point unloaded weapons at anyone."

"You're telling me those aircraft are armed?"

"As well as the Texas State Guard that has your flank on all four sides. So, Agent Hixson, if you take another step toward the capitol or fire those cannons into the capitol, the blood will actually be on your hands."

Hixson dropped off the two-way radio to contemplate his next move.

"Sir, we are prepared to proceed."

"I know, I know. Let me think for a minute!" barked Hixson. "Get D.C. back on the phone."

"Sir, the governor is trying to reach you again."

"Governor, I'm trying to reach D.C."

"Son, listen closely to me before your proceed. We have received evidence from an internal Department of Justice whistleblower that this whole Rash Sally conspiracy theory is a farce. Rash Sally acted on his own. He had ties to Iran. He was Muslim. His sister and her family were killed in Operation Python. The excerpts of his Master's thesis were contrived. He was sympathetic to the Tea Party's motives but in no way was he a Tea Party activist. Your boss and this administration are using this trumped-up investigation to demonize and eliminate the Tea Party. Before you give the order that is going to cost lives, I felt you should know this."

"Governor, if you had that kind of information, you would have released it."

"Agent Hixson, had you not shown up this morning with your contingent of federal jackboots, it would have been released at a press conference this morning."

Hixson was facing a real dilemma now. The news delivered by the governor was shocking, even unbelievable. What if he moved forward and this was all true? What if people were killed today after he had been made aware of this information? What if the governor was mistaken, or worse, lying?

"Get D.C. on the phone right now," Hixson ordered. While he waited for the connection to be made to Director Woodhouse, he could only pace and fume. When the agent who placed the call handed him the phone, he said, "Director, this is Agent Hixson…"

"Agent, we see what is happening on TV. Why haven't you moved on the capitol?" demanded an irritated Woodhouse.

"Sir, did you see the Apaches hovering above the capitol? If we move, I'll lose dozens of men. Rangers are at every window."

"Agent, I'm not asking you for an assessment. I'm ordering you to arrest the governor of Texas by any means necessary."

"Sir, I just spoke with the governor, and he told me some very disturbing information about an internal Justice Department whistleblower who had evidence that Rash Sally's motivation was his Iranian background, death of his sister and her family, and that the Tea Party is not connected."

There was a deafening silence on the other end of the line. "Sir, did you hear me?"

"Agent Hixson, who told you this and where did he get his information?"

"The governor himself, sir."

"Who is his source?"

"He hasn't told me. He just said it was an internal Justice employee."

"Shit," Woodhouse muttered. "Stand down for a few minutes and let me get with Mr. Tibbs."

"Please hurry, sir. The situation here is extremely volatile and could go off any second."

Woodhouse broke the connection to Hixson and turned to the rest in the situation room set up at the Department of Justice.

"Jamail, Hixson is telling me that he spoke to Cooper directly and was informed the governor had been given internal Justice information about a whistleblower."

"Son of a bitch! Goddamn Spilner, it's gotta be. Clear the room. Director and deputy directors only!" Tibbs was livid.

In thirty seconds, the ATF and FBI directors and their deputy directors had the situation room to themselves.

Tibbs continued, "Okay, is he bluffing? I need input here!"

"I don't think he's bluffing. We know Spilner copied files and got out with them somehow."

"But how in the hell did he get them to the governor?" asked Tibbs.

"Spilner must have shipped the files when he left work. He was dead within a couple of hours after he left the DOJ. I can't imagine he acted that quickly but, if he did, we are in serious jeopardy," said a somber Adamson.

"Well, his unfortunate *accident* apparently didn't happen soon enough," barked Tibbs.

"Hixson has got to follow through. Maybe those in the know will be caught in the crossfire," said Adamson hopefully. "Otherwise, everyone in this room is toast, as is the president."

"Why hasn't the governor gone public with this?" asked Tibbs.

"Who the hell knows? Maybe his info is incomplete or he is trying to verify it independently. We don't know what he knows," said Woodhouse.

"Too much time has passed. He would have gone public if he had the goods. It's been over a week since Spilner died," said a visibly concerned Tibbs.

"What do we have to lose now? Have Hixson move forward with orders to shoot to kill everyone who resists. Maybe the information will die with the scumbags in Texas," retorted Adamson.

"Well, you have a point, but we only have minutes to decide this," responded Tibbs.

"We know Spilner copied *every* file on Sally. I mean every file," stated Woodhouse.

"Order Hixson to proceed with unequivocal shoot-to-kill instructions for any resistance whatsoever, and that includes the governor himself," declared Tibbs.

"Sir, I have Hixson back on the phone." A deputy director handed Tibbs the phone.

"Agent Hixson, this is United States Attorney General Jamail Tibbs. The governor of Texas is lying to you to escape capture. He has nothing. You have my assurances that nothing he is telling you is even partially true. Do you understand me fully?"

"Yes, sir, but..."

"Hixson, if I don't hear an affirmative from you that you are going to immediately proceed with the planned operation, you will be replaced in thirty seconds. Do you understand me?" Tibbs' voice was quietly threatening.

"Affirmative, sir. Understood," said a reluctant Hixson.

Hixson hung up the phone and took a long look at the situation on the capitol grounds. Two Apaches hovered over the capitol with rocket launchers and Gatling-gun high caliber rotating machine guns ready to mow down his agents and troops.

Texas Rangers sat in the windows with old-school 30-30 Winchester saddle guns. The Texas State Guard, growing by the minute, were poised on nearby rooftops and some areas near the iron fence surrounding the capitol grounds. They now outnumbered his combined interdepartmental agents and U.S. Army troops. Hixson was about to make a career-defining decision.

"Get the governor back on the phone, right now!" yelled Hixson.

"Are we moving yet?" asked Agent Barnes, who was next in charge.

"I said get the governor on the phone. Don't make me repeat myself."

Agent Barnes glared at Hixson. "Yes, sir!" he said with a hint of insubordination. He called the governor, and handed the phone to Hixson when he had the connection

"This is Governor Cooper," the governor said.

"Governor, you have made claims about a Justice whistleblower."

"Yes, I have. I'm sure you talked to your superiors and they denied it."

"Yes, sir, they have."

"Agent Hixson," the governor said quietly, "listen very carefully to me. We have the evidence."

"I would like to see it."

"If that will avoid an armed conflict," Cooper said, "by all means, get your ass in here and see what we see."

"I will bring two men with me. We will be unarmed."

"We will be prepared to show you everything, but you will need about thirty minutes to see the entire content. Can you get your people to stand down that long?"

"Governor, my ass is on the line here. I need your word this information truly exists."

"Get your butt in here, Agent Hixson."

Hixson turned to his chain of command, "Stand down everyone. Pull back one hundred yards. Turn all weapons to the ground immediately."

"But, sir..." Barnes sputtered

"Did you not understand my orders, Barnes?"

"Yes, sir," Barnes said stiffly.

"Williams and Jennings, lose your weapons and come with me. We are going to pay the governor a visit."

Chapter 41

"I happily cling to my guns and my God, even if President Johnson thinks this is a simpleminded thing."

~ *Rick Perry*

Back at the DOJ, news channels reported that federal government forces were pulling back and three men in suits were entering the capitol building with their arms in the air.

"What the hell is going on there?" demanded Tibbs.

"Sir, we cannot reach Hixson on the command phone."

"Get somebody on the phone now! What the fuck is he doing? The operation should have started, goddamnit!" yelled Tibbs.

"Jamail, command there is telling us he went in to arrest the governor and bring him out himself."

"What? That was not the plan. Why can't this motherfucker follow orders? Did I not say commence the operation?" Tibbs ranted.

"We have just lost any chance to keep that information from breaking. There needs to be casualties and they need to be the governor and his staff. Son of a bitch!" yelled Adamson.

"We need to be working on contingencies, denials and counter-propaganda," Tibbs sounded panicked. "Get your teams on this now. If he walks out with the governor, you can be assured this information was passed on to others to make public." Tibbs glared at the directors and deputy directors in the room who seemed to be stunned into silence and unable to act.

"Goddamit, didn't you hear me?" he raged. "All of you are complicit in this! Need I remind you of that? Now get your people moving! We have very little time."

"Sir, are you going to call the president?" asked Woodhouse.

"No, not yet. Let's see what happens."

"Sir, just a suggestion... but can't we make something happen right now? Right now!" suggested Adamson.

"I'm listening."

"Let's get the operation launched and see where the chips fall. What do we have to lose at this point?"

Tibbs sat there rubbing his chin, then massaged his face with both hands as he thought about the consequences. "Make it happen," he said. "How do we commence with our people in the capitol?"

"Make it so those damn Texas State Guard troops get overzealous. That should be easy to do. They're so damn stupid."

Tibbs announced, "We will have to pass the chain of command to someone else."

"Done," said Woodhouse. "Orders have been passed to Agent Barnes."

"So what's the plan?"

"I've instructed the Army Rangers to remove the threat of the Texas State Guard troops positioned on the roof of the Texas Law Library," said Woodhouse smugly.

Agent Barnes was informed that Hixson had been officially relieved of command and that Barnes was in charge of the Austin operation. Barnes instructed an ATF unit of twelve agents, supported by twenty-five Army Rangers, to clear the rooftop by any force necessary.

The ATF and Army Rangers checked weapons, assembled and spread out in two groups to approach the Law Library, which was positioned opposite the southeast corner of the capitol grounds. As they approached, Texas State Guard troops demanded they halt. The ATF unit kept coming. The State Guards raised their weapons and again ordered them halt, but those instructions were ignored. Seeing weapons raised at their advance, the ATF opened fire. The State of Texas was being fired upon by federal forces. The ATF agents and Army Rangers fired as they advanced, taking positions behind lamp posts and trees, and dropping to the ground.

The Travis Rifles, named after Alamo hero William Barrett Travis, were extremely proud of their namesake and made it a rite of passage for nearly all their members to qualify as expert marksmen. Corporal Adams, the state guardsman in charge on the ground, commanded, "Travis Rifles, return fire!"

Even though the ATF unit and the Army Rangers had superior and newer weapons, the Travis Rifles decimated the unit. ATF agents in their trademark black paramilitary outfits and Army Rangers in digital camo littered the block and corner of the capitol grounds with slumped and motionless bodies. Several wounded troops screamed for assistance. One Texas State Guardsman was wounded in the upper arm.

The governor was operating out of a state senator's small staff room adjacent to his offices to review the evidence with Agent Hixson. Hixson and the governor had just exchanged introductions, and Hixson started to review what the governor's staff was presenting when all hell broke loose.

"What the hell is going on out there?" Hixson yelled into his radio.

"Sir, the director has relieved you of your command. Agent Barnes is in charge. He was instructed by the director to clear the Law Library roof."

"Are there casualties?"

"It appears so, sir."

"Get me Barnes. Right now!"

Meanwhile, the governor's staff and the Texas Rangers were receiving word from their communications staff that the ATF had attacked a position held by State Guardsmen.

"Dammit, Hixson, what the hell? Can't you get control of your folks out there?" demanded the governor.

"I've been relieved of command, sir. Orders are now coming directly from D.C."

Scattered gunfire could still be heard on the southeast corner of the grounds.

"Hixson, this is going to escalate. Why would they do this with you in here?"

"Governor, I'm disobeying orders. I've just committed career suicide. I wanted to see this evidence myself before things got out of control, but it may be too late. Dammit, I just need fifteen or twenty minutes to review this stuff."

One of the Apaches moved adjacent to the Law Library, now hovering barely fifty feet above the street. Barnes ordered more units to respond to the building and to provide cover for those agents and Army Rangers pinned behind obstacles. Other buildings occupied by state guardsmen were being drawn into the conflict as ATF units opened fire on adjacent buildings. A full-scale battle was escalating quickly.

An aide handed the U.S. attorney general a phone. "Mr. Tibbs, President Johnson is on the phone."

Tibbs walked away from his staff into an adjacent room to update the president, including telling him the news of the supposed whistleblower leak. Tibbs spent five minutes explaining the escalating scenario in Austin to the president. The president was livid.

In Austin, Gene Foster yelled, "Hixson, tell your folks to stand down. Tell them the governor is coming out. That's the only way to stop this thing."

"Barnes, this is Hixson. Stand down. The governor is coming out. Stand down. Do you hear me?"

"The governor is coming out?" Barnes asked incredulously. "You mean he is surrendering?"

Hixson looked at the governor to affirm that was what he intended.

"Yes, provided I get a news conference first," Cooper said. "I want this information out and I want it out now."

"Barnes, the governor will surrender if he gets to make a statement to the news agencies. Stand down everyone before we have more casualties. Do you understand me?"

"Sir, I'm sorry, but I'm under direct orders..."

Hixson shouted into the radio. "Goddammit, Barnes, listen to me. Justice wants the governor. He is surrendering. The violence is going to escalate, so stand down now! The governor is ordering his folks to do the same. I don't give a shit what Washington is telling you! Stand down now!"

The governor's staff received an update from DPS headquarters north of Austin.

"Damn, Governor, Pops' crew at DPS is completely surrounded in the maintenance building."

As soon as the ATF advanced on the Texas Law Library, word got to the ATF units at DPS surrounding the maintenance building. Somehow, confusion reigned about who was shooting at whom.

"Federal agents are being fired on! Advance now!" came an order on the radio.

"Shit! Okay, boys, this is for real. These guys are likely not going to surrender either," Agent Masterson shouted to his leadership at the DPS compound.

"Sir, I'm getting news there are dozens of ATF and Army Rangers down or killed," yelled an Army Ranger sergeant.

Pops was on the phone with the governor's staff. Since the violence had escalated, Pops figured it would at DPS also.

"Governor, ask those air boys to take out the two choppers sitting on the ground. I don't believe they think we will use them. We will do it here. Do the same at the capitol. Tell them to send flares at the choppers to move the pilots from harm's way."

The two Apaches at the capitol moved to the parking lot where the two UH-60 Blackhawks were positioned to ferry Brent Cooper, Gene Foster and the Texas Rangers after their arrests to destinations unknown. The pilots of the Apaches moved their attack choppers to near ground level opposite the two Blackhawks and transmitted repeatedly from their loudspeakers, "Pilots, abandon your aircraft.

You have fifteen seconds before we fire."

Both Apaches fired flares at the Blackhawks. One pilot who had remained near his Blackhawk ran to get clear. After the last pilot got clear, the Apaches launched one Hellfire rocket into each Blackhawk, creating two huge explosions. The Apaches then faded back to the capitol. If anyone doubted the Apaches were armed, they didn't now.

At DPS, the lone Apache lowered to near ground level and made the same announcements and shot flares with the same results. The pilots standing by abandoned the Blackhawks. The Blackhawks were then destroyed in giant fireballs from two Hellfire rockets. The Apache at DPS moved to the front of the maintenance building, creating an ominous sight for the federal agents and U.S. Army Rangers.

Cell phone traffic downtown and near DPS headquarters overwhelmed local cell towers. The federal government was communicating by satellite phones and radios while the Texas forces were forced to rely solely on two-way radios.

The next move was up to the United States government. The State of Texas had sent a clear message after the assault on the Texas Law Library. Texas would use force if necessary to repel the feds.

At 4:00 p.m. Eastern time, Fox News opened its broadcast at the top of the hour with Shepard Smith: *"Tonight, chaos in the Lone Star state. In what may be the most serious Constitutional crisis since the civil war, the State of Texas is seemingly at war with the United States government. In scenes that appear reminiscent of Chechnya or Georgia in the former Soviet Union, chaos has erupted. What you see on your screen is not a break-away Soviet republic but may be the beginning of a break-away Texas republic. The billowing smoke you see comes from United States Army Blackhawk helicopters destroyed by the 4th and 8th Regiments of the Air Wing of the Texas Militia. News reports have confirmed 18 ATF, FBI and U.S. Army Ranger troops are dead after a federal assault on the Texas capitol. The Texas governor has activated units of the Texas State Guardsmen, a state militia, and its air wing, which is controlled by the governor. These two units are typically only used for natural disaster relief.*

"In a dramatic response to the Texas Rangers arresting federal agents responsible for the highly controversial recovery of Tea Party activist Chuck Dixon, who was being held by the ATF, federal agents supported by U.S. Army Rangers descended on the Texas capitol and the Texas Department of Public Safety this morning to execute arrest warrants for the governor of Texas and members of the elite Texas Rangers. In what appears to be a tit-for-tat response, the feds were also executing warrants for the Texas lieutenant governor, various members of the governor's staff, and Pops Younger, the legendary Texas Ranger who led the now infamous raid at Ellington Air Force Base to free Dixon. During that raid, an ATF agent was shot and wounded.

'We are continuing live coverage from our affiliate in Austin. Less than fifteen minutes ago, four U.S. Army Blackhawk helicopters were destroyed by Texas militia rockets fired from their Apache helicopters. We are expecting word from President Johnson at any time. Meantime, we will go back to live coverage."

Chapter 42

"Don't Mess with Texas!™"

~ *Originally an anti-litter campaign by the Texas Department of Transportation in 1986, this became a Texas cultural phenomenon used by all Texans as a symbol of Texas pride; the motto was later adopted by the USS Texas nuclear submarine.*

The southeast wind blowing in Austin that afternoon blanketed DPS headquarters with thick dark smoke from the burning Blackhawk helicopters. The smoke was so thick the feds could not see the DPS maintenance building clearly.

Masterson was on the phone with Henry Woodhouse. "Director, this is Agent Masterson at DPS headquarters. I'm sure you know this by now, but that Apache is armed. It just took out our Blackhawks."

"Masterson," Woodhouse said wearily, "stand down for the moment. We will have new instructions very shortly. Do not let those Rangers escape."

"With all due respect, sir, the Rangers now have air cover. We are sitting ducks. Obviously, that Apache is fully armed and I would suspect the F-16s that continue to buzz our position are, too. Without our own air cover, we are sitting ducks."

"Agent, I am communicating with the Pentagon," Woodhouse said. "We will get you air cover shortly. As soon as we confirm air cover is en route, we will instruct you when and how to proceed."

At the situation room in Washington, D.C., the DOJ leadership was in a panic. All directors were called immediately to the White House where a new situation room to monitor both Austin hotspots was hurriedly being readied. The president was going to dive head first into the situation. The White House issued a brief statement saying, "It's time for the state government of Texas to lay down their arms, surrender and cede to federal authority. All those responsible for the casualties suffered by federal agents and U.S. Army personnel will be held accountable."

President Johnson convened an emergency meeting with Chief of Staff Radford, Secretary of Defense Will Benton and the Joint Chiefs of Staff. The situation in Texas was very delicate. If Johnson escalated the aggression at the state level, U.S. troops could be engaging the state government of Texas, the Texas militia and Texas citizens, widely known to be well-armed and fiercely loyal to their state. It was unclear how the country would react, but even less clear was how military personnel might respond when asked to shoot at Texans.

"I want air support immediately for the federal agents on the ground," instructed Johnson.

"Mr. President, does that mean you are instructing us to engage those F-16s and Apaches and take them out if necessary?" asked the Air Force general.

"I'm telling you they have already fired on our agents and are preventing our lawful mission to arrest federal fugitives."

"With all due respect, Mr. President, the Texas aircraft have not fired on our units, even though they have had plenty of opportunity. It appears they have only taken out the Blackhawks to make it more difficult to extradite the suspects once they are arrested," returned the general.

"I have eighteen dead."

"Mr. President, the casualties aren't from their aircraft. In our brief review of the events of the last few hours, the chain of command was abruptly changed at the capitol and the new agent in charge gave instructions to move on the building adjacent to the capitol where Texas State Guard troops and militia were positioned."

"I know Tibbs is not here yet, but why was the chain of command transferred in the middle of the operation?" Johnson asked.

"The agent in charge inexplicably went into the capitol building to talk with the governor."

"Why?" wondered the President.

"We think the governor is surrendering, but the agent has been in the capitol for almost an hour and a half, probably negotiating. However, these were not his orders from Tibbs. His orders were to advance on the capitol and take the suspects. Apparently, when the leadership changed, there was a lot of concern about these weekend warriors staring down our agents from a rooftop with automatic weapons pointed at them, so they advanced to remove them. Apparently they were not successful."

"Who fired first?"

"Somewhat unclear, Mr. President, but initial reports are that we did."

"Do not broadcast or repeat that without my *personal* clearance," the president ordered. "You said it's unclear; let's leave it at that. Hell, for all we know, one of these cowboys could have taken the first shot and that will be our position. Is that fully understood by *everyone* in this room?"

"Yes, Mr. President," they answered.

"Sir, we have just scrambled various Air Force fighter units stationed at Ft. Hood and Lackland Air Force Bases in Killeen and San Antonio. They are literally minutes away once airborne. They have been instructed to arm, take flight for Austin and await specific further instructions."

Texas would have an answer. The Texas State Guard was divided regionally into six regiments and all have specific historical names: the *Alamo Guards* in San Antonio and south Texas, the *Travis Rifles* in Austin and central Texas, the *Panther City Fencibles* in Fort Worth and, in north central Texas, *Terry's Texas Rangers* in Houston and east Texas, *Parson's Brigade* in Dallas and north Texas, and the *Roughnecks* in Midland, west Texas and the Panhandle.

Within minutes after the joint chiefs issued the order to scramble fighters at several bases in Texas they, and in particular the four-star Air Force general, were receiving emergency communications from multiple air stations in Texas.

With a look of disbelief, the general said, "Mr. President, I have urgent reports from Dyess, Lackland and Fort Hood that Texas Air National Guard and Texas Guard militia troops have either secured the fighter aircraft and attack helicopters or have disabled them across all our air bases in Texas. Our people are outnumbered. As you know, some of these bases only house a small unit of attack aircraft. The Texans are literally guarding the aircraft with weapons. It would appear that somebody figured out ahead of us that this would be our counter to their Apaches. What instructions should I provide?"

"Are you telling me, general, that once-a-month reservists and weekend militia men have rendered the United States Air Force impotent in a time of greatest need?" the president demanded. "How is that possible? What security is in place that would allow these people to waltz right in and seize your aircraft? Who is so incompetent that they have allowed this to happen?"

"Mr. President, many of these people work as Texas Air National Guard reserves and are as familiar with our operations as our people are. It's definitely an inside job. They are also telling me there are several Texas Rangers on site with these troops at each base."

"Son of a bitch, do you mean that ignorant cowboy governor has outsmarted you guys again?"

"Mr. President, with all due respect, we weren't briefed on this operation or the likelihood of this escalation by the DOJ. I would venture to say that Texas had its contingency plans in place well before your operation. The scope and breadth of their ability to shut down air operations at all Texas bases doesn't come easy and it doesn't come without advance planning. I wish your folks would have briefed us on this. We likely would have been able to prevent it."

The president paced back and forth across the room with his arms crossed, deep in thought.

"Do we engage these guys at each base?" he finally asked.

"Well, we could, but that would involve casualties on both sides, and it doesn't immediately address your concerns at the two Austin sites because we don't know how long it might take to re-secure those aircraft and resume full flight operations," replied Secretary Benton. Then he added, "I'm not sure how something like that plays out. I mean you have Americans firing at Americans."

Tibbs, the directors and deputy directors arrived in the situation room just in time to hear the news. For Tibbs, the sooner the situation escalated and the larger it became, the more likely the evidence could be destroyed or pushed aside for the larger story, if there was one.

The finger-pointing in the situation room at the White House grew more intense as debate raged on how to quell the insurrection in Texas. Neither the secretary of defense nor the joint chiefs knew what Tibbs and the rest of the leadership of the Executive Branch, including the president, knew regarding the real facts about the Sally investigation.

"No, you have Americans firing at Texans," President Johnson said emphatically. "Nobody in the rest of the country gives a *shit* about them; in fact I would venture to say it's about time to punish that braggadocios state once and for all. Don't forget: they have already killed eighteen Americans."

While waiting for instructions from D.C., Agent Masterson sat in his command post three hundred yards from the DPS maintenance building, glancing every few minutes at the building, trying to make out any movement.

"What the hell...?" said one of the ATF agents.

As clouds of smoke drifted across the compound, Masterson could make out a lone figure standing approximately forty yards in front of the building.

"That's Pops Younger!" shouted an ATF agent.

"Why the hell is he standing like that right out in the open?"

There stood Pops, all six foot three of him, long and angular, wearing matching holsters carrying Colt .45 revolvers attached around his waist, Stetson cowboy hat slightly cocked to the left, cowboy boots, rolled-up sleeves on his white pearl snap western shirt and a handlebar mustache. Even from that far away, Masterson could see Pops spit his smokeless tobacco on the ground.

"Should I shoot the son of a bitch?" asked another agent. "Maybe he's ready to surrender," he added hopefully.

"They blow up our choppers, then surrender? I'm not buying that theory. No, I'll go talk to him. Looks like he has something to say," said Masterson.

Masterson asked a fellow agent to accompany him. Both of them walked directly toward Younger but left their pistols in their holsters as it was obvious Pops was carrying. FBI and ATF agents momentarily ignored their posts to watch. They were awed by the Texas law enforcement legend who defied the federal government, standing amid the smoke of the destroyed Blackhawk helicopters, looking like he walked right out of the 1880s.

"Mr. Younger, seems like you would like to speak. Are you ready for this ridiculous confrontation to end?"

Pops removed his Stetson and swatted it twice on his right leg, seemingly to remove dust or particles, before answering Masterson.

"Yes, I think we should end this confrontation now before you boys get hurt."

Masterson looked at Pops incredulously. "Mr. Younger, need I remind you that your fellow Rangers are surrounded by a hundred or so highly trained FBI and ATF agents as well as Army Special Forces? How do you propose we end this confrontation peacefully?"

Pops paused, adjusted his hat one more time and prepared to answer Masterson in his own time, which was much slower than Masterson appreciated.

"I suggest you instruct your folks to lay their weapons down immediately," Pops said calmly.

"What?" Masterson said, half-laughingly. "Pops, I appreciate your substantial cojones and I know you have that Apache hovering over there, but that will not deter us. We will also have air support shortly. I have orders and I intend to fulfill them."

"Agent Masterson, I'll give you this last opportunity to surrender peacefully or you are going to lose a whole gaggle of your boys."

Masterson got a sickening feeling deep in the pit of his stomach as he surmised Pops knew something he didn't.

"How do you figure that, Pops?"

Pops spit on the ground again, then slowly stated in his signature slow Texas drawl, "Son, please take a gander at your flank."

Masterson and the agent accompanying him spun around to look at their fellow agents and the Army troops positioned behind and to the side of them.

"Holy crap…"

Texas Guardsmen and Texas Rangers who were not in the headquarters building when the fray started had mustered blocks away and waited for the perfect moment to silently position themselves on the flank of the feds. Most of the Guards were still in street clothes, called into emergency duty to report from their day-to-day jobs. There were now several hundred weapons pointed at the feds. Those watching the meeting with Pops still hadn't noticed the movement when Pops swatted his leg with his Stetson. Immediately, the Apache banked steeply, positioned itself fifty feet over Pops and began rotating its machine guns without firing them.

The feds watching Masterson could not hear the conversation but, based on his reaction, got very nervous now that the Apache had moved into an aggressive position. Masterson, seeing the advantage the Texans now had, grabbed the radio from his fellow agent. "This is Masterson. Stand down. I repeat, stand down," he shouted to be heard over the noise of the Apache's rotor blades. "Lay your weapons down. I repeat, lay your weapons down now."

It took a few minutes for the rest of the feds to grasp the situation. Slowly, agents and Army Rangers began laying down their weapons, some of them cursing because it was obvious that a citizen militia had taken down three highly skilled and professionally trained units.

"Now, Agent Masterson," Pops drawled, "please call your superiors up in Yankee-land and let them know your entire outfit will immediately be arrested for trespassing and other miscellaneous grievances against the citizens of Texas."

In Washington, a defeated Woodhouse hung his head dejectedly as he got off his phone.

"Mr. Tibbs, Agent Masterson just called in from DPS headquarters. They were forced to surrender to the Texas Guard and Texas Rangers. They have all been taken into custody. There are no casualties on either side."

"What? Surrender? Didn't you have a couple of hundred agents and Special Forces there? How is that even possible?" President Johnson barked.

"Well, sir," Woodhouse said, looking embarrassed, "apparently they mustered hundreds of citizen militia, coupled with the fact they had the Apache with no air support from us and somehow they outflanked the federal forces on the ground. According to Masterson, Pops Younger just outmaneuvered them."

Chapter 43

"The only maxim of a free government ought to be to trust no man living with power to endanger the public liberty."

~ *John Adams*

At the capitol, Agent Hixson finally got Agent Barnes to have his agents and troops momentarily stand down. The governor had gotten word to the news crews parked blocks away that he would accept one news crew from each major affiliate and named several new media outlets that would be allowed to participate in a spontaneous press conference including Breitbart, The Daily Caller, The Blaze, Drudge, Newsmax, Politico and several others. The news conference was to be held in fifteen minutes inside the capitol building. Both NBC and CBS declined invitations, citing concerns over reporting crews' safety with both sides armed and poised to erupt at a moment's notice.

Twenty minutes later, approximately sixty people were escorted through the line of agents and troops on the capitol lawn to the steps where Texas Rangers and DPS troopers opened the double doors to allow them in. The reporters were allowed to set up their cameras in the famous rotunda of the Texas capitol building, with images of Crockett, Travis, Bowie, Houston and others looking down upon them.

"Governor, please allow me a few minutes to call Tim Spilner's dad. I promised myself he would hear from me how much of a hero his son was before this became public. I won't take long," Chuck Dixon said.

"All right, but we have two sides pointing guns at each other outside. Make it quick."

Fifteen minutes later, Lieutenant Governor Foster kicked off the presser:

"Ladies and gentlemen, fellow Texans and Americans. First, let me say here, right off the bat, that it is unfortunate people were killed here today. This is a direct result of the federal government's actions and they should be held accountable for these deaths. In Texas, we believe in putting things in the simplest, most straightforward terms. The federal government attacked Texas militia. They shot first. Texas shot back. It's really that simple. We regret the loss of life; however, the federal government is sadly mistaken if they think Texas is just going to roll over and take these jackbooted tactics from the Department of Justice and this administration.

"In addition to these actions, the Texas Rangers and Texas Guards have arrested one hundred twenty-nine federal agents and U.S. Army troops for similar tactics engaged in at the Department of Public Safety headquarters just north of downtown Austin. Pops Younger and his Texas Rangers, with assistance from the Texas Guards, have quelled the incursion into and the invasion of Texas property. There were no casualties reported at this location; however, as most of you saw live here downtown, two government helicopters were destroyed on location at DPS and two were destroyed just blocks from the capitol. Now, I would like to bring up Governor Cooper, who will reveal shocking evidence of a mass administration cover-up that has led to the events you see here today."

Murmurs and sidebar conversations escalated the decibel levels inside the capitol rotunda. The governor stepped to the microphone, slowly surveying the audience. Standing behind him was Agent Hixson.

"What I am about to share with you, Texas and America, is shared with the deepest regret. It is a most shameful chapter of American history. I really don't know how to couch it any other way.

"Several days ago, Texas Attorney General Jeff Weaver received a package via FedEx from an attorney employed at the Justice Department who was an investigator assigned to the Rash Sally assassination and conspiracy investigation."

The crowd in the rotunda tried to edge closer, the interest more intense.

Cooper continued, "Rash Sally was not a Tea Party member. Yes, he was doing a Master's thesis on the Tea Party about the Tea Party's attitudes towards Muslims and other ethnic groups. Rash Sally empathized with most of the Tea Party principles, such as fiscal conservatism and adherence to the Constitution. He never became an official member of any local or national Tea Party. The fact is, we have evidence from this Justice Department whistleblower that Rash Sally was, in fact, an Iranian Muslim. Sally's sister and her family were all killed in Operation Python, the raid carried out by the U.S. and Israel on Iranian nuclear sites. After the raid, Sally regularly communicated with known extremist terrorist cells in the United States, Canada, France, Iran, Syria, Egypt and other countries. He was motivated by this administration's actions in Iran."

The crowd of reporters began to shout questions and buzz inside the rotunda was palpable.

"Hold your questions, please, and let me finish," requested the governor.

"This administration, particularly United States Attorney General Tibbs and most probably President Johnson, used the assassination attempt as a method to destroy political opposition, namely the Tea Party patriots in Texas, Arizona, Oklahoma, South Carolina, Alabama and Georgia. This administration literally has blood on its hands for the unconstitutional raids on Texans and others simply for their political beliefs. Stan Mumford and others died unnecessarily.

"Now, the same day this package was sent, Justice attorney Tim Spilner and his wife were inexplicably killed in a suspicious car accident in Georgetown, D.C. Draw your own conclusions. At a minimum, I would think an expanded investigation of Tim Spilner's death is warranted, considering the magnitude of evidence we are making available to you shortly.

"The State of Texas now calls upon Congress to deal with this calamity expeditiously. Texas and the American people deserve answers. According to the evidence we have, the administration has known, from shortly after the assassination attempt, that Sally was neither an agent nor a member of any Tea Party. These actions, including the blatant cover-up, are criminal and should be punished to the fullest extent of the law. As I speak to you now, federal ATF and FBI agents, along with U.S. military troops, stand poised on our capitol lawn to aid this administration's cover-up of its crimes. My first and foremost responsibility is the safety of Texans. Let me assure the United States Congress and the Executive Branch that Texas will not—I repeat WILL NOT—stand for jackbooted thugs encroaching on our God-given rights. If Congress will not act, I assure you Texas will. The individual sovereignty of Texas is not open for debate and will be defended to the last man standing.

"Now that clear evidence of this administration's crimes is public, I fully expect the troops positioned around our beloved capitol to be withdrawn at once.

"Next, I would like to introduce to you FBI Agent Hixson, who was presented this same evidence over the last hour. He has a few words to say."

The governor stepped aside as Agent Hixson approached the makeshift podium.

"Governor Cooper and his staff have shared the information received from a Justice Department staffer who apparently died on the same day it was sent. I have had less than an hour to review the documents and emails. I cannot independently verify that this is, in fact, the same evidence the Justice Department has in its possession; however, what I will state is that there is enough evidence here to warrant a full congressional investigation of the Executive Branch of our government. Over the last few hours, I have been removed from command of the federal government operation here at the capitol that initially called for the arrests of Governor Cooper, Lieutenant Governor Foster, various staff members in state government and the Texas Rangers involved in various operations in conflict with the FBI and ATF.

"Given this new set of evidence, I call on the Justice Department to end this operation on the capitol grounds and for the FBI, ATF and U.S. Army Special Forces to back off, retreat and let this play out through appropriate channels. Further bloodshed is unnecessary and, from what I have seen here, could have been completely avoided. I know making these statements will likely end my FBI career; however, it is hard to argue with the evidence the governor has given me the privilege to inspect. I am convinced he also wants the bloodshed to end.

"At this time, I am going to ask FBI Agent Barnes to stand down and remove all federal agencies from this state's property. Agent Barnes, if you can hear me now, stand down. Remove all troops and agents immediately."

Most of the federal agents and troops did not have access to the press conference broadcast. At various times during the broadcast, the Texas Guards sitting atop buildings surrounding the capitol grounds could be heard yelling and cheering. Agents who had access to monitors in nearby news vans, radios and other sources began spreading the news about what they heard.

The morale of the feds positioned at the capitol quickly deteriorated. What was once anger for their brethren cut down in the two blocks around the Texas Law Library now became feelings of disgust for most of them. Still, some of the hard-core feds were fully prepared and ready to go into the capitol building and arrest the governor at any cost.

Chapter 44

"A revolution is an idea which has found its bayonets."

~ *Napoleon Bonaparte*

Agent Barnes heard the broadcast and, not willing to make a career-ending decision on his own, called FBI Director Henry Woodhouse in D.C. Barnes had a very hard time reaching his director, as he and many other directors were sequestered with the president in the situation room at the White House.

There were multiple 42-inch LCD television screens throughout the situation room. Each one had a different channel on, broadcasting the live telecast from the Texas state capitol building. The entire room sat quiet as Governor Cooper and others spilled the news to the rest of the country. The president was the first to speak when the press conference was over.

"Gentlemen, we have to attack this head on. We need to bring Smith and Gould in here now!" he said firmly as he motioned to Cliff Radford to summon them to the White House immediately.

Tibbs sat in his leather chair with his head in his hands, looking up every now and then when someone made a suggestion, hoping the suggestion would make this story go away.

"When Smith gets here, we will get our talking points together and get them distributed throughout the administration," the president said. "In the meantime, let's turn up some of the news coverage so we can see how much damage control is going to be necessary."

Finally, Barnes got through to Woodhouse, who put him on hold to ask Tibbs and the others what the agents on the ground in Austin should do. They all looked at each other for a few brief seconds before the president spoke. "Tell them to get the hell out of there. We need to regroup to find out what our next move will be. I don't want any press releases, interviews or comments made by anyone on the staff or anyone on the ground in Austin. Tell them I am issuing a gag order on the whole event. Is that understood?"

"Yes, Mr. President," replied Woodhouse.

He was on the phone for a few more minutes before he put his hand over the mic of the phone, cleared his throat and asked, "Sir, the agents and troops want to know how they will get a ride out of there. Their transportation... the Blackhawks were destroyed."

"Son of a bitch! You guys fail the operation then you want me to figure out how to get your guys out? Tell them to take taxis, for all I care," the president yelled. "If they would have gotten the governor out when they were ordered to, that press conference would never have happened."

Tibbs nervously stood up and offered, "Mr. President, they got this news from this Spilner guy. Chances are that the governor isn't the only one with this information. If it hadn't come out now, it was going to."

"Yes, and how the hell does a DOJ employee just walk out with highly classified information? Who is going to brief me on exactly what he got? Does he have director or above level memos or emails?" a visibly irritated president asked, glaring directly at Adamson.

"Sir, we know he copied Sally files and Sally emails, but there were no internal or inter-departmental communications on those particular servers, so we are confident that's all he has."

"Confident? You're confident?" asked the president sarcastically.

After several conversations with Woodhouse, Agent Barnes radioed Agent Hixson.

"This is Barnes, We are being ordered to stand down. However, the crowds and that militia in the blocks around us are getting agitated and may provoke further clashes. I also have some gung-ho guys who lost some friends. We need to defuse this as soon as possible."

"Well, let me consult with the governor. I'll get right back to you."

A few minutes later, the lieutenant governor came on Barnes' radio, "This is Lieutenant Governor Gene Foster. Agent Hixson passed the radio to me."

"Hello, sir, this is beginning to escalate out here. Your folks are yelling at mine and there is still a tremendous amount of friction out here. You guys took out our ride," said Barnes, referring to the destroyed Blackhawks.

"Agent, the governor is sending four school buses to the east side of the capitol building as we speak. You and your crew are to board those school buses. We will arrange for the wounded and dead to be transported as well."

"Sir, where are the school buses going?"

"We will allow your folks to bring in one C-130 aircraft to transport all of you, but you will have to leave Texas. That plane is not going to be allowed to land anywhere in the state except Austin Bergstrom International Airport. We are also loading school buses at DPS headquarters building with those who were arrested there and they will meet you at the airport. Agent Hixson is arranging the C-130 with Washington as we speak.

"You are to instruct your unit that all weapons are to be left in a pile. If they do not follow these instructions, your men will be arrested. Also, before boarding the plane, each of them will be required to swear never to enter Texas again, and that they will never take up arms against Texas or Texans again, ever."

Barnes was silent for a few minutes. Then he blurted, "Are you fucking serious? We aren't surrendering. We are simply being called back by Washington and have been instructed to stand down."

"Agent Barnes, you and your men will either accept these terms or you will be arrested. This isn't a negotiation and our terms are not up for discussion. Your entire premise for being here is a lie. The sooner you accept that this administration is corrupt and is responsible for the deaths of your agents, the sooner you can get out of here."

"There is no way in hell all of my men are going to accept those terms," Barnes said flatly. "In fact, there's probably a few of them that are from Texas originally."

"Agent, it would be hard for us to believe any Texan would assault the capitol or support the unconstitutional actions your department has waged against the average Texan, but those terms apply to all of your men, period."

In the time since the governor's news conference, the number of Texas Guards had more than doubled to nearly one thousand troops surrounding the feds, who had pulled back to the northeast corner of the capitol grounds. The feds worked through the night with emergency medical personnel who were allowed in to stabilize those who needed emergency medical care and transport them to area hospitals. The state wanted the feds to take with them the injured that had been treated at hospitals and were not critically wounded.

By 3:00 a.m., the feds were loaded on the school buses but were awaiting the arrival of the C-130 transport plane to land at Austin Bergstrom International. The C-130 had to be brought in from an Oklahoma air base because all U.S. Air Force bases and their respective flight operations had been locked down or disabled by Texas Air National Guard and the Texas Guard.

A very long day and an equally long night were almost over for all involved in Austin. At daybreak, DPS vehicles and Texas Guard Humvees arrived to escort the school buses to the airport. The school buses at DPS headquarters were already rolling with a huge escort of state law enforcement vehicles and Humvees.

As the school buses meandered through downtown with the sirens and lights, an outpouring of people came to the street curbs to see the spectacle. The worldwide news coverage had gone uninterrupted through the night. It was likely everyone in America knew about the scene that had unfolded in Texas the day before.

Along the route to the airport, Texans turned out by the thousands at 6:30 a.m. Families waving Lone Star flags and homemade signs were everywhere. Some waved the famous yellow Gadsden Flag. Many yelled profanities at the buses and a few even threw rocks.

All the media was covering the 'retreat' of the feds, who arrived in Blackhawks but were leaving in yellow school buses. Many news feeds showed recurring images of the piles of weapons on the capitol lawn that the feds and U.S. Army Rangers were forced to give up. The Texas militia was celebrating near the capitol.

At the situation room in the White House, the mood was both somber and angry. Smith and Gould stayed with the directors and president through most of the night, watching news coverage and getting updates from Barnes on the scene.

Gould was furious when he learned about the state of Texas requiring the agents and Special Forces to swear an oath promising non-aggression and no re-entry into Texas.

"Who the hell do they think they are?" Gould swore. "This is a good example why nobody in the country likes those dumb-asses. They are so damn full of themselves!"

Smith was worried. "Mr. President, we need to do some quick polling to see how the country is reacting to this to make sure our talking points are in line with public sentiment. That means you may not be able to make a statement for a few hours. We may want to put out a couple of benign sentences, but we really need to know where we stand with the rest of the country on this issue. I think they will be behind us, sir, except for the rednecks south of the Mason-Dixon Line, as usual."

Chapter 45

"And what country can preserve its liberties, if its rulers are not warned from time to time, that this people preserve the spirit of resistance? Let them take arms."

~ *Thomas Jefferson*

The headlines in newspapers the next day were an interesting study in contrasts from a red state vs. blue state perspective:

Texas Commits Treason, Kills 18 Feds
— The Boston Globe

Texas Militia Under Governor Kills 18 Federal Troops
— NY Times

High Noon in Texas; State Repels Arrests; Kills 18
—Washington Post

Texas Governor Responsible for 18 Deaths
— San Francisco Examiner

Treason in Texas! State Kills 18 Feds
— Philadelphia Inquirer

Texans Kill 18 Feds While Serving Warrants
— Chicago Tribune

Feds Attack State Capitol, 18 Die, Feds Surrender
— Houston Chronicle

Feds Fail in Attempt to Attack Capitol – 18 Dead!
— San Antonio Express

Constitutional Showdown at Capitol – 18 Die
— Dallas Morning News

Feds Clash with Texans – 18 Feds Die
— Daily Oklahoman

Constitutional Crisis in Texas – 18 Die
– Atlanta Journal Constitution
Texas Repels Federal Invasion; 18 Dead
– New Orleans Times-Picayune
Texas Embarrasses Feds & Justice at State Capitol
– Orlando Sentinel

The vivid scenes played over the next twenty-four hours on every news channel and Internet new media websites included personal recordings from cell phones at street level and from adjacent rooftops to the Texas state capitol building. Images of dead federal agents and U.S. Army Rangers invoked anger from many parts of the country, where citizens didn't understand that the unit attacked the Texas militia position and fired first.

Images of the feds surrendering and being placed on school buses, along with images of the piles of surrendered weapons, ran repeatedly. There were also scenes of patriotic Texans who showed up on the streets of Austin by the thousands to voice their support for their governor, the Texas Rangers, the Texas Guard and militia for thwarting what they felt was a clumsy attempt by Washington to embarrass the governor and the state.

Images of the few isolated youths throwing rocks at the school buses were played mostly by MSNBC, who gave the impression that the buses were pelted by angry Texans during the entire trip to the airport.

At the airport, six ATF agents, four FBI agents and six Army Rangers refused to sign the non-aggression and no re-entry agreement documents that conditioned their release and were arrested and taken into custody. Their comrades were escorted to the C-130 for transportation to an Air Force base outside of Texas to be determined by the Department of Defense and the Justice Department.

The announcement of a government cover-up amidst new evidence was the secondary story, but many of the traditional mainstream media were not expanding coverage on that monstrous topic and were instead focused on Texas and its state government as having committed treason for its use of a state military to resist the execution of legitimate federal arrest warrants.

Governor Cooper issued a press statement shortly after the C-130 took off from the temporarily shut-down Austin airport:

"In light of the events of yesterday, the federal government's encroachment into Texas sovereignty, and this administration's refusal to acknowledge the U.S. Constitution, I am hereby calling a special session of the Texas Legislature, effective the day after tomorrow."

The events of the previous twenty-four hours gave every talking head, no-name congressman, political pundit and self-proclaimed historian a platform to either condemn Texas or condemn the administration. Although most Democrats condemned the state, even Republicans as a whole were deeply and angrily divided over how the issue was handled, with establishment Republicans primarily believing the state should relent, offer up the intended targets of the federal arrest warrants and let the courts sort it out.

Naturally, the Tea Party and ultra-conservative base of the GOP wanted the administration to be punished for its incursion into state sovereignty but, even more importantly, they wanted more information about the Rash Sally cover-up and the persecution of their grassroots movement.

Steve Milford, who had to literally scare his wife to the point of sheer terror to get her to immediately drop what she was doing and get their family to Reagan National Airport by 8:30 a.m. that fateful morning, was trying to explain the circumstances in more detail to his wife and several of Governor Cooper's state staffers on the Hawker 800 jet that picked them up.

At approximately 10:00 a.m. CST that morning, news came over the pilot's radio of the events that were unfolding in Austin. The pilot was instructed to divert from Austin and land at Hooks Airport, a small private airport northwest of Houston in a small bedroom community called Tomball. Texas Rangers met them there to escort them to safety, just as they had Chuck Dixon's family. Hours later, the Milford family was introduced to the Dixon family at a large, private and secure ranch just west of Austin in the Texas hill country.

Governor Cooper's office began systematically releasing the documents and files provided by Tim Spilner to news-friendly organizations such as Fox News, Breitbart, The Daily Caller, The Blaze, Rush Limbaugh, and others the very next morning following the two major incidents in Austin. Later that afternoon, the same files were released to the mainstream media, including MSNBC, CBS, ABC, Politico, Real Clear Politics, the BBC and others.

By that evening's news cycle, the released files were blowing up the worldwide news. There were calls for the impeachment of Tibbs and Johnson from conservatives and even from some moderate Democrats. The mood at the White House was not gleeful.

That same evening, President Johnson summoned those involved in the Department of Justice raids conducted by FBI and ATF, as well as Homeland Security, his chief political advisors, the Democratic National Committee chairman, Smith, Gould, McDermott, Radford and various White House attorneys.

Smith led off the meeting. "Gentlemen and ladies, we have a monumental problem. We need to figure out how to respond to this leak of classified documents and we need to figure it out this evening. The news media is bombarding us for a response from today's official leak of the documents. We have the usual nutjobs running around in Congress pandering to the hysteria. Now, make no mistake, we have some serious problems here. One: How do we diffuse and discredit the nature of the documents leaked and two: How do we deal with Texas?"

"I'll start," said Tibbs. "First, the leak and publishing of classified documents is a breach of national security. Those responsible should be punished to the fullest extent of the law, including Governor Cooper."

"Okay, we can deal with that after we have our full response and talking points figured out," responded Radford. "First and foremost, we should categorically deny all allegations. The best defense is a good offense. The documents have been altered, and they are also not complete. This is an attempt to embarrass the administration, pure and simple."

"Okay, I like that so far," beamed Smith.

"We also should demonize Spilner. What dirt do we have on him? Paint him as a disgruntled employee or someone with extreme ideological proclivities," added Tibbs.

"Does he have any Tea Party ties?" asked Gould.

"Well, interestingly enough, his dad has some," added Woodhouse.

"Good, follow up on that. Even the slightest and most remote thread of relevance to the Tea Party should be used," noted Tibbs.

"Damn, Jamail, you would have made a good propagandist back in the old Soviet Union," laughed Gould nervously. Tibbs didn't look too pleased at the comparison and didn't know if it was a back-handed compliment or a slap.

Writing on a large whiteboard that had been brought in for the meeting, Smith continued, "Okay, so what I have so far is that we are going to do the following action items:

"One: Attack the validity of the documents. We should claim there are more documents and these particular documents were taken out of context.

"Two: Destroy Spilner's credibility. State he was under investigation for spying and treason. Dig up any dirt you have. Arrests, employee reviews, I want to know what kind of positions he and his wife had sex in. I want to know what porn he watched. Also, dig up the Tea Party ties. It's very important we tie him to a motive or an extremist agenda.

"Three: Lean on congressmen and senators who aren't towing the party line. They know we have been through significant attacks before, especially Justice," Smith glanced accusingly at Tibbs, referring to the fact Justice always seemed to be in the headlines, with gun running to Mexican cartels, voter ID registration laws and immigration. "Let them know that to bet against the administration could be their political suicide. And I do mean lean on them heavily, Radford! Now is the time to call in any and all markers.

"Four: The staff will continue to work through the evening to put together talking points. Once these talking points are established and approved, I want them out to all of you. You should be taking any opportunity you have to go on talk shows or broadcasts to counter this leak, but stick to your talking points.

"Five: Any talk of impeachment needs to be met with a vast amount of incredible disgust, surprise and political rancor. Dismiss it outright; laugh in its face, do not let it grow legs. We will provide you information to counter any questions regarding the legitimacy of any requests for impeachment and those impeachment suggestions need to be turned around and pointed at the governor of Texas."

Tibbs dismissed several in the room at that point, saying the next topic needed to be addressed only by cabinet and director-level staffers. Only senior staff aides were allowed in the room. Once all other staffers had left, Tibbs had the floor.

"Okay, now on to Texas and Governor Brent Cooper," he said, looking like he was very anxious to get into this particular topic. The governor and state of Texas had foiled every move by Justice and had made the DOJ, the FBI and ATF look amateurish.

"The acceptance of and the distribution of classified material related to national defense is a felony. This needs to be fully demonstrated to the press. If the strategy mentioned previously is to attack the validity of the information in regard to context, this should dovetail with that strategy."

"Okay, so the governor committed a felony. We've tried to arrest him once. Now, it would appear the entire state is behind him. Let's face it. He embarrassed us and embarrassed some very proud departments and this administration," commented Homeland Secretary Sarah McDermott.

"We need to reverse the trend and make him as unpopular in Texas as he is in the Northeast or on the West Coast," said Smith.

"How do we do that? What do you suggest? We don't have a lot of time here," Tibbs said.

"How do we normally topple a regime? With both external and internal pressures," said Secretary of Defense Benton.

"Okay, let's talk about external pressures," said Tibbs, as he stood and began pacing.

"Normally, we put in sanctions first. So let's figure out how we sanction an entire state," said Radford.

"First, cut off any and all federal funds. I'm talking education, highway, Medicare!" Tibbs yelled.

"I like the way you're thinking." Johnson lounged in his chair, more relaxed than his staff.

"The next thing we would do is blockade the country, so let's do the same to Texas," said Radford.

"Blockade? That's extreme, but we have some extreme circumstances. We're already hearing rumblings from other states. We can't let this defiance spread. If we put Texas in its place, the other states won't challenge federal authority. We need to make an example of Texas," Tibbs contributed.

"That's right. We'll block all incoming and outgoing traffic on every road on every Texas border. We'll shut down aircraft coming in and out, and we will not provide FAA support, effectively grounding all air traffic. We'll shut down their ports in Galveston, Houston, Corpus Christi, Port Arthur and Brownsville. Also, we can turn off the Internet to Texas," offered Radford.

"I'm really starting to like this!" smiled Johnson.

"Next," said Gould, "we shut off the banking system, not allowing incoming or outgoing transactions. I also propose we suspend their congressional and senatorial seats."

"Can we do that?" asked Johnson, sitting up straighter and taking notice.

"If Texas is in a state of war against the U.S., we can do anything. I think we can make that claim based on their actions in Austin," responded one of the senior White House attorneys.

"Those are some very effective external pressures," laughed Johnson.

"Oh, there's more!" exclaimed Gould. "We shut down all telecommunications in and out. Also, by blockading the highway system, rail and shipping, we can starve them out. And yes, we can shut down and suspend all federal payments of any kind, including Social Security and Medicare payments."

"Yikes, now that starts to get personal. Are we sure we want to start to affect individual voters?" asked Johnson.

"Absolutely. That's where internal pressure gets applied to remove the governor. When you start impacting people's daily lives and start making life hard for basic necessities, they will start to put pressure on their leadership to get things right with Washington. Hell, they may arrest him themselves and hand him over to us. This may take a shorter amount of time than you think," Gould said gleefully.

"Okay, I'll leave it to the staff to plan this," said the president. "I'll need the public statements discussed as soon as possible. Do we need to draft executive orders to effect these maneuvers?"

"It depends. Several of these items may; some may not," replied Tibbs.

"All right, we have a plan. I want a direct call placed to Governor Cooper to tell him what's going to happen. Avery, can you do that?" asked Johnson.

"I think it needs to come from an administration official," Tibbs stated. Smith shrugged, like he didn't care who made the call.

"Well, it sure can't be you, Jamail. He'll probably just hang up on you. He hates you," laughed McDermott.

"The feeling is mutual."

"I can make the call. He'll know that I can and will shut off all federal payments. At the end of the day, he'll know he has limited time before his constituents start beating down his doors for their lives to return to normal," explained Gould.

"This is a good plan," affirmed the president. "Can you guys wrap this up? I have a tee time in about thirty minutes. Just call if you have any questions." He beamed at his personnel.

Within the hour, the White House issued a press statement:

"Despite repeated attempts, the State of Texas, in particular its state government, certain Texas law enforcement units and the governor have thumbed their nose at the rule of law.

"The state has unlawfully arrested federal agents and military personnel and has refused to comply with legally issued federal arrest warrants. This criminal activity has led to the deaths of eighteen Americans serving their country in law enforcement or the military, with at least eleven more wounded and still in hospitals.

"Texans must decide if they will continue to allow this current state government to set policies that are detrimental to the people of Texas and their fellow Americans. If the state does not begin complying with federal laws, including the voluntary surrender of the governor, lieutenant governor and the Texas Rangers involved in the operations at Ellington Air Force Base, the federal government will commence actions to force the state to comply with federal law.

"We have reached out to the governor to explain the actions we are going to take that, unfortunately, will likely affect every Texan. The governor must decide if he is a governor for the people and turn himself over to federal authorities by noon tomorrow, or the federal government will start imposing sanctions on Texas."

Some of the more liberal Democrats in Congress from Texas and the Texas State Legislature immediately called for the impeachment, recall or removal of Governor Cooper and Lieutenant Governor Foster. Several state legislators indicated they would file bills to force a recall election in the upcoming special session called by Governor Cooper.

Firearms dealers throughout Texas reported record sales. Many sporting goods retailers had bare shelves where inventories of guns used to be. Not since Johnson's first election had dealers seen this type of a run on firearms and ammunition.

Although many editorials and op-eds in major Texas newspapers were critical of Cooper, Texans showed support for their governor and anger at Washington, D.C. Those feelings were overwhelmingly strong and getting stronger.

Texas and Washington, D.C., which had been polar opposites for years on a multitude of policies, but which had gotten further apart during the first term of the Johnson administration, were now accelerating to an unavoidable collision of historic proportions.

Chapter 46

"The liberties of a people never were, nor ever will be, secure, when the transactions of their rulers may be concealed from them."

~ Patrick Henry

"The beauty of the second amendment is that it will not be needed until they try to take it."

~ Thomas Jefferson

At the state capitol building in Austin, hundreds of reporters gathered for a news conference called by the governor to detail the findings of the Rash Sally investigation. Also on hand were Chuck Dixon and Steve Milford, who were prepared to make statements to the press and answer questions.

"Thank you for coming." the governor began. "We are faced with the most outrageous form of tyranny our country has known in one hundred and fifty years."

Governor Cooper paused and took a long, slow look at the audience, allowing people to settle down as reporters and news crews were still filing in, finding space hard to come by.

"This administration knowingly used the Rash Sally assassination attempt on President Johnson to further a political agenda. That political agenda was to pin the attempt on the Tea Party, many of whom are citizens of Texas.

"This administration lied to the American people. It covered up the facts of the assassination. Because of the administration's lies, people have died in the riots immediately following the assassination attempt, as have innocent Tea Party members at the hands of federal agents who acted in a criminal and unconstitutional manner.

"This administration has no regard for the United States Constitution. It is made up of former hippies, illicit drug users, terrorists, socialists and communists. As you saw two days ago, this administration tried to trample the truth with an unprecedented military operation against a state capitol and a state government not seen since 1860.

"An American hero named Tim Spilner who worked on the Rash Sally investigation was killed, along with his wife, in a highly suspicious car accident on the very same day he distributed this incredible cover-up evidence from the Department of Justice to Texas Attorney General Jeff Weaver.

"One of the gentlemen sitting behind me was a friend and co-worker of Tim Spilner. Standing by him is Tim Spilner's father. Also standing with me is Chuck Dixon, whose home was terrorized and whose best friend, Stan Mumford, was killed in an unprovoked shooting by federal agents."

Cooper paused again and his serious look was replaced by a defiant scowl.

"Today, I call on Congress to appoint a special investigator, totally independent of the Executive Branch, to conduct a special investigation into the cover-up of information that resulted in the deaths of innocent Texans and Tim Spilner, who was also an innocent. Let me emphasize that this investigation must be conducted outside of the FBI, ATF or Homeland Security. I also demand that the U.S. House of Representatives bring impeachment charges to the floor for a vote immediately, ultimately to be tried by the U.S. Senate.

"Let me state for the record, the citizens of Texas have let it be known to their elected officials, me included, that they will NOT stand for a federal leviathan in Washington, D.C., especially this administration that is corrupt and uses thug-like tactics to attempt to bring a sovereign state into line with a misguided and criminal notion of federal authority.

"Today, in a special session of the Texas legislature, we will adopt measures to deal with this issue. I have had many conversations with fellow governors across the country who are appalled at this administration's criminal behavior and who back Texas one hundred percent.

"Let me remind those in the rest of the country a little about Texas history. In 1836, the tyrannical ruler of Mexico abandoned the spirit and intent of the Mexican Constitution of 1824. At the Alamo, a flag flew from inside the walls with the year 1824 on it, reflecting the Texians' desire to return to that constitution, or else. They didn't and Texas became a free republic because of it.

"We expect Congress to take appropriate and immediate action to return this country to our Constitution and to impeach the criminals who sit in our federal government, specifically this administration, including the president of the United States, Tyrell Johnson."

The press conference continued with the personal testimonies of Chuck Dixon, Steve Milford and Tim Spilner's father. All three were believable, personable and displayed a significant grasp of the facts surrounding the Tea Party raids. Steve Milford attested to the credibility of Tim Spilner.

Tim's father had a hard time getting through the press conference, still visibly shaken by his son and daughter-in-law's tragic deaths. He made no bones about the fact he believed the government was somehow involved. He also explained that his son and he were not of the same ideology and that Tim had voted for Johnson twice.

At the end of the press conference, Governor Cooper, Lieutenant Governor Foster, Texas Attorney General Weaver, and Pops Younger stood at the podium for questions.

"Governor, you were accused of fanning the flames of secession a few years ago, which you walked back. Are you threatening secession again?" asked a liberal media reporter.

"Let me say this: I will always follow the will of the people of Texas, whom I serve."

"Are you saying you believe the people of Texas want to secede?"

"What I'm saying is that the people of Texas will watch very closely how Congress acts, how the rest of the country responds, and what is done to bring the criminals in this administration to justice."

"Are you going to turn yourself in?" yelled a reporter in the back.

"No, but I will accept President Johnson's resignation," said a defiant Cooper.

"What is the status of the arrested federal agents in Austin and in Houston?" asked a West Coast reporter.

"I will defer to Mr. Weaver, our state's attorney," said the governor. He stepped back momentarily to allow Weaver to get to the mic.

"Those agents arrested from both operations are making their way through the Texas justice system. Unlike the process Chuck Dixon and others from the Tea Party went through, these folks were read their rights, provided access to attorneys, and given normal due process. They have all had initial hearings in front of a judge; however, no judge has granted them bail."

"Do you think the Department of Justice will try to arrest you again?" asked another reporter.

"I doubt it," smiled the governor. Many in the audience laughed.

"Are the U.S. air bases still locked down?" asked a seasoned reporter from New York.

"Yes, but I can't get into specifics on that issue," said the governor.

"Has anyone in the administration tried to contact you in the last twenty-four hours?" asked the same reporter.

"Yes, I received a call from Benjamin Gould this morning. Basically, his call pertained to threats the administration was making to the people of Texas.".

Now the press crowd really clamored for more information about the Gould conversation. What threats could he possibly make? Was this going to escalate?

"Can you be more specific, Governor Cooper? What were the

threats?" asked a reporter as he pressed forward to try to get to the front where reporters were held back by DPS state troopers and a rope.

"I can't go into specifics but let me just say that, instead of working with Texas to resolve the issues, this administration has once again resorted to Chicago thug-like tactics. I told Mr. Gould that, if the administration attempts to follow through with threats to isolate Texas, we will respond in kind."

The reporters yelled and screamed for more information, to the point where the crowd was almost unruly.

"Sir, Mr. Governor, we notice the American flag is no longer flying on the capitol grounds nor is it displayed in the rotunda. Why is that?" asked a young woman reporter.

"No comment," the governor said wryly. "I'm sorry. I have to go now and get ready for the special session of the legislature. I again call on Congress to start impeachment proceedings immediately. You should be asking Johnson and Tibbs for many answers regarding the Rash Sally information and the evidence of the cover-up this hero Tim Spilner brought to light. Thank you."

By the time the sergeant-at-arms called the special session of the Texas legislature, leading legislators were announcing they were going to pass a resolution supporting the governor and condemning the administration. It took less than forty-five minutes after the legislature convened to condemn the administration with a 91 percent yea vote:

TEXAS JOINT RESOLUTION No 2216

WHEREAS, the federal government of the United States has mislead the American public about the motives of presidential assassin Rashid Safly-Allah; and

WHEREAS, the administration has blamed the Tea Party for the assassination attempt although it had clear evidence that the motive for the as-

sassination attempt was the U.S. government's unconstitutional interdiction into Iran during Operation Python; and

WHEREAS, the Justice Department and President Johnson purposely withheld such evidence from the American people to pursue a political agenda; and

WHEREAS, the federal government has conducted unlawful search-and-seizure raids in the State of Texas, which caused material harm to Texas residents; and

WHEREAS, the federal government suspended habeas corpus and due process rights of Texas citizens in violation of the United States Constitution; and

WHEREAS, the administration ordered the illegal missions of federal agents acting under the authority of the Justice Department that resulted in the unwarranted deaths of certain Texas citizens, the destruction of personal property, the unlawful seizure of certain properties; and

WHEREAS, under orders from the administration, the federal government conducted illegal operations against and in the State of Texas, including military operations at the state capitol and Department of Public Safety headquarters; and

WHEREAS, illegal arrest warrants were issued for various Texas residents and government officials that were not signed by the appropriate authorities and were ultimately executed purely for political purposes; and

WHEREAS, the State of Texas demands the United States Senate conduct immediate impeachment proceedings against the president of the United States, the vice president, the U.S. attorney general, the treasury secretary, the directors of the FBI, ATF and Homeland Security, the White House chief of staff; and

WHEREAS, the State of Texas demands that a criminal investigation be opened by an independent counsel not appointed by the Executive Branch of the current administration into the criminal conduct of the president of the United States, the vice president, the U.S. attorney general, the treasury secretary, the directors of the FBI, ATF and Homeland Security, the White House chief of staff, the Democratic National Committee chairperson, and various *presidential advisors; and*

WHEREAS, the State of Texas demands that a criminal investigation be opened by an independent investigator not appointed by the Executive Branch of the current administration into the death of Justice Department whistle-blower Tim Spilner and his wife Mary Anne Spilner.

NOW, therefore, be it RESOLVED, that the Joint Texas Legislature, on behalf of the People of Texas, demands the recognition of the covenants of this Joint Resolution and that the federal government recognize the Tenth Amendment to the United States Constitution and the Executive Branch's violation of the rights of Texas under the same Tenth Amendment.

After this resolution was made public, the mainstream media downplayed it as just theatre, with no real meaning or purpose. MSNBC went so far as to call it a "feel-good" piece from the Texas legislature to justify the unlawful acts by state leaders regarding the events at Ellington and in Austin.

The Democrat-controlled House and Senate made it clear they were not going to bring impeachment hearings for a full floor vote, despite the fact that several influential Democrats sided with Republicans that more investigation into the Sally documents was needed. The administration, as part of its stated game plan, put immense and unprecedented pressure on Democratic leadership as the Sunday talk show guests seemed to be repeating verbatim the talking points the White House team had drawn up. There were questions to be asked: With Justice controlling the law enforcement arm of the Executive Branch, who could act on any investigation? Was this an issue the founding fathers never foresaw? Who enforces laws when the Executive Branch is corrupt?

President Johnson wasted no time. The staff had mobilized quickly to respond to the leak of the Sally files and to the Texas legislature's resolution. On a Friday afternoon, which was when the administration typically issued bad news to the country because of the reduced exposure, Johnson placed direct orders with the Treasury, Homeland Security, FAA, FCC, DOJ and various other federal agencies.

The Executive Branch was going to lock down Texas, force her to her knees to comply with federal authority and arrest Governor Brent Cooper.

Chapter 47

"A state of war only serves as an excuse for domestic tyranny."

~ *Aleksandr Solzhenitsyn*
Soviet Writer & Dissident

"Experience hath shown, that even under the best forms of government those entrusted with power have, in time, and by slow operations, perverted it into tyranny."

~ *Thomas Jefferson*

A coordinated plan by the Department of Defense landed helicopters and U.S. Army troops at seven locations where interstate highways crossed Texas borders. In addition to those seven sites, dozens of other cross-border highways on the New Mexico, Arkansas, Oklahoma and Louisiana borders with Texas had caravans of Humvees, troop transports and helicopters blockading the roads. Within forty minutes, the U.S. Army and Homeland Security had shut down traffic entering and leaving Texas on most major roads. The Army was not letting Texans cross the border out of the state and was only allowing those into Texas who had valid Texas driver's licenses. The traffic began to back up for miles each way, especially on interstate highways.

At the ports in Galveston, Corpus Christi, Houston, Port Arthur and Brownsville, U.S. Navy ships lurked five miles offshore and began intercepting cargo ships and turning them back, effectively creating a naval blockade. Ships that were leaving the harbors with Texas goods were ordered to return to the port they just left. Pleasure boats were not allowed to exceed a five-mile limit.

At the Federal Reserve, inter-bank electronic money exchanges were halted for the banks that had routing numbers identified with Texas. No money was allowed in through check clearances or money transfers. The Fed only allowed amounts less than $5,000 to be transferred out, and only if it was going to a U.S. bank.

Where the FCC could, it shut down Internet points of presence, gateways from major Internet providers to access the worldwide web. Internet traffic in Texas slowed to a crawl.

The FAA redirected all flights headed to Texas to alternate airports. The FAA was not allowed to clear any flights for take-off out of Texas airports. The FAA regional headquarters in Houston and Fort Worth were allowed to continue to direct traffic already in the air. The TSA at all airports was advised to turn back travelers who were Texas residents and only board residents from other states and countries. When the airports were cleared, the TSA was instructed to shut down its imaging machines, close the lines and empty the airports of travelers.

Firearms dealers in Texas were not given access to the electronic gun registration approval process. If a dealer wanted to sell a gun, it was now a federal crime to do it without the necessary background check.

Federal employees with the IRS, FBI, Homeland Security, FAA, ATF, HHS and hundreds of other organizations were distributed a communique from the White House, letting them know the actions against Texas were not directed at them and, if they wanted to leave Texas, they would be given special privileges as loyal federal employees.

Local law enforcement was notified of the operation once it started. They were advised not to interfere whatsoever with federal operations, that they should keep normal operations functioning, help keep the population calm and continue to enforce state and federal laws.

The IRS was one of the few federal agencies instructed to remain open. The feds wanted payments to continue to flow from Texas to Washington, despite the fact that no federal money was coming to Texas. The IRS was supplied with a special "list" of Texas residents and businesses for whom the agency should commence immediate comprehensive tax audits. The governor's office scrambled to respond to the feds' actions.

The Johnson administration announced a live television statement to be made that evening by President Johnson from the Oval Office.

President Johnson walked into the Oval Office to deliver his address to the nation. The teleprompters on both sides of his desk and behind the main camera were ready.

"My fellow Americans," he began, his face somber, "today my administration was forced to make some difficult decisions regarding the actions of the state government of Texas and, in particular, its governor.

"As all America knows, eighteen of our fellow Americans who were just doing their jobs died at the state capitol in Austin." The president's tone became almost sorrowful. "These men were there to help serve perfectly legal arrest warrants for the governor of Texas, who ordered an operation conducted at a U.S. Air Force base that violated federal law, and others who were involved in that operation, where a federal ATF agent was shot.

"Texas is illegally holding federal law enforcement officials and U.S. military and has wrongly pressed charges against them.

"As we speak today, the State of Texas has still shut down flight operations at United States military bases in Texas. This is an act of treason. Some of those involved in this shut-down are military reservists in the United States military. These are serious actions, treasonous actions against the government they swore to obey. Having flight operations shut down over a large region of this country jeopardizes our national defense and readiness.

"Now," the president said emphatically, "I could have authorized a full and overwhelming military action to restore flight operations at these bases. That possibility has not been ruled out. Let me remind the governor that those are United States military bases and those are United States military aircraft.

"Since the Texas state government has not shown any proclivity for ending the confrontation with federal authority, my administration has consulted Congress, constitutional law experts, my cabinet, the Joint Chiefs of Staff and other leaders in America to determine the best way to end this crisis without further bloodshed.

"Make no mistake. Governor Cooper, Lieutenant Governor Foster, the Texas Rangers and others who have had federal arrest warrants issued for them must turn themselves in at once. We call on the American citizens in Texas to put pressure on their state leaders to turn themselves over to federal authorities and to restore American military bases in the state to the Air Force and Army.

"While the actions we have taken may seem extreme to some, they are necessary. But let me state for the record and emphasize that these actions are not directed at the American citizens of Texas."

The president directed his gaze to the teleprompters. "First, we have shut down all travel to and from Texas, both via our highway system, by air, by train and via Texas ports. Travel to Texas will be restricted to residents of Texas who need to return home. No commercial carriers will operate to or from Texas during this crisis, including buses, airlines, cruise ships, trains or otherwise.

"Second," he said sternly, "we have suspended all federal payments of any kind to Texas. We cannot continue to support a state government that is defiant to federal authority. Banking transactions to Texas have also been suspended."

President Johnson leaned forward. "My administration is taking other significant but necessary steps to end this crisis, but let me be perfectly clear: Governor Cooper, Lieutenant Governor Foster, the Texas Rangers and Texas Guard could end this crisis at any time by surrendering to federal authorities.

"Mr. Governor, my phone is open. You can call me at any time and end this crisis. I am hopeful that this government can return to normal relations with the State of Texas.

"To the people of Texas, I implore you to contact your mayors, your city council, your state legislators and the governor's office. Your state government's actions are affecting you and, the longer this goes on, the harder it will be for your individual lives to return to normal. The rest of America is watching and expecting you to live up to your American heritage.

"God bless you and God bless America. Thank you and goodnight."

Two large screen projection TVs had displayed Johnson's speech to the large crowd assembled on the capitol lawn. They booed Johnson constantly during the speech.

Governor Cooper promised to have a response to Johnson's message within thirty minutes of the speech. Cameras and the press were set up on the capitol steps with a large crowd awaiting his reply.

Right on time, Cooper walked to the podium, flanked by Gene Foster and Jeff Weaver. Cooper looked grim.

"My fellow Texans, the president of the United States has effectively waged war on Texas. Not only did he send fully armed military troops to our capitol, he also sent federal agents to terrorize our citizens, detain them unlawfully and without due process, caused several unnecessary deaths and now has increased the stakes to dangerous levels.

"This president has enacted measures that would only be used when you are at war with another country. He has stationed federal troops at our borders with other states, stopped the flow of commerce which, by the way, includes food and medicine. He has blockaded our ports. This is not how a president should govern or resolve conflicts with a state."

Reading from his prepared statement, the governor continued, "What President Johnson did not mention in his speech tonight is that the federal payments he referred to also include payments of

Social Security and Medicare.

"This is another example of how this president views federal authority. Those checks are earned by citizens who paid into the system. The federal government owes them those payments. This is an attempt to put fiscal pressure on Texas to succumb to his version of federal authority. Instead, he is hurting the people of Texas.

"Also, what the president didn't mention is that, by shutting down the transfer of funds between banks, he is essentially suspending the paychecks of millions of Texans whose payroll is processed in any other state by employers out of state. These facts were confirmed late this afternoon with the Comptroller of the Currency and with the Social Security Administration. But President Johnson is still finding a way to pay federal employees in the state. This is yet another example of this administration's priorities of federal employees over private enterprise and non-government workers.

"I once again call on Congress, and specifically the U.S. Senate, to start impeachment proceedings immediately. If the Senate conducts a vote on impeachment for the president, vice president, U.S. attorney general, secretary of the treasury and others, I will happily turn myself in to federal authorities. This administration has so blatantly violated the United States Constitution that Texas cannot and will *not* recognize its authority. The U.S. Congress and our fellow states should be demanding these actions."

Several Texas state senators and state representatives had announced earlier in the day they were introducing bills in the special session that the governor had called to put a referendum on a statewide ballot for Texas independence. Texas could hold a special election for voters to *secede* from the United States.

The sentiment throughout Texas against the federal government had grown angrier by the day. What started as a general distrust of federal authority, taxes and government incursion into states' rights had reached a fever pitch with the actions against Chuck Dixon, Stan Mumford and the Tea Party patriots.

Anti-Washington rhetoric escalated because the evidence showed these attacks were politically motivated and involved a cover-up at the highest levels of the Executive Branch. The attempted paramilitary action by the Justice Department, carried out with the president's approval on their state capital of Austin, pushed the average Texan to sentiments not seen since 1860.

Whether the sentiment was powerful enough to carry through on a special referendum by Texas voters to secede was yet to be seen.

Chapter 48

"They who can give up essential liberty to obtain a little temporary safety, deserve neither liberty nor safety."

~ Benjamin Franklin

The governors of Oklahoma, Louisiana and Arkansas registered formal protests with the administration for stationing federal troops at their borders with Texas and for the disruption in commerce and travel caused by the shutdown of major and interstate highways. Senators and house representatives from all three states began lobbying the administration and congressional leaders immediately for re-opening those highways. Even family members were not allowed into Texas to visit relatives living there.

On the national scene, despite heavy criticism from the mainstream media regarding the sudden boldness of Texas against the administration, news reports were having little effect outside the normal liberal bastions on the West Coast and northeast United States. According to polling data, there was a growing surge for impeachment proceedings, enough so that even some leading Democrats were willing to split with party lines to call for an independent counsel to investigate the cover-up. Almost half of Americans now thought the federal government likely had something to do with the deaths of Tim Spilner and his wife.

Debates raged on both the Senate and House floors about the appropriate action needed regarding the "Texas problem." The elder statesmen and women of both parties called for calm and for the fed to ease up or tensions could reach a point where a formal split occurred or full-scale military action was warranted. Tensions reached a new high when the Texas governor ordered the Texas Guard to the same choke points where federal troops were stationed.

The next morning, America woke up to breaking news coverage of a live statement from the Texas governor.

"The administration has ordered military troops to our state borders and has created a naval blockade in the Gulf of Mexico," Governor Cooper stated. "The Fed has shut down banking transactions for private citizens, stopped the flow of commerce into and out of Texas, and has ceased federal payments of any kind to Texas citizens who have paid into federal programs with their taxes. It has created a run on Texas banks and could put many Texas-chartered banks out of business. There has also been a run on food, medicine and gasoline."

The governor paused for a few seconds to confer with an aide standing by his side, then continued, "As of today, I have ordered all oil and natural gas pipelines to be shut down. There will be no Texas oil, natural gas or gasoline flowing out of Texas to the rest of the country until this administration opens the highways and lanes of commerce.

"I have also ordered the Texas Guard to position themselves at the border choke points where federal military troops are illegally blocking free access to Texas highways and ports. Let me state emphatically," the governor punctuated his comments by pointing into the cameras, "I am not dispatching troops for armed conflict with U.S. troops. These troops are to be positioned for defensive purposes only in the event this administration launches a federal incursion into the sovereign state of Texas as it has already attempted. Once again, and I will do this daily until this crisis is over, Congress must act at once with impeachment proceedings. This crisis will only escalate without congressional action to protect the United States Constitution."

For the first time, it appeared Governor Cooper had little hope that a crisis could be averted.

"Governor," shouted a reporter, "is Texas going to secede?"

"Let me be clear," the governor said, "I have stated years ago and in the past that I have always felt any state had the right to secede. However, Texas will follow the will of its people as a sovereign, freedom-loving state." He directed his comments to the large group. "As you are aware, there are bills right now in the special session of the Texas legislature calling for a referendum on that topic. The longer the administration follows its punitive actions against Texans and the longer Congress fails to act on clearly impeachable offenses, the more likely Texans will feel compelled to follow Constitutional principles."

"Are you dispatching the Texas militia to fight U.S. troops to open those highways?" yelled another reporter.

The governor answered the question patiently, even though he'd already responded to it, and went a step farther. "The troops I have ordered to those choke points are defensive only—for now. They are moving into position to prevent another federal incursion into a sovereign state."

"Will they fire at U.S. Army troops if they come into Texas?" was the follow-up question shouted by the same reporter.

"Any unlawful incursion into Texas will be met with armed resistance. Yes."

"You mean you will fire at fellow Americans?"

"I think you need to ask that question to President Johnson. Will American troops fire on fellow Americans who happen to be Texans? Will American troops follow an unconstitutional order to invade Texas?"

The national news, already reporting the story since the capitol incident as a "crisis," were now buzzing over the increased stakes put on the table by both sides. Several offers came in from state, church and business leaders to mediate the crisis.

At the White House, President Johnson's indignation with Texas reached unprecedented levels.

"I'm tired of that bozo thinking he can dictate to us," he told Radford, Tibbs, Gould and Smith.

"The more this crisis with Texas dominates national news, the less attention people will focus on the Rash-Sally investigation," said Smith.

"Okay, so we have an escalating crisis. What are our options?" asked Johnson.

"The first option is to launch a full-scale military operation to crush the Texas Guard, then capture the governor and have him do his perp walk in handcuffs for all the nation to see!" shouted Tibbs.

"God, how I would love to see those images," replied Johnson.

"Or, we let nature take its course and literally starve them out. Conditions should deteriorate so fast Texans will want to lynch their governor soon enough," laughed Tibbs.

"I would like to wait them out; however, the drums of impeachment proceedings have gained some strength, although we still have the majority in Congress, so it may not go anywhere," stated Smith.

"Are we using sledgehammers to get our folks in line?" asked Johnson.

"Yes, Mr. President. We have a few stragglers that in due time will be punished; however, we still have a clear majority and nobody is going to get the votes for an impeachment hearing in this Congress," affirmed Radford.

"This is exactly why we work so hard for a political majority at any cost," the president commented. "A fully Democratic Congress is the only way we collectively retain power. I want you to keep reminding our people of that!"

Senate Minority Leader Mitch McConnell in the U.S. Senate received a request from the governor of Texas for a conference call with Republican leadership in the House and Senate, as well as some in the Republican National Committee.

Mitch McConnell weighed his options, then agreed. He set up the call. "Hello, Governor, this is Mitch. Are we all on the call?"

A collective yes came from more than two dozen participants. After the participants identified themselves, the governor began the call.

"Mr. Leader, when is the Senate going to bring impeachment up for a vote? You know this crisis will escalate and this proceeding needs to happen sooner rather than later," Cooper said.

"Governor, we still don't have the votes," McConnell said. "Right now, we can't even get it out of committee. We are trying…"

"Trying?" The governor was indignant. "Ladies and gentlemen, I have federal troops on my borders, I have a banking system shut down, and we are effectively being blockaded."

"Our founding fathers didn't give us much wiggle room," responded the new senator from Texas, who'd been elected in a landslide Tea Party-backed vote in the general election and an exciting run-off election to win the Republican primary. "I assume they never thought our entire Executive Branch of government could be corrupt."

"Who do I send to arrest the president?" McConnell asked. "Justice won't do it. Anything short of that is a coup and is unconstitutional."

"Mr. Leader," Governor Cooper addressed McConnell now, "are you telling me that our government can do nothing about crimes that are committed by the president and his staff?"

There was an uncomfortable silence before McConnell answered. "As you know, Governor, the Justice Department holds all Executive Branch law enforcement jurisdiction in this matter. Without the Senate's affirmative vote for impeachment proceedings and the appointment of a special prosecutor, we are at a loss how to proceed."

"Hold on! Hold on just a minute," Cooper roared. "I've just been informed that shots are being fired by Texas Guard and U.S. Army troops in Texarkana. Damn!"

"Governor, we understand your plight. I assume there is no way you would consider turning yourself in?" asked the governor of Utah.

"Tell me how that solves anything relating to the impeachment proceedings. I'm sure by now that you have all read the documents and have seen the testimony, yet what I am hearing from you and

other constitutional experts is that without Justice or an impeachment vote, there is nothing we can do."

The young senator from Texas was considered a constitutional expert himself, having tried cases in front of the Supreme Court. He
agreed with the governor. "Folks, the governor is likely correct. The
situation in Texas may be the only leverage we have. With the Executive Branch involved both in the conspiracy and cover-up, there will
likely be no movement to clean up their own house. With Congress
in a Democratic majority, even if we had the votes to bring impeachment to the floor, it wouldn't pass. I have never been so disappointed
in our system as I am today."

"Well, then, we have a different kind of constitutional crisis going
on here in Texas. My legislature is going to bring a referendum for
secession to the floor any day now for a vote. Our sources tell us it
will pass. The next step is for the citizens to vote on it. What if that
passes?" questioned the governor.

"Governor, there are sixteen other governors who are making a
joint statement tonight about the federal government's recent actions with troops and federal payments. They are going to condemn
the president," said a fellow governor from a southern state.

"Jim," Cooper said, "I appreciate the support. We all know that
may move positive polling a point or two, but it doesn't get them off
our borders or restore our sovereignty."

When the governor hung up the phone after the hour and fifteen
minute conference call, he was dejected. The call began with the
governor hopeful that certain actions could be taken to lift the federal government's foot on the neck of Texas economic survival, but
ended with him realizing Texas was probably on her own.

In Texas, banks stayed open, even though initially there was a run
on all Texas-chartered banks as word spread that the feds were looking to shut those down. The state government allowed the banks
to close temporarily to allow for panic to subside somewhat while
they began broadcasting messages of calm. The national banks with

locations in Texas were not hit as hard, because the Johnson administration had clearly identified Texas banks as targets. Many of the independent Texas banks were on the brink of collapse as funds were withdrawn at a dizzying pace.

Food stock on grocery store shelves began to disappear, mostly by Texans who began to stockpile and hoard food as a result of the blockade. The Texas agriculture commissioner indicated to the governor that, between existing inventories of the many grocery distribution centers throughout Texas, Texas farmers and co-ops, Texas would not run out of food and could self-sustain indefinitely. However, he indicated Texas could run out of certain specific items during a long-term blockade. One huge concern was for medical supplies or drugs that were imported. The state was still studying how long it could sustain public health without certain supplies like insulin and other important medicines.

Of greatest concern was the blocking of federal payments, particularly direct payments to Texas citizens. Texans began losing Social Security payments, disability checks, Medicaid and Medicare payments to doctors and hospitals and funds that went directly to schools.

The Johnson administration had calculated that, by impacting Texans' daily lives, they would put pressure on their state government to cooperate with the feds. This was a huge miscalculation.

Thousands of Texans organized a rally in front of federal buildings in Houston, Dallas and San Antonio. In Austin, the rally was held in front of the regional center of the IRS. Crowds were angry, and they were angry at Washington. Local law enforcement officials had to call in off-duty officers to help with the sizeable demonstrations. Federal employees who left their jobs after work were jeered at and had profanities hurled at them. This was especially true of IRS employees leaving their jobs at day's end in Houston and Austin. Texas was mad at anyone and everyone associated with Washington.

In the Texas legislature, three competing bills from the Texas

House were merged into a single bill from the Texas Senate, calling for a statewide emergency referendum for Texas independence. Many Democrats who opposed the governor throughout his tenure in the governor's mansion were now poised to support him. The few who opposed the vote, who were extremely liberal Democrats and several moderate Republicans, were castigated heavily in the press by colleagues, citizens and the Tea Party. It appeared that Texans had become singled-minded and banded together by a common enemy—Washington, D.C. and the Johnson administration.

A Gallup poll indicated 61 percent of Texans supported secession and independence.

The Texas governor issued a recall for the two senators and thirty-two members of Congress to come home to Texas for a briefing on the independence referendum vote. It was unclear how all members of Congress were going to return with roads blocks and the FAA shutting down air lanes and outbound flights to Texas airports.

The governor issued a statement: "The State of Texas has recalled its entire congressional delegation to meet with state officials and their constituencies in Texas. What is not clear is if and how the Johnson administration will allow them to return to Texas to address this growing crisis of an unconstitutional and criminal administration. We demand that this administration allow free and uninhibited travel of these publicly elected officials to return to their home state safely and unimpeded."

The Johnson administration kept the pressure on the governor, demanding that the Texas Guard release control of flight operations at various Texas Air Force and Army bases. Texas refused.

The Johnson administration countered by ordering B-52 Stratofortress bombers, which are the United States' largest and can carry nuclear weapons, to make training runs over Texas and her capital. Johnson also ordered full flight operations off the decks of three aircraft carriers moved into the Gulf of Mexico. Johnson was buzzing all major cities in Texas with F-15s, F-16s and the bombers.

This intentional show of force ahead of the Texas legislature's vote on an independence referendum was designed to intimidate. But each time Johnson made a move to intimidate Texas, it back-fired and only seemed to galvanize Texans from all political and socio-economic backgrounds.

Chapter 49

"All political power is inherent in the people, and all free governments are founded on their authority, and instituted for their benefit. The faith of the people of Texas stands pledged to the preservation of a republican form of government, and, subject to this limitation only, they have at all times the inalienable right to alter, reform or abolish their government in such manner as they may think expedient."

~ The Texas Constitution (Article 1, Section 2)

Introduced by the Texas Speaker of the House, Chuck Dixon walked to the podium to be introduced to the joint Texas legislature. In attendance were twenty-six of the thirty-two Texas members of the U.S. House of Representatives. Six members of the Texas Congressional Caucus who were extremely liberal Democrats boycotted the vote and planned a press conference at a local hotel.

The two sitting U.S. senators from Texas were in attendance, along with many dignitaries and celebrities from the state who sensed the historic nature of the upcoming vote. News crews from affiliates across Texas were on hand, with at least fifty news and satellite trucks parked just beyond the capitol grounds, near where eighteen federal troops and agents lost their lives attacking Texas Guard troops at the Texas Law Library. This event was broadcast through local affiliates and the Internet across the world. What would Texas do?

As Chuck Dixon was introduced, the joint legislature and all in attendance rose to their feet and applauded him with a standing ovation that lasted a full eight minutes. At Chuck's side were his wife Christy and son Colton.

Chuck Dixon began: "First, thank you so much. God Bless Texas!"

The crowd erupted again, with louder yells, cheers and another standing ovation that lasted a full five minutes.

"Wow. Thank you again. Unbelievable," said Chuck as he swiped at tears. He took a few seconds to gather himself.

"My fellow Texans, I wasn't born here. I am not a native Texan, but I got here as fast as I could!" he said, smiling as the audience laughed with him. "But, even though I wasn't born here, let me tell you one thing. I am a Texan!"

The crowd burst into more applause.

"Now, I would never compare myself to these great Texans but, as we all know, Houston, Bowie, Travis, Crockett and many others weren't born in Texas but Texas got into their hearts. It got in their hearts enough to die for." He could barely finish sentences before the crowd applauded again.

"I'm not any of those great men. I am a simple man. Beside me is my wife Christy and my son Colton. Several years ago, I was a frustrated, middle-aged business owner and entrepreneur. I believed for a long time that our country was headed in the wrong direction. More importantly, I felt that the United States Constitution was slowly being eradicated one day at a time. It didn't appear to me that most of the country held that sacred document with the same reverence I had growing up and still maintain to this day," Chuck told the crowd.

"I saw the growth of socialism and government dependencies damage American and Texan values of the individual liberty I grew up with. I saw free enterprise under attack from undue federal regulations and crony capitalism.

"I'll never forget the night I received a phone call from Stan Mumford, a long-time friend and business associate." Chuck paused for a long time, finding it hard to continue to speak about his good friend. The crowd responded with more applause, almost reverently.

"Stan wanted me to go to a small meeting of the Tea Party. He said they were just like us. We both believed the federal government was out of control, that Congress was inept and that our country was headed to a cataclysmic failure.

"So, I went. I met people just like me who thought just like me. Average folks in a sense, but not average when it came to their dreams for their children and grandchildren and the direction of our country.

"Before I knew it, I was part of the Tea Party. Before I knew it, Stan and I were organizing a local chapter where I lived. And, before I knew it, our small volunteer effort started to make a big impact on local elections. And we all know what happened in the last mid-terms."

Again, applause interrupted Chuck. He waited for it to die down, then continued. "During all the time I have been associated with the Tea Party, I can honestly say I haven't met the so-called racists and extremists that those on the left say permeate this purely grass roots organization. To be perfectly honest, they simply aren't true and, if these people would just attend an event or meeting of these Tea Party activists, they would know that for themselves!" Chuck said, his voice rising toward the end of his last sentence.

"What my family and many others like us have done is actively participate in our freedom. We got involved. We organized and spent precious time that none of us really had to get this country back. We met so many great people who shared the same dream we have."

Chuck paused for a moment as he looked out at the enthusiastic crowd, then began again. "The federal government started attacking the Tea Party. Never before in the history of our country has there been such an organized attack on free-thinking, freedom-loving pa-triots in this country by their own government.

"Under the Johnson administration, our fellow Tea Party patriots have been harassed, audited, terrorized and even killed!" said Chuck forcefully. "When I received the call to rush home one day, I had no idea what I would find. When I arrived, it was chaos. Christy and Colton were being held prisoner. My American government terror-ized me and my family, destroying my home, terrifying my family and doing all of this under the ruse of the NDAA—the National Defense Authorization Act. Those in Congress who voted for this despicable legislation should be tried for treason!"

The crowd rose and applauded wildly. Some of the congressional delegation in attendance who voted for the NDAA clapped politely but appeared stoic and self-righteous about their vote in favor of the act.

"Yet I was lucky," Chuck said. "My best friend, mentor and fellow Tea Party member was murdered by federal agents right in front of his family and neighbors. I don't care what you read. I know the truth and the truth is they shot Stan Mumford without cause!" shouted Chuck to roaring applause.

"I was held for days with limited food and water. I was spit on, cussed at and not provided an attorney, nor was I read my rights. The worst part of my time being held at Ellington Field was not knowing about these two standing beside me. They didn't know where I had been taken, or if I was dead or alive." Chuck wiped away tears.

"I will never forget the Texas Ranger who first entered the room where I was being held," Chuck recalled as the crowd laughed. "I will be forever grateful to Pops Younger and his Texas Rangers."

The crowd again stood and began chanting, "Pops, Pops, Pops."

Standing off to the side out of view was Pops Younger. When he stepped out and waved to Chuck and the audience, everybody went crazy.

"We are also infinitely grateful to Governor Cooper. He took a gigantic risk, a risk that he and our beloved Texas is still dealing with today by authorizing the raid to free me at Ellington."

Chuck turned to look straight at the governor and said, "Thank you, Governor Cooper. I thank you from the bottom of my heart."

Once again, the crowd rose to hugely enthusiastic cheers and applause. Chuck and his family clapped with the crowd, pointing to the governor and showing their appreciation.

"I want to also thank all of you, Texas. Your incredible outpouring of support and love will never be forgotten."

The crowd remained standing, cheering wildly.

"Now I will turn this back over to the Speaker. I am eternally grateful and humbled that a simple middle-aged husband, father and businessman was asked to address this special body of Texas patriots. When you cast your votes in a few minutes, I ask you to remember Stan Mumford and his family. I ask you to uphold the most basic form of a republic. I ask that you let Texas decide on her own what our course is. Let the rest of the United States government and Congress know today that, for Texas, it's the Constitution or a free Texas Republic!"

The crowd in the gallery overlooking the chamber burst into applause first and loudest. The outburst lasted nearly ten minutes.

Next, the Speaker came to podium to take the roll call on the vote for a referendum to be put in front of Texas voters in two weeks for Texas independence, contingent upon Congress appointing a special prosecutor of Johnson, Tibbs and others in his administration and for a Senate vote to impeach the president and others in his administration.

The roll call vote passed the Texas legislature unanimously with sixteen abstentions.

The United States Congress was now "on the clock."

Chapter 50

"If by the mere force of numbers a majority should deprive a minority of any clearly written constitutional right, it might, in a moral point of view, justify revolution."

~ Abraham Lincoln

The Texas vote rocked the country. The next day, gas prices went to all-time highs. The stock market lost 9 percent of its market value in one day. Congressional leaders called on their caucuses to either support impeachment proceedings or to call Texas' bluff.

Media outlets asked Americans on camera all across the country one of the most interesting questions in American history: "Would you rather have your president impeached or would you rather keep Texas as a state?" Support for Texas had been strong, especially from the South and Mountain West states; however, the thought of Texas actually seceding made many pause.

Texas was castigated unmercifully by the mainstream media and leftist organizations, many who were calling for Texas to go ahead and leave, saying that the United States would be better off without it.

The problem with that strategy was it helped galvanize an already united Texas. Despite the embargo on shipments and the blockade, Texas was holding up well. Neighbors were helping neighbors. Texas lenders were suspending mortgages and other payments due by Texans while the banking crisis was holding up paychecks. Food banks and charitable organizations saw donations to their inventories swell to unprecedented levels. Hospitals and doctors took patients for urgent or critical care with no Medicare or Medicaid payments. School districts still operated without federal government subsidies although, as typical with the teachers' unions, there was much consternation about what would happen to their pay and less interest in what capacity students might suffer. Governor Cooper ordered all Texas schools to conduct a class on the Constitution and explain why Texas was at this crossroads with the United States government.

The eyes of the nation now fell on Congress. Would Congress act on Texas' demand for an impeachment vote and the appointment of a special prosecutor? Both the GOP and Democrats counted their votes to bring impeachment proceedings to the floor for a vote. If the vote passed, the Senate would actually try the impeachment.

Word came from Congress that the House would bring an impeachment vote to the floor the next morning. Americans planned their workdays around the vote so they could see it live. Was the president of the United States facing impeachment charges and a trial in the Senate? Was the governor of Texas really going to turn himself over for arrest to federal authorities if the impeachment vote carried?

Leaders in the GOP were skeptical they had the votes to carry the day, but the Democrats were under increased pressure from their constituents in moderate districts to move forward with impeachment in light of the evidence produced by Tim Spilner. The White House and the administration put extreme pressure on House Democrats to vote "nay." The Johnson administration, famous for cutting back-room deals and making good on political threats, was in hyper-drive, leaning hard on any and all Democrats and even some moderate Republicans. One sixteen-term Democratic House member said, "The administration is promising to break our legs if we vote for impeachment, and I believe them."

The next morning, Americans woke up to the news that skirmishes had broken out at two blockade points on the Texas-Oklahoma border, apparently by Oklahomans supportive of Texas agitated that federal troops were blocking two major highways and Interstate I-35 that connected Oklahoma City and Dallas. No casualties were reported, but it was announced that more troops were being sent to the area.

The White House issued a statement the morning of the vote stating, "It's time America moves on to more pressing issues with the economy, healthcare and jobs. The vote scheduled in the House today is pure partisan politics. Regardless of this vote, Texas needs to stand down and those leaders in their state government who have arrest warrants pending need to surrender and end this crisis."

The statement was issued to put increased pressure on the vote. The White House was watching and, if a representative was on the wrong side of the vote, there would be hell to pay. The GOP had no chance without some Democrats crossing the aisle and voting to impeach the Democratic president.

When the House vote was in, the nays won, 294-140 with one abstention. President Johnson would not be impeached.

The White House situation room where the president and his staff were watching the vote broke out Dom Perignon champagne and started celebrating, even though it was only 10:45 a.m. Eastern time.

In Austin, the governor's staff assembled in the governor's mansion to watch the vote was disappointed but not surprised. They had been informed by the Texas congressional delegation that they didn't have the votes and the only way the impeachment would happen was if enough Democrats crossed. They didn't.

Chuck Dixon and Steve Milford had been invited to the governor's mansion for the vote. Although some in the room were dejected, Steve Milford stood up and asked, "Ladies and gentlemen, do you know where I might find a job in this new Republic of Texas?"

At that point, many in the room realized what was upon them. The citizens of Texas had their destiny in their own hands. There was both exhilaration and trepidation. All across the state, Texans experienced the excitement of a new republic and the unknown of how the United States government would react to the vote. Would the measure pass? Would the United States government unleash the full force of the military to hold onto a breakaway state?

The mainstream media continued to bury the story of Rash-Sally and the evidence of the cover-up. The Democrats were glowing in their impeachment victory and became emboldened regarding the upcoming Texas referendum. Many Democrats called for Texas to be "punished." Governors of several states offered to broker a mediation between the state and the Johnson administration, but only if Texas suspended the referendum on the vote.

Polling data was scrutinized by the Johnson administration to see if Texas voters would really approve a referendum for secession. The voting demographics in Texas had changed with more Hispanics and transplants from other regions of the country who perhaps did not have the same pride and loyalty to Texas that native Texans had.

The Johnson administration, with its Chicago-style politics, wasted no time in pouncing on an opportunity to sway the Texas vote. Johnson's minions began rattling sabers. The administration had given specific talking points addressing the use of and the right of the United States government to use military force to quell an insurrection.

There was no organized political party supporting Texas' secession internally or externally in Texas. The GOP found itself in a quandary. Although Republicans completely backed the impeachment vote and most of the Texas leadership, the establishment in the GOP was against the secession of Texas or any other state for that matter.

If Texas was going to approve secession it would, like the Tea Party, have to be a totally grassroots movement with precious little time to organize. Because the vote was so soon, there was no time to organize. However, TV stations in Houston, Dallas, Ft. Worth, Austin, Brownsville, Corpus Christi, Amarillo and Lubbock were all hosting local debates over the issue on live broadcasts.

In an interview with a San Antonio television station, Governor

Cooper seemed at ease with the vote and confident the state would move forward, whatever the outcome. Pressed for particulars on how Texas would establish a government, the governor said, "This is Texas. We know how to get things done. I have complete faith in the people of this state to do the right thing and to follow through. We will be fine either way."

The day before the polls opened, Pops Younger walked right into the governor's office without knocking, barging right through the double doors. The governor stood up from his desk, knowing that Pops wasn't one to mess around. He obviously had something to share.

"Governor, I just received this fax from a buddy at Langley. Instead of explaining it, I'll just let you read it," said Pops.

The governor took the two pages stapled together and sat down to read it.

"Oh, my God," he exclaimed.

"That's what I said, but damn, Governor, we knew this was probably the case; we just didn't have proof."

"Well, we do now."

The governor called an immediate press conference, just in time to make most evening news broadcasts.

"I have just submitted a report conducted by two sources, including the CIA and an independent investigator regarding the car accident that claimed the lives of whistleblower and patriot Tim Spilner and his wife. Two separate investigators were provided access to the vehicle without the administration's knowledge. In both reports, it is conclusive that Tim Spilner's car was tampered with, particularly with the vehicle's acceleration. According to this report, Tim Spilner and his wife were murdered. On the day Tim Spilner blew the whistle on the Justice Department, he and his wife were murdered. This administration had the motive and the means. Once again, I call on Congress to act on this knowledge. Maybe the impeachment vote was a few days too early."

Immediately, congressional leaders in both parties were quick to denounce any immediate conclusions and both parties claimed there would not be an immediate call for another impeachment vote. That news was huge the day before the referendum went out for Texans' votes.

One Texas senator and fourteen Texas representatives announced their resignation from the Republican Party.

"We no longer share the same values as our Republican counterparts," stated the new senator from Texas as he stood with his fellow former Republicans at a news conference the morning of the vote. "Regardless of whether we move forward as the Republic of Texas or Congress acts responsibly and holds this administration responsible for its crimes and returns to the Constitution, we will not move forward as the status quo. What you see before you are the founding members of the Constitution Party. Our charter will be to follow either the United States Constitution or the Texas Constitution under the premise of individual liberty, fiscal sanity and a small and very limited government."

The polls closed at 7:00 p.m. County election boards throughout Texas reported record turnout. Exit polling indicated the vote was very close.

By 8:10 p.m., most news organizations had called the election. Texans had voted by a 68 to 32 percent margin to secede! Secession parties were underway all over Texas. Several governors called the Texas governor to congratulate the state. Several state legislators from other states indicated bills would be introduced in their state legislatures for the same type of referendum.

President Johnson walked to the East Wing of the White House to read a prepared statement.

"Fellow Americans, the people of Texas, led by a radical state government that has defied federal authority, have voted tonight to secede from the Union. This has happened before. It didn't work then and it won't work now. The United States has no intention of allowing this to happen. To leave the United States is treason, pure and simple."

Chuck Dixon, who was with the governor's staff and Pops Younger when the race was called, watched Johnson's statement from the White House.

A reporter turned to Chuck and asked, "The president of the United States claims Texas has committed treason. What do you have to say to the president?"

"Well, in that case, we are in good company with Washington, Jefferson, Patrick Henry, Adams, Bowie, Travis, Crockett and Houston. I guess we are all **Patriots of Treason!**"

"Texas will again lift its head and stand among the nations. It ought to do so, for no country upon the globe can compare with it in natural advantages."
~ *Sam Houston*

CPSIA information can be obtained at www.ICGtesting.com
Printed in the USA
LVOW132043141112

307268LV00003B/3/P